CROSSING FIRE

R.K. LILLEY

This book is for the OG Breathing Fire fans. I wrote this one for you. There aren't a ton of you, but you're my favorites. I'm so thankful for your patience and your grace while it took me for-fucking-ever to finish this.

BOOK TWO
IN THE HERETIC DAUGHTERS SERIES

JILLIAN

It had always been clear to me that we had different
songs playing in our heads. My music was usually
more a of death metal battle march that involved a lot of
blood being spilt. Dom's. . . Dom's music was
something that a romantic Irish bard would listen to,
whatever the hell that might be. He was a warrior, but
i'd always known he had a poet's soul. There could be
no denying that it was one of the things I loved most
about him. Still, it had always made everything hard.
It wasn't easy to be the other half of someone's perfect,
immortal love story when you were as imperfect as me.
I'd always known I'd mess it all up. It had only been a
matter of time.

DOM

It had always been as clear as day to me that it was fate
that brought us together. Our love was written in the
stars as clearly as ink on paper, but I knew she couldn't
read it. She was no star gazer. And certainly no dream
chaser. Her feet were planted too firmly on the ground.
Except, of course, when she turned into a dragon.

CHAPTER ONE

HOT MESS

The house was small and nondescript, and right smack in the middle of a shockingly populated area. This, though, was the best thing about the hot mess that was Las Vegas. Hiding in plain sight. Mixing in with loud, messy crowds of strangers. Conducting top secret meetings in rows of cookie-cutter houses.

I parked my black, brand spanking new Dodge Challenger at the curb and approached the house cautiously. My two-handed, double-bladed battle axe stayed in the trunk, unfortunately. I had a small pistol strapped to my ankle, hidden under the hem of my boot-cut jeans. A large knife was strapped to my other ankle. I wasn't expecting trouble at this meeting, but ruling the idea out completely went against every instinct I had.

My weapons were a considerate gift from my ex. *Ex-ish*? Hell, I didn't know what he was, but he'd supplied me with everything he thought I'd need on short notice.

It had been a nice thought, but I was already itching for my old, familiar arsenal, which had been lost when I'd been captured by my deranged relatives. I'd escaped, but hadn't been exactly in the mindset to find my confiscated stash as I'd bolted from the place in my dragon form, then promptly flown far, far away.

I knocked softly on the light blue door of the tiny stucco house. It was the darkest house on the street, the porch lit only by the streetlights. From what I could see of the inside from the small, twin front windows, every light inside of the house was off, as well.

The place looked deserted. There was even an old for sale sign in the tiny desert landscaped front yard.

I wondered briefly if I was somehow at the wrong address when the door flew open and a hard hand yanked me inside. A harsh voice that I recognized well kept me from lashing out at the sudden contact. "About time," Caleb told me, shutting the door quietly, then dragged me further into the dark house.

I shook him off, waving him ahead of me when he shot me a glance.

I certainly didn't need the sociopath chameleon alien to hold my hand.

He led me down a dark hallway to a door with faint light showing through the bottom. I was surprised, when he opened it, that it led to a basement. Basements were hard to come by in Vegas, especially in a tiny house like this one. But it did explain why the rest of the house was completely dark.

Caleb waved me down the narrow stairway first, closing the door very quietly behind us.

I just blinked for a moment when I saw the inhabitants of the top secret basement meeting place, and what they were doing.

Christian and Luke both rose as I entered, but I didn't miss what filled their computer screens, the bright colors vivid even across the room.

Christian was the dragon slayer to my dragon, we were an odd pairing but it was hardly the oddest thing about me.

In fact to me it made a strange sort of sense to my way of thinking.

I've never needed an archenemy, I've always had myself.

So of course I made my natural enemy into my best friend. It was decades ago and he was one of a very small number of dragon slayers that lived in the States. When I'd found out he was living in my city, I'd scoped him out and even befriended him just to keep eyes on him and suspicion off me and my sister, but the calculation had ended there. Everything that our friendship became I attributed to enjoying each other's company and making each other laugh. Normal friendship stuff had superseded all the natural instincts. I personally thought it was a heartwarming story even if he had tried to kill me once he finally found out what I was.

Christian positively beamed at me, rushing forward to lift me up in a bone-crushing hug, spinning me around and talking all at once. "We missed you, girl. And you're all glowy and golden. Pretty. Is that what color your dragon is?"

I didn't answer, since he was both squeezing the air out of me and not stopping long enough to let me get a word in.

Caleb managed to cut in with an answer. "The pictures I saw of her landing on the roof looked to be pale gold, or even silver, in the dark."

"Ohhh," Christian said, setting me down to study me. He took a lock of my hair between his fingers, rubbing it. "It's so bright, it looks like it could rub off."

I shrugged it off, not really worried about the after-effects of my dragon trance. I knew that they would fade away, eventually. I pointed at his computer. "How's WoW treating you these days? Is that a new patch? Please don't tell me that you made me come here for a top secret World of Warcraft party," I told him archly. If they had, I was going to be royally pissed.

Christian waved a cursory hand at the gaming computers set up in the corner. "That? Naw. That was just to kill time."

I looked at Caleb. He met my gaze with a very blank expression. "No, Jillian, we did not invite you here for a gaming party," he said, his tone slightly disgusted.

I supposed that, while I could have expected something that silly from Christian, I should have known better with Caleb involved.

I was suddenly distracted by Luke, who had moved close behind me and gone to his knees, his head lowered.

Now Luke, he wasn't a friend but a strange complication.

Oh Lord, he was still doing that.

I sighed.

"Um, hey, Luke. How's it going?" I asked, patting his head rather awkwardly.

"Good, Mistress Jillian, now that I've gotten to see you again. My Mistress is even more beautiful than I remembered."

Christian giggled like a school boy. I glared at him. I had no idea what to do with a submissive man. Generally, the men I hung out with were sarcastic, crude, dominant, aggressive, borderline or not so borderline psychotic, violent to the bat-shit crazy degree, and sometimes just plain obnoxious. *None* of those qualities could be called submissive. Frankly, I didn't even know what to do with a man that didn't give me shit just for breathing. Which reminded me. . .

I pointed a finger at Christian. "You need to stop baiting Dom. It's gotten old already."

His giggles died until he was just smiling at me, an almost

fond expression on his face.   "You know I'd do almost anything for you, girl, but I won't do *that*."

I closed my eyes and counted to ten. This meeting was not off to a productive start.

Caleb spoke, finally bringing up the reason I had come. "Tianlong is still in town, though the rest of his people left months ago. Luke here has joined his household, becoming one of his favorite pets. He overheard news of another dragon visiting Vegas, one of the Chinese, and he thinks it might be Drake. Luke needs to get back undercover very soon, but he refused to go without getting to see you, since he unfortunately overheard us talking about your return."

Caleb gave Luke a very unfriendly look. "Well, here she is. Anything you want to say before you go back?"

Luke just shook his head, darting a quick glance at my face, then looking back down at my feet. "No. Everything I need to say to Mistress Jillian I've said in the letters that Christian is holding for her. And I have gazed upon her beauty. I can go back to my duties with a light heart."

I shook my head at him, exasperated, but still, I tried to be nice. I could do nice. Sort of. "You're, um, doing a good job, Luke. Thank you for helping us."

He kissed my feet suddenly, and I backed hastily away, the room filling with Christian's most obnoxious laugh.

"I am not worthy of your thanks," Luke said, prostate on the ground.

I cringed, but tried to talk some reason into him. "You are, Luke. Of course you are. I'm proud of you. It sounds like you're doing a really good job, and it's a very selfless thing that you're doing to help my sister."

He turned his head until his cheek lay on the basement's concrete floor, a look of near bliss on his face. "Mistress is so kind. I live to please you, Mistress Jillian," he said.

I sent Caleb a wide-eyed help me kind of look. Luke's kind

of adoration made my skin literally crawl, and I didn't know what the hell to do with it, especially since I owed the strange hunky sub so much for his unexpected help.

Caleb gave me his little shrug. That shrug said it all: *Who knows? Who cares? Not me. Deal with it.* It was Caleb in a nutshell.

And Christian was even less helpful, of course, just clutching his belly and laughing at me. If he'd been a few feet closer, I'd have kicked him.

"Get going, Luke," Caleb finally said, after an awkward pause. "You know how to contact me if you learn anything useful."

I breathed a sigh of relief when he finally made his embarrassingly adoring goodbyes.

Caleb seemed unaffected by the uncomfortable exchange, getting back to the point after Luke had gone. "We're as sure as we can be that Tianlong doesn't have Lynn. And we're nearly positive that the Chinese took her. That makes Drake our most likely suspect. He's due in town in five days. We need to have a plan for when he gets here. I say we kidnap him, torture him for information, and get this mess figured out, once and for all."

I processed the information while he paused for long moments.

Christian showed considerable restraint, being that he was a dragon slayer and we were talking about an enemy dragon. For all of a minute. "And then we slay his ass!"

I sent him a baffled look, opening my mouth to retort. Caleb beat me to it. "No. We keep him until we have Lynn back. After that, whatever. Who cares? But we use him *alive*, as a hostage, until we get her back."

Christian just sighed, not a bit surprised. "A slayer's gotta try, ya know?"

I rolled my eyes. "It's easy to say we'll kidnap him.

Harder to do it. We have a plan for that?"

Caleb smiled, his cold, creepy smile. "Yes. You owe Tianlong a date. It's time to deliver."

I groaned. I had been a tiny bit busy since I'd made that promise. I had completely forgotten the stupid thing. "It's not a date. I promised him a meeting."

He gave his little shrug. "You need to set it up, in six days, with the druids to act as intermediaries. I'm sure you can talk Dom into that, for your own safety and all. Drake won't want to come anywhere near that meeting, being that he has to know that you'll suspect he has your sister."

"This will hopefully tie up Tianlong and the druids for a few hours, leaving Drake to Christian and me. And since the druids clearly won't approve of kidnapping one of the few dragons that they aren't actively warring with, you need to get as many of them involved with that meeting as you can manage. Make it real official, real political, and real long-winded. Hell, work the jealousy angle with Dom. If he knows that Tianlong wants you to have his dragon babies, that mess could last for days. If we really luck out, the whole thing might dissolve into outright war. You just have to get your psycho ex mad enough. You seem to have a talent for that. The more time you give us to work, the better our chances are of snatching Drake."

Christian finally piped in, helpful as ever. "We'll call it, 'Operation: Baiting the Bear and Snatching the Dragon.'"

"We're not calling it that," I retorted instantly.

I closed my eyes, rubbing my temples. Caleb's plans were usually solid, but this one already made me want to beat my own head against the wall. There was no question that I'd rather be in on the kidnapping part, as opposed to the whole meeting fiasco.

"Fine," I said finally, "I'll talk to Dom."

"Good. And while you're at it, get him to set up a meeting

for us with their captured dragon."

My eyes snapped open. Dom had mentioned something about that. . . and then promptly distracted me. "Who is it?" I asked Caleb.

His mouth hardened. Touchy subject. "We don't know. We don't know *anything* about him, and we haven't been allowed to speak to him. They have him held in some sort of underground compound in the desert, but I haven't been able to get close enough to check it out. Dom won't tell us a thing. He wouldn't even discuss the prisoner with us, until he saw you again."

"Bastard thought we knew where you were," Christian piped in. It *had* been an unusually long period of silence for him. "He thought that we just weren't telling him." He sounded disgruntled, his English accent growing thicker, at the thought.

I had to smile just a touch at that. Everyone in this room knew that if they *had* known where I was, and I hadn't wanted them to tell Dom, there's no way in hell that they would have, so him getting defensive about it was just good comedy. And very typical Christian.

"I'll talk to him about that, too," I assured them.

"Make sure to stipulate that we *all* get to talk to the dragon," Caleb said, a hard glint in his eye.

I arched a brow at him. He was very much overestimating my skills of persuasion, but I supposed I'd try. "I'll see what I can do. In the morning. Dom didn't seem too happy with me when I left. I'm going to give him some time to cool off before I start asking for favors."

Caleb shrugged. "No one knows how to play Dom like you do, so I'll leave it to your discretion."

I gave him a very hard look for that one. "That's going a little far. I do not *play* Dom."

Christian coughed slightly, muttering, "*Like a fiddle,*" under his breath.

I didn't look away from Caleb, who had started it, but I suddenly had the strong urge to deck Christian.

Caleb met my eyes steadily. "Just calling a spade a spade. You can look at it through the filter of your emotions, if that makes you feel better, but I see it solely for what it is."

I felt my temper boiling, though I knew Caleb well enough to see that he could never understand my feelings for Dom. "And that would be?"

"Extremely useful. I don't see that as a bad thing. On the contrary. Wrapping one of the most powerful druids around your littlest finger is a very good play. But we're getting off track. If you won't ask him tonight, I have something else planned."

I stayed silent, just waiting for him to continue.

I was trying real hard not to be pissed about his assessment of my relationship with Dom. I had never been so mercenary, never set out to make him utterly obsessed with me. And I certainly hadn't chosen to stay just as obsessed with him, though no one ever seemed to notice *my* feelings.

I knew that the druids saw me as the cold bitch that had played with Dom's emotions. I was used to that. Having my own friends thinking that. . . stung. But that was just how Caleb's mind worked, so how upset could I get about it, really? And Christian was, well, an ass, likely giving me grief just because it tickled his fancy. I should have been used to them both, but I struggled for endless moments to stifle my rage and hell, my hurt.

Why was I being so sensitive? Was it the dragon trance, still keeping some hold on me? Was I feeling a sudden bout of postpartum depression? I really didn't know.

Finally, when I thought I had a good handle on it, at least enough to drop the subject for the moment, I spoke. "What did you have planned?"

Caleb smiled his cold little smile. "A surprise. I'll ride with you in your car. Christian, you follow us in yours."

Christian was nearly vibrating in anticipation. "I love surprises."

"It's not for you," Caleb said coldly.

Christian shrugged. "So? I still like surprises."

I wondered, not for the first time, how these two men could be friends, spend significant time with each other, when they were very nearly polar opposites.

"I *don't* like surprises," I told Caleb. He knew that. Hell, *everyone* knew that.

He gave me his little shrug. "This surprise is unavoidable, so you might as well get it over with."

I studied him closely, though I knew that was pointless. Caleb was exactly as readable as he wanted to be. It could have been a mimic thing. I had no idea, since I'd never met another of his kind. I mused that it may not have been a bad thing. The thought of more than one Caleb in the world just boggled the mind.

Being enigmatic and hard to read was one thing, expecting me to go blind into some surprise situation was quite another. "I'm not walking into anything blind, Caleb," I told him frankly.

In a way, I trusted Caleb. He'd played reliable backup for me too many times to count, and he had obviously been actively involved in trying to find my sister, even without my having to ask. I had also played his backup many a time, so you could say we were even-steven.

Yes, I trusted Caleb to do exactly what he said he would, but only that. His keeping secrets left too many gray areas for my peace of mind. I wasn't playing along until the rules were very clear. He knew me well enough to get that.

Finally, he caved, but he didn't look pleased about it. Like I cared. "Christian and I were in on the raid. You know, the one that attempted to rescue you. We found some of your goodies there, and we were also nice enough to scour the desert for you, at the spot where you were taken. We recovered most of your weapons. They aren't here. I'm keeping them at another location. Would you like to go get them?" He showed me his teeth in what the twisted bastard probably thought was a smile.

Now that was more like it. I nodded. "Let's do it."

CHAPTER TWO

SOCIOPATH CHAMELION ALIEN

I have a druid tail," I told Caleb as I pulled away from the house. Christian was parked in the back of the house where a small alleyway was attached to the garage. I'd heard his loud race car speed away before we'd even gotten into my car.

"Of course you do," Caleb responded, his tone dry. "And if I know anything at all about Dom, your gear is covered in tracking devices, and so is this car. We'll take care of it."

I sent him a look. Caleb's plans usually worked for what he intended them to, but I couldn't exactly count on him to take Dom's reaction into account. In fact, considering their history, I could pretty much assume that pissing Dom off royally would make Caleb's day.

"Is there a reason why we have to lose them so fast tonight?" I asked. I didn't like being tracked or followed either, but I wanted the trouble I would get for going straight off the radar even less.

"Your things are at a location that I would like to keep private. The druids keep enough damned tabs on me. My biggest weapon stash in town is not their business."

Fair enough. Couldn't blame him there. Knowing Caleb, he'd have things in that stash that would get him imprisoned or worse.

Of course, that didn't mean I wouldn't be catching all sorts of hell for losing my tail later. I would be worrying about that *later*, though, since I very much wanted my weapons back. It wasn't even a question.

"Make a left at the next light," Caleb told me.

I did, watching the car that followed rather closely behind me. Whoever had been put on tailing duty wasn't even bothering to be subtle about it. They must not have heard much about me.

"Make a right, here," Caleb said as I drew almost even with a small side street.

I had to swerve rather crazily to make the turn, since he'd given me so little notice. "Maybe *you* should have driven," I told him as I evened the car out, watching the dark SUV behind us careen wildly into the turn just behind us.

"This is more entertaining," he told me dryly, and I shot him a look. His expression was deadpan, of course, but I knew that he was being very literal. Caleb did seem to find it endlessly entertaining to mess with me. And the annoyed druids behind us would certainly be icing on his cake.

"Right," he said, and I had to make another sharp turn, even going slowly.

"Right," he said again, maybe two minutes later.

"U-turn," he said, when I had nearly passed another street.

"Dick," I muttered, but I followed his instructions.

"Wouldn't you like to know," he shot back without expression.

Actually, I kind of would. I couldn't even be sure what sex the sociopath chameleon alien was, really. His preferred form was male, but that didn't mean a damn thing. I'd seen Caleb mimic me with perfect accuracy, and his sexuality, hell, that was anybody's guess. We'd known him for years, decades even, and he'd only ever showed a leaning towards the A-sexual variety. Was there a specific sexuality for people who only got a hard-on for super badass weapons?

"Not firsthand, that's for sure," I shot back. Never hurt to be perfectly clear about things like that.

He snorted, an unusual noise from his usually stoic self. I shot him a look. His little smile was as good as a shit-eating grin on somebody else. "Trust me, you're safe there. There's only one thing I want your body for."

My mind flashed back to the night before I'd done my little disappearing act. He'd been mimicking me then, wearing an obscene outfit that still made my cheeks heat in embarrassment.

"I really don't like the sound of that," I told him, my tone hard.

He gave his little shrug. "Nothing is free, Jillian. I know you know that. Don't balk at my methods. There may come a time that I'll need to mimic you perfectly. It may make all the difference between success and failure. You are a complicated woman. Complicated takes practice, even for me."

He was full of shit. I just knew it. The bit about needing practice, and the implication that he'd been mimicking me for fun. I tried to level with him. "You are not allowed to mimic me for anything…bad. Got it?"

His smile was chilling. "I can live with that. That gives me a lot of wiggle room, though, you understand?"

I sighed. "I understand that your help isn't free. Getting the best gun in the world at my back will cost me. That I understand."

"Yes," was all he said to that.

"Left," he said, a few minutes later. I didn't even know

where we were anymore. The small streets in this area were barely lit, and huge concrete barriers lined the streets, small, dark houses nearly hidden on the other side of those barriers.

"Pull into this parking lot," he said, and I did.

It was a small, deserted lot. The large, nondescript warehouse attached seemed disproportionately large for the lot. Caleb pulled something out of his pocket, pointing it at the building. A large panel that I hadn't even realized was a garage door slid open smoothly and quickly. I pulled in without a word. It shut directly behind us. The druids would be getting pissy in a hurry about that one.

"Take off your jeans, shoes, and your bra. Leave your phone in the car, too, of course," Caleb said brusquely, opening his door and getting out.

I did so, sighing. The repercussions were probably going to suck, but he was right. The druids would have slipped tracking devices into all of those, and taking the time to find them would only aggravate things. "You have more clothes for me, perchance?"

"Nope," he said without a hint of remorse.

Braless, shoeless, and pant-less, I followed Caleb out of a door on the opposite side of the building from where we'd entered.

Christian was there, car running, door opened.

I got to crawl into the cramped back of his super tiny sports car.

Christian hooted at me. "Looks like I missed the party. I suddenly feel overdressed."

I rolled my eyes at him.

Caleb got in quickly behind me. "Drive fast," he said brusquely, shutting his door very quietly.

Christian took off like the hounds of hell were behind us. That, or some very pissed off druids.

"I at least need pants," I complained, after we'd raced

through half of the city, Christian finally driving rather sedately, for him.

"I'll have something at the house," Caleb said. "No bras, though," he added.

Beggars couldn't be choosers, and I'd be happy just for some pants. I was surprised that Caleb even had those, since he had no need for clothing that I'd ever seen. As he could mimic people, so could he mimic clothes. I'd asked him once if he ever got cold. He had simply said no, without elaborating. Typical Caleb. I was lucky to have gotten an answer at all.

Lynn had told me that she'd tried to touch his clothing once, to see if it actually felt like clothing, since it was obviously mimicked. She'd told me that I should never ever try that, and that the only thing she'd learned from the experiment was not to mess with Caleb.

I'd had plenty of casual contact with him, grabbing his arm, or having him adjust a weapon's harness for me here and there, but I'd heeded her words. Leave his clothes alone. It was sort of like asking me or Lynn about our age. A touchy subject all around. No possibility of getting a useful answer and endless potential to piss us off. Lose, lose.

We ended up in a neighborhood much like the one we'd begun in. A smallish house on a street crowded with cookie-cutter houses. It was a quiet neighborhood, the area neither particularly good or bad. Which, being Vegas, made it kind of bad. But only one meth-house on the block was not as bad is it could be. Yes, I know, I'd make a horrible Las Vegas realtor.

I didn't mention that Caleb hadn't bothered to blindfold me, or that Christian had obviously known where this place was without needing directions. Either Caleb was growing more trusting, or he was planning to ditch the house soon. I didn't ask which, since he'd never give me a straight answer for a question like that.

Christian pulled his tiny car into the carport, and we filed out silently.

No one said a word as we entered the dark house. Like the other house, this one was completely dark, and Caleb didn't turn on any lights as he led us through it. He told us to stop in the hallway, approaching a door about six feet away by himself. He typed in a code, then did a tongue scan to open the dark steel door.

Yes, a tongue scan. Only Caleb.

He pointed a finger at me. "No one is to know about the tongue thing," he told me.

I just nodded, eyes wide in the dark. Weird sociopath chameleon alien. So there was something distinctive enough about his tongue that it could be considered identifying. I hadn't particularly wanted to know that, in fact I found it disturbing, but I still made a note of it. In the very small mimic file in my brain, it went under the tab: More weird shit I've learned about Caleb.

Caleb led us into another basement, only turning the light on when we were all inside, and the door was shut behind us.

I started to walk down the stairs ahead of him once the lights were on.

"Wait," he called, his tone casual. Still, I stopped on a dime. In the world of heinously scary, crazy booby traps, I imagined that Caleb was King. And I didn't imagine for a second that what he claimed was his biggest weapons' stash in the city didn't have a failsafe, or ten.

He led us down the stairs, his steps very calculated. I watched his feet, seeing that he seemed to be stepping out a sort of pattern on the stairs as we descended.

"Do we need to follow your steps?" I asked him, hesitating behind him.

"No. Just don't go ahead of me. The system is set up to

allow me two companions."

"What happens if there's less than two?" I asked.

"Nothing."

"What happens if there's more than two?" I tried.

Christian must have already known all of these answers. Otherwise, I couldn't have imagined him not asking at least some of these questions himself.

"Boom," Caleb said.

"Boom?" I asked.

Christian snorted. "Boom is a horrible explosion noise. It's too simple. At least say Kaboom! Or make a cool noise accompanied by a gesture." Christian demonstrated enthusiastically, making his hands into a ball that grew bigger and bigger, finally throwing his arms out in the universal sign for *explodes.*

I laughed. Caleb just gave his little shrug. "Boom gets the point across. If this house is breached, no more house."

I arched a brow at him, trying not to get mad. "Just the house?" I asked.

He gave that evil little shrug. "No more block."

I shook my head at him, my face tight. "You can't put the entire neighborhood at risk just to keep your secrets." My tone was hard.

"You can't stop me," he said, his own voice just as hard. He must have some very nasty secrets here indeed, to go to such lengths, and be so open with me about it. "Trust me, if this place is breached, this block going down is the least of our problems."

Is ignorance bliss? Hell no. But I still didn't want to know any more about this Pandora's box of a house. Uncharacteristically, but not all that surprisingly, I stopped asking questions after that.

The basement was spartan, seeming almost empty, though it was a very tiny space considering the size of the house. I saw why before I could think much about it.

Caleb used his creepy tongue scan to access a panel in the smooth, dark gray wall. He very deliberately angled away from us so we couldn't get a good look at his tongue while he did so. Fine by me.

An entire section of the wall just sort of lifted, and I stepped back, startled at the unexpected moving wall.

There was some kind of closet set up inside, though all I could make out was one large silver chest and a smallish black dresser. Other than that, it seemed empty.

"Your weapons' stash doesn't play well with others," Caleb told me idly, stepping into the small space.

Perhaps my mind had been shying away from it. Perhaps I was very, very good at denial. Perhaps it was the dragon trance that made my mind forget the little things, like, oh, say a blood drinking war-axe that liked to get into my head, aggravating my already unhealthy bloodlust to a fever-pitch within a small amount of time, chanting kill, kill, kill until I fed it the blood that it craved.

Whatever it was that had made me very conveniently forget about the pain in the ass that was Torst, Caleb's words quickly made me remember.

Right on the tail of that thought was another. If Caleb had recovered Torst for me, the damned axe would be in my head by now. But he wasn't. Did that mean that Caleb *hadn't* recovered the cursed thing?

That possibility was almost worse than the thought that he had. If he hadn't recovered Torst, that meant that it was either lost in the desert, which was bad, bad, bad. Or else it meant that my deranged relatives had ahold of it, which was worse, worse, worse.

Caleb relieved my mind (kind of) when he opened the silver chest.

CROSSING FIRE

CHAPTER THREE
EXACTLY LIKE A NUTCASE

I saw the thing in the chest and braced myself for the onslaught.

I was both relieved and chagrined that Caleb had in fact recovered my bastard of a blood-thirsty axe. Or at least, it looked like he had…

I shot him a look. "What the hell? That looks like Torst, but he's not talking. Torst never shuts up."

Christian snorted. "You sound like a nutcase. An axe can't talk."

I rounded on him. "Torst can. He's in my head if I'm even in the same building." As I spoke, I pointed at my temple, showing him where Torst 'talked to me.'

Exactly like a nutcase would do.

Christian's brows shot up into his artfully messy blond hair. "I knew that *you* talked to Torst, but this is the first I've heard of him talking back. And here I just thought you were being funny when you had one-sided conversations with your bloodthirsty pet axe." I could tell by his cheerful tone that he was making fun of me, which wasn't a shocker. Christian would stop giving me shit at about the moment his heart stopped beating. He continued, "And what does the chatty axe say to you?"

I glared, but it was half-hearted at best. Having a talking pet axe did qualify me as at least borderline crazy.

"He says, 'I thirst,' a lot. And threatens to kill me. And threatens to kill *you*."

Christian pointed at himself, letting out his most infectious laugh that was hard not to at least smile with. *"Me?* What did I ever do to Mr. Thirsty?"

I shrugged, not even trying to keep my smile back now. "It's not personal. He threatens to kill all of my friends. And ya know, enemies, of course. He's not particular."

Christian tapped his temple in exactly the same spot that I had. "You should get some help for those voices in your head."

"Yes. If by help you mean someone that can dispose of magical, immortal, bloodthirsty axes," I shot back, unfazed, and not at all optimistic that I'd ever be so lucky as to actually find such help.

Christian opened his mouth, just the look on his face telling me that he was about to say something ornery, when Caleb cut in. "Trust me, this is Torst. Take him."

"Why is he so quiet?" I asked him suspiciously.

Caleb just gave me dead eyes. "Maybe you should just enjoy the silence, instead of *questioning* it. Take your axe."

I eyed the silver chest, taking a cautious step towards it. "Why does this feel like a trap?" I asked the room at large.

Caleb sighed, looking annoyed. He strode to the dresser, the only other thing inside of the strange closet. He opened the bottom drawer, pulling out a huge battle axe that shone even in the dim light of the closet, the brighter basement light behind me setting off the various jewels set into the handle in a rather dazzling display. It was pretty.

Warkitten was a showy axe, to be sure, but still a good one. It had been my favorite trusty weapon for over a decade, and if life sucked less, would be again. It was the weapon I preferred, the weapon I wanted. But I had promises to keep, and lives to save, namely those that Torst would take in someone else's hands. I couldn't trust anyone else to deal with the shit-storm that was Torst. I'd had a brief respite while it'd rotted in that storage unit back on Warm Springs road, but I knew I couldn't push my luck like that again.

Caleb held Warkitten out to me, gripping the middle of the oversized battle axe so I could take the hilt easily.

I grabbed her with a little sigh. Even her handle was perfect, the grip having been adjusted with the softest leather over the hard metal until it was literally made for my hand.

Christian snorted. "It's like Warkitten is your mistress, and Torst is your wife. You're in love with the one, and obligated to the other. Weirdo."

I had to laugh. And not even at his strange little analogy. "You dork. I'm a girl. Torst would be my husband, not my wife, in your screwed up little scenario."

He just shrugged. "If you say so."

"You have to take Torst. I've bought you about a week of its silence," Caleb said quietly, not enjoying our not so witty repartee in the slightest. "I can't keep that thing, as much as I'd love to. It's not compatible with the hammer."

I just blinked in surprise, because I'd forgotten about that cursed hammer, and also because what he'd just said was freaking strange. "Our weapons aren't compatible?" I asked him slowly.

He rolled his shoulders, looking way too agitated about it for my peace of mind. "One person having them both in possession is a recipe for disaster. One wants power, the other blood. It's been *bad*. The hammer is the safer bet for me. I don't trust myself with the axe. As I said, it is a *bad* combination."

I felt dread curl in my belly. That kind of a confession from Caleb hadn't come from nothing. If he said that it had been bad, and Torst was involved, then the gods only knew how much blood had been spilled.

"What happened?" I asked very carefully.

He grew still as a stone. "You see that he's silent. I don't like voices in my head. I've been *keeping* him silent. I'm sure you know what keeps him silent."

My hand tightened on Warkitten. "Not innocents," I said, trying real hard not to make it a question.

He shrugged that little shrug, and I wondered how hard it would really be to take his head. "Innocent is such a strange word. Such a strange concept. Who is innocent, really?"

"Most humans are innocent," I told him, my voice suddenly as cold as the grave. "And *all* children are innocent."

"If you take time-travel into account, no one's innocent on a long enough timeline," Christian said unhelpfully.

"Very funny," I said, rolling my eyes.

They looked intensely at each other and then at me.

"He's joking," Caleb said which made me think it actually wasn't a joke now. "And I didn't kill any children," Caleb added.

"But you did kill humans. Who and why? And what else?"

"Let's just say, Torst got to sample a little bit of everything. Even using your flawed logic on the issue, though, none of them could be considered innocent."

I looked to Christian.

He held up his hands defensively. "We've been together almost constantly. Things have been bloody, but he didn't kill anybody that didn't need killing, even with Torst in the mix."

I looked back at Caleb, far from appeased. Was he proving a point, trying to make me see that I needed to take Torst? He'd been riling me, and I wanted to know the reason. And of course, I still didn't trust him to use what he called my flawed logic correctly. Christian had said that the two of them had been together 'almost constantly,' which left some disturbing wiggle room.

"I'll take the axe, I always planned to, but why are you trying so hard to piss me off?" I asked him tightly.

"I just wanted to make sure that things are clear between us, in case you hear anything…later. Now you can't say that I lied to you."

I suddenly felt exhausted, just so impossibly tired that I couldn't deal with another moment of this pissing contest. "You know that won't mean shit if I find out you've done something that I can't accept."

He inclined his head. "I'm well aware. Take the axe."

With a sigh I ran covetous hands over my axe 'mistress,' wishing that I could have even one thing that I wanted in life, even if it was just this pretty axe.

Instead, I always just got a mix of hard choices that were bitter as hell to swallow.

I took Warkitten back to the dresser, pausing at the chest for a long moment, glancing between the two weapons.

Torst was a huge, plain, beast of an axe, not a pretty thing about him, and certainly not a jewel in sight. His handle was cold metal. If you tried to wrap it, or refit it, he just reshaped however he damn well pleased. He looked like he'd be uncomfortable to handle, but that wasn't really the issue at all. The issue was that when you were wielding him, you'd be so consumed with bloodlust that you wouldn't give a thought to how the grip felt.

I thought of all of my deranged relatives and how I didn't have a clue just how they'd gotten that way. I'd always stood by the idea that the family dementia was not a forgone conclusion, but what else could I do? I supposed I could have my BFF dragon slayer kill me, but that seemed like quitting. I was not a quitter, just a runner. There's a difference. Or at least I liked to think so.

No matter how I tried to spin it, though, I just couldn't imagine that becoming the warden for that axe again was good for my sanity. I wasn't exactly short on bloodlust to begin with. That's why the thing had stayed in a storage container for nearly a decade, but I couldn't do something like that again. It had been stupid, and irresponsible, and a punishment for the cursed thing. It had also been a miracle that nothing truly heinous had happened as a result. That axe in the hands of even the most harmless human on the planet was bad news.

With ill-grace and a bad attitude, I shut away Warkitten, and reached for Torst. I couldn't even feel too relieved about the fact that he stayed silent at my touch. That silence had apparently been bought with a lot of gods-only-know what blood.

Caleb emptied out the top two drawers of the dresser, filling two large duffle bags.

"Two goody bags to go for the crazy woman," Christian said cheerfully.

I punched him in the arm.

Caleb tossed me my axe shoulder harness, and I caught it, but just looked at it.

"We aren't sleeping here?" I asked.

Both men sent me a nearly identical, baffled look. That was a disturbing new development. The two of them had definitely bonded while I'd been away.

"You've become quite the copacetic pair. Will you two be sending out Christmas cards together this year?"

Christian laughed. "In a prom pose. I call big spoon."

"This is not a place to sleep," Caleb said, ignoring us. "This is a cover for a stash. I never stay here for more than twenty minutes, as I don't really feel like getting blown to pieces in my sleep if someone tries to breach the place."

Fair enough. "Lead on," I told them. I needed sleep.

CHAPTER
FOUR
TELEPATHIC EGG

W e wound up staying at yet another small, cookie-cutter house less than twenty minutes away. This one belonged to Christian.

"I wonder how many houses you have between the two of you," I mused as Christian pulled into a two-car garage.

I saw Christian shoot Caleb a glance. "I have six properties in and around the Vegas valley, but I think it's safe to say we'll never hear how many Caleb has."

"That would be a safe bet," Caleb agreed succinctly.

I wasn't surprised.

"Don't feel bad, Jillian," Christian said as he opened his door. "We have a lot of houses, but you have a brand new, shiny Dodge Challenger. Or at least you did, until we ditched it. Let's hope that Dom didn't tear it to pieces in a jealous fit of rage."

I grimaced. That wasn't going to go over well, but Dom really should have known better than to have me tailed.

The house was small, with three tiny bedrooms, and I crashed hard on the twin bed that Christian showed me to.

When I woke again it was light out. Still early morning, by

the direction of the sun. That was good, since taking all day to get back to my abandoned car would only aggravate things, I was sure.

Someone had left me jeans and even a sports bra that almost fit. It was downright sweet. I got dressed and grabbed my axe. It was still mysteriously quiet.

Christian and Caleb dropped me off a full block away from the garage where I'd left the car. Caleb handed me a garage door opener as I climbed out of the backseat.

"*Pussies*," I called to them loudly as they peeled away like they were being chased, but I couldn't really blame them. Dom wouldn't hurt me, no matter how mad he was. No one in their right mind could assume that Caleb and Christian would get the same treatment.

I was somewhat relieved when I arrived at the garage and found no Dom.

Of course, there *was* a team of druids swarming the place, and they converged on me the instant they saw me.

They flanked me, stopping about four feet away, all of them looking wary in their three-piece-suits.

I didn't recognize any of them.

There was one woman in the group. She had dark hair, a level stare, and she spoke for the lot. "Are you unharmed? The Arch was alarmed when we found your car abandoned, and your tracking devices. . . discarded. My first order is to ascertain that you are unharmed."

I studied her, wondering how to get out of this mess. But should I, really? We'd be working with the druids and getting higher up on their shit list was hardly a good idea. "I'm just fine. What was your second order?"

"To contact the Arch and update him."

I nodded at her. "Go right ahead."

She had her cell to her ear, her gaze unwavering on me.

"What's the third order?" I asked.

"To...escort you back to the casino."

I snorted. Escort, my ass.

"Sir," she spoke into the phone. "We found her. She assures us that she is unharmed." She paused. "She came back to her car. She's cooperating." She glanced at me, as though to make sure I hadn't bolted.

She answered a few more questions, then handed her phone to me.

I grimaced as I put it to my ear. This was the part I'd been dreading—facing him myself.

"Hey," I said quietly, not sure what else I could say.

"Hey," he repeated back, his tone icy. "Some foreign. . . diplomats are arriving in town today. We're assembling a task force to combat the rogue dragon threat. We're arranging a meeting this afternoon, and I'd like you to attend."

"Um, sure," I said, still waiting for the other shoe to drop. I couldn't believe that he would just let the issue of me disappearing for the night drop without a word.

"Caleb and Christian need to be there, too, since I assume they'll want to be involved."

I assumed the same. As much as the two of them couldn't stand the druids, they wouldn't be able to resist the chance to join a task force that would have the legal right to take out some dragons. I knew I couldn't.

"I'll let them know," I said.

There was a long pause on the other end. "Thank you." Another long pause. "And could you. . . please return to the casino posthaste. I've set up a secure room for our son, and I'd like you to approve it."

That surprised me, but I agreed to it readily enough.

My approval. . . What a strange way to word it. Dom had never needed anyone's approval for anything.

My security detail at least let me drive myself back to

Dom's casino, though of course they tailed me. I didn't even give them a hard time, driving straight there.

I parked valet, and three of the druids made it to the door before I did, holding it open for me.

Two others grabbed the bags out of my car, following me with them.

"We'll put your bags away for you, ma'am," one of the male druids told me.

Caleb had said he'd earned me a week of silence from Torst, and I tended to trust him about something that important.

"They'll need to be locked up tight," I decided aloud. "No one should have access to them but me." I figured that covered all the bases and bought me some time.

"We'll put them in a safe in your suite," he assured me.

My suite? I wondered about it but figured I'd save that question for Dom since it was a bit embarrassing that I didn't know where I was staying.

Was it his suite of rooms or had I been assigned my own?

I shook off the musings. Time enough for that later. "What are your official orders concerning me?" I asked the female druid.

"To assist you, if needed, and to protect you, if necessary," she answered quickly.

I rolled my eyes. Those duties were bogus, but she wasn't the one to take it up with. It wasn't her fault she'd been assigned as my babysitter.

I opened my mouth to ask her where to go, when the very air around us changed. I shivered, every hair on my body rising as a surge of power made its way to us.

I had no doubts about just who was approaching.

We passed through two sets of doors before we were in the casino. The normal sounds of slots clinking and music seemed drowned out, as though the man approaching had overwhelmed every sense with his overpowering presence.

I met the druid woman's gaze. "Is it always like this now? His power never calms down? He feels like a walking powder keg, and I can't even see him yet."

She looked puzzled by that. "He is the Arch," she said, as though that should explain it. I'd met an Arch or two, and the position most definitely did *not* explain it. I would have bet my life on the fact that there wasn't a druid alive more powerful than Dom, and that power just seemed to be growing.

His face was expressionless, his stance stiff, as he finally turned a corner and came into view.

I figured he was in a bad mood, though I couldn't read it, but something else instantly distracted me. There was a small black patch over his right eye, his wolf's eye. It was a small patch, and didn't seem to be attached by any strings. I'd never seen him wear such a thing before.

"Did something happen to your eye?" I asked him the second he was within ear shot.

One of his dark brows went up. "This way," he said, striding back the way he'd come.

"Is your eye okay?" I asked again, sincerely worried.

"It's fine. I wear this whenever I'm among humans."

"You never used to."

"Things change. Appearances must be kept. The eye could raise questions."

I didn't like that, hated that he had to hide even the physical aspects of who he was in public now.

"Fucking druid politics," I muttered.

I saw a corner of his mouth turn up, but he didn't comment.

"Stay here," he told the druids who had been trailing us as we approached a lone elevator. He used two keys before the doors slid open. I followed him in.

"I spoke to Caleb and Christian about the meeting this afternoon," he said idly as he punched the button on the elevator to send us to the bottom level. "They said they'd be there."

I was tense, waiting for him to say something about me ditching my tail the night before, but he didn't bring it up, and I sure wasn't going to.

"Thank you," I responded. Caleb had made me memorize his current number, but I hadn't had a chance to call yet.

"I know that you work best with those two, and the three of you will certainly be essential for the task force. If there is anyone alive with firsthand experience in dragon-slaying, they aren't on any of our rosters, so you three have a distinct advantage." As he spoke, he took off his eye patch, slipping it into his pocket.

I knew of at least one who had experience slaying nearly the entire female population of my family, though I couldn't imagine he'd be on any druid roster.

"The dragons have at least one slayer, as well," I told him as we disembarked from the elevator. "One with experience killing *many* dragons. He is my father's pet."

He sent me a startled look, and I thought I caught a hint of the worry in his eyes. "I'll need to know all about that. You'll brief me later."

I sighed, knowing I was about to piss him off royally, but unable to help it. "I need to talk to the dragon you have in custody. How about we exchange a briefing for a talking?"

His jaw clenched, but he took it better than I'd thought he would. "We'll discuss it later. For now, I need to walk you through the steps I've taken to secure our son before I have to leave on urgent business. Everything else can wait."

We passed two sets of guards in the hallway before we made it to the next door.

"There will be four guards in this hallway at all times," he explained, "as well as two to guard the elevator doors up top."

He walked me through a hand print scan, eye scan, and voice activated door, inputting my information into all three.

"Who all has access to the vault itself?"

"You, me, and my lieutenants, and one of the seven will be on active guarding duty at all times."

I didn't want to ask, but I couldn't help it. I would never trust the bitch. "I'm assuming Siobhan is the exception to that?"

He sighed. "She'll never be guarding our child, if that's what you're getting at. She's loyal, but I knew you wouldn't approve of that."

"She shouldn't have *access*, either. She'd harm him if she could. You're being naive if you don't believe that."

"She is exempted from guarding, and she would be unable to access the vault if she tried. I haven't even told her about it, though with this many guards, our child won't be a secret from anyone for long. I didn't see another option. Better to err on the side of caution than to rely on discretion alone. Any more questions?"

I glanced around, making sure we were alone. We were in a small, nondescript white room. "Where's your lieutenant now?"

"The next room. They will act as the last line of defense before the vault."

A nine digit code that I made myself memorize took us into the next secure room.

Collin was lounging on a low white couch reading a book when we entered.

He stood, smiling at the sight of us. "Dom! Jillian! Gods, it's good to see the two of you together again. Congratulations on the baby! What a shocker! You do know how to make an entrance, Jillian!"

I smiled, perpetually surprised to run into a friendly face among the druids. Collin always had been the most amiable of the bunch. "Thanks. If it's any consolation, the baby surprised me as much as anyone."

"A twelve year pregnancy!" he laughed. "I can see how that might surprise!"

Dom only nodded to his cousin/lieutenant, going immediately to the next door. Clearly, he wasn't in the mood to chat. "Jillian, come memorize this code."

I obeyed, watching him unlock the combination. I didn't have a photographic memory, by any means—there was too much random junk in my brain—but I could memorize a few nine digit codes if it was crucial.

The watermelon-sized egg lay on a small round bed that sat low to the ground, perched upright on soft white cushions. It was a paler golden today, setting off the metallic tones still present in my own skin.

I had it cradled in my arms before Dom had closed the door behind us. I traced my fingers over the patterns etched in its surface. They changed, I'd noticed, as the egg grew.

I did this for several minutes before I realized that Dom still stood at the closed door. He watched us, face carefully blank, though I saw something raw move behind his mismatched eyes as I studied him.

"Our telepathic egg," I said affectionately.

We shared a warm look.

"I need to go now. I'm late to an important meeting," he said, not moving.

I nodded, my attention going back to the egg.

Dom contradicted himself almost instantly, moving to kneel beside us. He touched one big hand to the egg, the other moved to cup the back of my head. "I've named him," he said quietly.

I shot him a startled look.

"He wanted me to." He sounded a touch defensive, which was downright strange coming from him. "Somehow, through his telepathy, he's picked up knowledge about druid customs. He knew it was my duty to name him, and so he asked me to."

"What did you name him?" I asked.

"Conan."

I nodded. It had been his father's name, and I'd half expected it.

"He told me that he has the wolf's eye. And he speaks Druidic."

That had me speechless for a moment, my mind racing with the implications. "How could he know what color his own eyes are? And how could he learn an entire second language?"

Dom looked less puzzled about that than I was. "The eyes would have a feeling—a changed nature. He says the beast-call wars with the dragon inside of him. You know as well as I that having two natures is a complicated balance. He'll have a bigger challenge ahead of him than most, but he's been given more power, so we can hope that it will balance out. And the Druidic...who can say? He was inside of you for twelve years, and conscious for at least some of it, and if there is a limit to his telepathy, I do not know it."

I knew I didn't need to tell him, but I said it anyway. "No one can know about the telepathy. The things he's picked up about druids already would make him such a target. . ."

He nodded. "I know. No one will hear it from me. I think our biggest concern is that he may reveal the secret himself. We don't know who he might try to contact."

"The girl," a small voice said in my head.

I looked down at Conan's egg, the voice now familiar to me. "What girl?" I asked him.

"The girl you met. The one with the lavender eyes. You need to

let her see me."

The girl from the club where I'd gone to look for Lynn, I recalled. I'd run into her briefly the night before I'd disappeared, and I'd known she wasn't human. I'd sent Luke to find her. If all had gone as planned, she should've been in druid protective custody.

I looked up at Dom. "Did a human named Luke bring you a little girl with purple eyes and dark blond hair?"

He nodded. "She doesn't say much, but we've put her in one of our schools. She's doing well, and she's safe, though we still know nothing about her."

"She's not human."

"So I gathered. What is she, then?"

"I don't know," I answered. The answer came from a different source.

"She's half-dragon kin, half-human. The dragons must not know you have her. She is ours. Her name is Yinlong."

"Ours?" Dom asked.

Somehow, Conan could talk to us both at once. It was insane. And good to know.

"A part of our family. You must let her see me. It is hurting her to stay away."

"I don't understand," I said slowly.

"Hurting her how?" Dom asked.

"I can't explain it. Bring her to see me. Let her have the codes. She is safe. She is family."

Dom and I exchanged a look.

"Not even born yet and already giving orders and keeping secrets," Dom muttered, though his tone was fond, and his mouth was turned up in a smile.

"Will you let her see him?" I asked.

Dom nodded. "I'll bring her myself as soon as I can. She must already know he's a telepath. They've clearly been speaking to each other so there's no reason to keep her away.

I'm not giving her any codes, though."

"You'll learn to trust her, and then you'll give her the codes."

Dom and I shared a look that said *not likely.*

"I have to go. The meeting is in four hours. I'll see you then," Dom said.

He kissed my forehead, then Conan's egg, said something softly in Druidic, and left.

I lay down on the tiny bed with Conan, content just to be near him for a while.

I was not a peaceful soul. I rarely sat down, rarely rested unless it was for required for sleep. But being near Conan was different, or rather, I was different when I was near him. I could lie beside him for hours, doing nothing but tracing his beautiful golden shell.

My world was in chaos, but one thing was clear. Motherhood was changing me.

CHAPTER
FIVE
BAGGAGE-FREE VERSION

Whoa, there. I haven't seen you dressed like a girl in so long, I forgot that you *were* one," Christian said as I stepped off the elevator. He didn't faze me. He usually didn't. But especially not right now. I'd just spent hours with Conan, and it had put me in a good mood.

I was dressed in a short, floral summer dress that I'd picked up at one of the dress boutiques in the casino. It was white with large violets painted across it. My sandals were tan and ridiculously high heeled, considering that I was tall barefoot. Most days I was in the mood for a black T-shirt and jeans but today, apparently, I was feeling my feminine side. I couldn't deny that had a lot to do with the fact that we were meeting with Dom, and this dress showed plenty of skin, from some impressive cleavage, to my shoulders, arms, and a whole lotta leg. It might be too much skin for a business meeting, which was where we were headed, but it made me feel good, so I'd worn it anyway. I'd even made the rare effort of having my hair curled into soft waves. I'd only worn a tiny bit of makeup, but black mascara'd lashes, and pink glossy lips had a dramatic effect with my still gold-touched skin.

I nodded at Caleb and Christian. They were here for the meeting with Dom and the other members of the task force, as well. I welcomed the help. I wouldn't have made this mess the druids' fight, but since my family had done that, I was happy to work with them now that the battle lines were drawn.

I strode through the casino toward the bank of elevators that led to the office wing of the vast building. Caleb and Christian fell into step on either side of me, naturally flanking me. The casual observer probably thought they were my bodyguards.

They were both wearing suits, Caleb all in black, Christian in flamboyant pale gray with a matching shirt and vibrant violet tie, as though we had matched on purpose, the weirdo.

Caleb stood behind us in the elevator, and I didn't have to wonder why for long. We were about halfway to the top when I felt a surge of power behind me.

I turned, looking back.

I cursed.

Christian grinned. "*This* is why I love hanging out with you," he told Caleb.

I rolled my eyes, turning back around. Caleb had grown more powerful while I'd been away. I was sure it had something to do with him owning the hammer. Now it only took him a few seconds to shift forms. No more needing privacy or time for him. And so a black suit clad version of me stood behind me. As much as I wanted to put a stop to it, I let it go. I had strong backup. So they were a little eccentric. He claimed he was practicing playing me. I could see how that might come in handy for the challenges ahead. The *after*, well, that I would worry about *after* all of the dragons that needed killing were killed.

I was very good at prioritizing disasters, and the disaster of Caleb could be handled later.

"Wanna tell me why you're mimicking me when I'm right here?" I asked, just for the hell of it.

"Not really. The main reason is for practice. If I can fool Dom, I will know I have perfected you."

I shivered. That creeped me out. "We need to set up some boundaries about that. Immediately following this meeting."

"Perhaps."

I left it at that. The last thing I wanted to do was rile him up when he was mimicking me at a meeting with Dom. And the only way you ever found out that Caleb was riled was after he had paid you back tenfold. Anyone who spent much time with him learned to tread carefully.

"So how is your egg today?" Christian asked as the elevator reached the top floor. I'd given the boys a brief version of the story about my unexpected child the night before. They were both suitably surprised by that development.

I couldn't keep in a loud, happy laugh. "He's great. His name is Conan. Dom named him after his father. It's a warrior's name."

"Yes, I know." Christian shook the geas on his wrist at me, a carefree smile on his face. "I heard it from Dom when they were adding his name to my geas."

Of course. I didn't know how they'd squeezed that in, but Dom thought of everything. It was his best and worst quality. I was, however, happy about it at that moment.

We headed to reception, the men naturally flanking me again. I assumed we would be waved through, as the sulky ginger girl downstairs had done, but this receptionist held up one finger for us to wait to enter the office.

I raised a brow at the attractive receptionist. She was giving us a perplexed look. Seeing two of me had to be a little confusing. She raised black brows over her stylish glasses at us. She looked like a sexy librarian. I didn't think there were good odds on Christian *not* hitting on her.

"He'll let me know when he's ready for you," she addressed me and Caleb, obviously confused but not asking about the odd situation.

Christian started up a strong flirt with her. She was amenable. He had her severe look turning to a flirtatious smile in under a minute.

I rolled my eyes.

Caleb imitated my expression perfectly.

Shit, he was practicing. I had the thought again that having someone as dangerous as Caleb studying my every move this closely, no matter the reason, was sure to be a double-edged sword, but then again, befriending him had always been a dangerous endeavor.

I froze at the sound of Dom laughing from his office. It was a rare sound, at least as of late. I wondered at the cause of it. Was he wandering around like a giddy fool today, as I was, because of Conan? The thought warmed me.

As Dom's office door started to open, I was surprised when Caleb laced his/my fingers through my own, pulling me a little as he stepped forward toward the door.

Dom stepped through with a tall blond woman, smiling warmly down at her. She could have been my sister, looks-wise. She was tall and thin, with generous curves and long, ash-blond hair. Even her face was similar, with even, Nordic features and blue eyes. They were a much darker blue than mine. But, still, the resemblance was startling. She wore fashionable business attire, her skirt tight and reaching her knees. Her white dress shirt was tucked in snugly, and unbuttoned far enough down her chest to reveal a generous amount of cleavage. Her emerald stiletto heels made my own look like flats, they were so high. Her wavy hair hung long down to her mid-back. She was stunning and beyond polished. And she was certainly Dom's physical ideal.

I should know, since I was the prototype. But perhaps she was the baggage-free version of me.

He'd given her such a warm look.

I stopped moving at the sight of them, forcing Caleb to halt as well. He did so without protest, stepping back until we were side by side again, still holding my hand firmly.

Dom froze as well when his brilliant gaze fell on us, a matching pair of Jillians. His eyes went to our joined hands, and the warmth in them turned instantly chilly. My eyes went to Dom's solicitous hand on the woman's elbow. I knew my own gaze hardened as well. I glanced at Caleb.

He shared my expression. *Damn*, he was good.

"Helen, these are some of the other members of the task force," Dom began without preamble. His tone was icy. Somehow I didn't think that ice was directed at Helen. "The one flirting with my receptionist is Christian."

Christian walked to the woman, straightening his tie. He held out a hand to her, giving her a smile full of all his usual charm. "Pleasure to meet you, Helen." His English accent was more apparent than usual, his voice silky smooth.

She shook his hand, giving him a cool nod. Dom and Helen looked at Caleb and me at the same time, as though they were in sync. "The blond in the dress is Jillian." His voice was impersonal. I felt a stab of something unpleasant in my chest. I schooled my face into its best impassive mask. It came very natural even when I was upset.

I looked at Caleb. *Dammit*, he had that expression down perfectly, too. "The one holding Jillian's hand and mimicking her for some mysterious reason is Caleb. Everyone, this is Helen. Please come in and have a seat, and I will explain."

"Nice to meet you," Helen said in a cold, crisp, British accent. She turned and headed to the large conference table in the office they had just come out of.

Dom stepped to the side, waving us in so that we had to walk past him. In a playful mood, Christian skipped over and grabbed my other hand.

Oh, lord, what was he up to?

He swung our joined hands, grinning. "I felt left out," he explained to the room at large, shrugging.

Caleb and I rolled our eyes. The boys were messing with Dom. What else was new?

I sighed, walking toward the conference room.

The guys walked with me as though it were something we did all the time. Walking hand in hand, the three of us...*Yeah, right.*

We stopped at the doorway. Dom had it blocked so that the three of us couldn't enter all at once. Christian relinquished my hand without protest, gliding to the table and smoothly pulling out a chair with the back facing us, waiting.

Caleb let me enter first, keeping our hands linked and letting me file in ahead of him. It was surreal. Caleb was the least affectionate creature on the planet, possibly every planet, and suddenly he wouldn't stop holding my hand?

I barely made it a step into the room before I was stopped by Caleb's grip.

I glanced back with a questioning look.

I hadn't even sensed Dom moving, but he had a death grip on Caleb's wrist that looked like it might snap it in half.

Caleb's free hand moved instinctively to a spot on his lower back. "Don't," I warned him, knowing he always had nasty tricks up his sleeve. Literally.

"If you pull a weapon on me, you'd best be certain that it is something that can kill me." The hair on the back of my neck stood on end at Dom's dangerously soft growl.

Power crawled along my skin. It was such a strong wave

of it that I wondered if every druid in the building felt the punch of it.

Caleb's hand lowered back to his side, empty. His mouth tightened, and something I'd never thought to see swam behind his eyes.

He was scared of Dom, I realized, stunned. Was fear the thing that made him feel the need to rile the Arch? He had always been like that with him. He loved to rattle the tiger's cage.

Caleb finally released my hand, and I took a few steps back, further into the conference room. Dom still kept hold of his wrist, squeezing so hard I couldn't believe it hadn't snapped like a twig yet.

It was more than a bit odd watching Dom handle a Caleb who looked like me that way.

"I'm not sure if you've heard," Dom said, his voice bleeding like murder into the room, "but touching her has a very steep price. I tore the last man I thought was sleeping with her into little, tiny scraps of flesh. It wasn't a fast kill. I toyed with him. Tortured him until he bled out, and I drank his blood, ate his heart, and took his life's power. I *bathed* in the wreckage of his flesh. I've never enjoyed a kill so much in my life. Even now, knowing he was set up, his death is a fond memory for me, *because his hands were still on her in those pictures.* You don't want to die like that, trust me."

Oh Lord, I thought.

Caleb's little joke had put Dom in a dangerous mood.

"Dom," I spoke up. "You misunderstand." I put a hand on his arm, and he shuddered.

"Sit down, Jillian. That isn't helping," Dom thundered. But moments later he released Caleb, who whipped away from him, sitting down quickly at the seat beside the one Christian held out for me.

CHAPTER
SIX

HERETIC DAUGHTERS' PET

I sat, thanking Christian. He pushed my chair in like the perfect gentleman he wasn't and took the seat to my right.

Dom sat on the opposite side from us, Helen taking the seat to his right.

Who was she? *What* was she?

Dom pointed a finger at Christian. "The same goes for you."

I rolled my eyes. Caleb was back to normal, and I saw him copying me out of the corner of my eye. "I swore a blood oath about that, Dom," I began. "This is all—"

"See now, Jillian," Dom interrupted me, tone black and full of scorn, "that's the problem with being an unrepentant oath-breaker. It makes it so *none* of your oaths have any meaning at all. Especially your oaths to *me*."

Ouch. But, okay, I could see his point there. I inclined my head, my expression perfectly blank.

"What gave me away?" Caleb asked Dom unexpectedly.

"How'd you know I wasn't Jillian?" he clarified when Dom didn't immediately answer, instead just stared at him like he was contemplating how best to slowly dismember him. .

Finally Dom sighed and said, "You were looking at *her* more than at me. She rarely looks away from me. And if she does, it's up or down, but not at other people. At least, not for long. Not when I'm around."

I glared. Arrogant asshole. I tried to keep from cringing. I did not like the way that sounded, but I could hardly dispute it.

"Let's move on, please. Who is Helen?" I asked rudely, as though she wasn't even there. The guys' shenanigans had quickly absorbed my good mood.

Dom raised a brow at me. "Helen is an old friend and a business associate of mine. She's worked closely with the druids for many years now, over in London. But that's not really the pertinent question for this task force. You should be asking, *what* is Helen. Or can you guess?"

I studied her. I still didn't like what I saw. An old friend, huh? *Barf.* Suddenly, Helen sent him a warm glance. Her eyes ran over his body in a familiar, possessive way. And from that knowing look I just suddenly knew for a fact that they'd slept together. She'd tapped that. It was all over her smug, not quite as good-looking as me face. Gods, was it an old fling or something ongoing?

I felt bile rise. I knew about his legion of indiscretions after I'd left him, but seeing it firsthand affected me all over again. I wanted to kill her. I wanted to kill him. It was ridiculous, but that didn't make the rage or the hurt go away.

I had left him, I had courted this, and I had no right to take exception to the things he had done after I was gone, but it didn't make it any easier to live with. Not then and not now.

She cast a look at Christian, and it was disdainful in a way that had my hackles rising. As though I didn't already have a list of reasons to hate her.

She'd taken a particular sort of dislike for him, giving him a look that you would give a traitor to your cause.

A switch clicked on in my brain. The realization of what she was came to me then.

I looked at her slender, elegant wrists. How had I missed that there was a *geas* on one of them? I'd been distracted by the force of nature that was Dom, obviously.

My horrified eyes shot to Dom's. His dazzling blue and gold eyes were studying me intently. "Don't you think you should have warned me first?" I asked him, feeling fury creep up over my body. Fury and a sense of betrayal. My voice was barely more than a whisper.

"What is it? What is she?" Christian and Caleb asked at the same time.

I glared at Dom. He looked down suddenly, but quickly up again. He was uncomfortable, but not nearly enough so.

"She's a slayer," I said, each word forced out of a suddenly tight throat.

"What kind of slayer?" Caleb asked.

I shot him a look, one brow raised. He annoyingly copied it just out of habit. Usually he was quicker on the uptake. "What kind do you think?" I had the rare pleasure of watching an actual expression come over his sociopathic face. Surprise. Being as it was my face and my mood had swiftly turned to shit, it was not as enjoyable as it should have been.

I went back to staring Dom down while Christian had the loudest reaction. "Bloody hell, I've heard of you, come to think of it!"

"Well, I have certainly heard of you," Helen responded dryly. "The Heretic Daughters' Pet is what the other slayers call you now."

My furious gaze shot to her for that. "You don't even

know what that means. I've seen what you call a *pet* firsthand. Christian is *not* enthralled. He's one of my dearest, oldest friends. I would never do anything to mess up his mind. He's not my *pet*."

She gave me a very unfriendly look, but stayed silent.

"You wanted me to walk in on this blind, Dom? Really?" I asked him, venom in my tone, bile rising.

He cleared his throat, looking more uncomfortable by the second. "The geas protects you. We thought of every eventuality."

I felt my skin start to steam with my temper. "*We*? Who is this *we*?" I asked softly.

"Helen and I," he answered.

Bravely, I thought.

I stood, almost too furious to speak.

"She knew that *I* was coming into this, but you kept *me* ignorant, Dom? Have you so little care for my welfare?"

The boys stood up with me.

Christian placed a restraining hand on my arm. I knew it burned him on contact, but he didn't even flinch. "Let's take a walk, Jillian. Cool off a bit."

Dom pointed at Christian. "You, out. I warned you not to touch her," he had the audacity to say. "In fact, everyone leave us. The others aren't expected for another half an hour. Jillian and I need to speak privately for a moment."

Helen placed a familiar hand on Dom's shoulder, and he looked at her questioningly. But he did not remove her hand.

He had the nerve to threaten my boys, but let her touch him like that?

My fist slammed into the thick granite that topped the oversized conference table. With a loud crash, it cracked down the middle. The dumb bitch didn't have the sense to remove her hand even then. "Do you really think that's necessary?" Helen was asking Dom.

Dom saw my intent before anyone else and made a lightning quick move to intercept me. He had me in a rock hard embrace, pinning my arms to my body, before I made it to them. "Out! All of you! Just shut up and get out!" His shout held all of his power to command.

Finally, they listened, making a hasty retreat.

I shook for a good five minutes before I could speak. "How could you, Dom?" I whispered. "I'm vulnerable now that I'm out in the open, and you *invite an extra slayer to town without warning me?* You let me walk into this room blind. How could you betray me like that? Do you want me *dead*?"

A powerful shudder wracked his body, and I could tell by the punch of magic in it that it was the power of the *beast-call* running through him. I wasn't the only one in this room on the verge of losing control of their temper. "Of course not. I do not believe her a threat to you. The geas is foolproof. Just look at Christian. She is only interested in slaying the dragons who've given in to their baser instincts." I thought that was a diplomatic way of putting it. "She's said so, and she has been a trustworthy ally for a very long time."

I laughed bitterly. "And you believed her? At the risk of my *life*, you believed that? She must be an amazing lay."

His expression froze, and it made him look guilty as hell. I started to struggle out of his hold. It was damn near unbreakable.

But I would break it. I was very good at breaking things. It was, in fact, my most notable talent.

"Dammit, Jillian, I told you about all of that. It's in the past. Our relationship is completely platonic and professional at this point. I did not put your life at risk. My former sexual relationship with her has not affected my judgement."

"Former?" If true, that was something, at least.

"Yes. Former. Ancient history, as far as I'm concerned. I

have something else to discuss with you. She's not the only slayer coming to town."

I suddenly knelt in a flash, my body escaping his arms. I pushed back and kicked up high with the same motion. My other heel was barely on the ground, so when my kick connected solidly with his jaw, it threw me back and down. I slid across the floor, gliding until my head connected with the wall across the room from Dom. I stood quickly, preparing to defend. I had probably hurt myself as much as I'd hurt him, but it had been worth it.

Dom just rubbed his jaw, looking at me. "That smarts."

He took one cautious step forward. He reached a careful hand out to me. His devastating eyes were focused, trying to capture mine.

I shook my head at him. "Do *not* touch me. If you lay one finger on me, I'm going to leave. And anyone who tries to stop me will suffer. Call them back in."

I was still furious, but I felt that at least I had my temper under control. Ish. Jealousy and righteous fury combined were a hell of a combo to walk away from clean.

The others came back in. The table was set aright in a long process that involved planks being brought in and nailed along the wooden base table. It was a temporary solution. I had ruined that table. I was hoping it was the most destructive incident in this meeting but it was a fact that we hadn't even gotten started, so that seemed a little too optimistic.

Everyone resumed their seats.

"I'd like to start with a suggestion," Helen began before we'd even settled in again. "I know you insisted on this geas for me," she shook her wrist to illustrate, "but to put one on *everyone* on my half of the team seems excessive."

Dom gave her a look so unfriendly it instantly brightened my mood. "It is *not* negotiable. *Every* single team member will have a geas. In fact, it's a done deal. My second has been performing the ritual even as we speak. And there won't be a *your half* of the team. It will be one team with one lead. If you can't work with Jillian, Helen, you won't be useful on this task force. She's taking point on this one. Jillian's in charge."

Helen's eyes widened in dismay. This was news to her. To me, too, for that matter. "Do you really think that's wise, Dom? I have much more experience heading druid task forces. Have you led even one, Jillian?"

Dom spoke before I could give her my succinct answer. "Jillian knows the enemy in a way no one else could. She knows their names and faces. Their weaknesses and strengths," I didn't know about that one, but I wasn't going to argue with him when he sounded like he was making such a good point on my behalf. "And she is the only dragon who has not gone actively rogue or been captured at this point in time. She is their leader, as far as the druids are concerned. So she is clearly the ranking member of the force. Not only is it a wise choice, Helen, it is the only choice I would consider. If you cannot accept this decision, I suggest you walk away now. A soldier who can't follow orders in battle is useless."

"Dom, you're letting her lead you around by the—"

I stopped her, tired of the sound of her voice. "Have you ever killed one of my kind?"

Her eyes narrowed, and her mouth tightened with temper. "Not yet."

I waved a hand at the men beside me. "Well, we have. We are the only ones to have successfully done so since 'The Purging.'" At least, on this side of the world. I had no idea what had been going on with any of the dragons from the east, but adding that would sort of shit on my point, so I didn't.

And of course that had gotten everyone's attention. "What

is 'The Purging?'" Dom asked me.

My answer was interrupted by Dom's intercom buzzing. "Sir, the other members of your meeting are all here."

Dom ignored it. "Well?"

I shrugged. "It can wait. Show me our backup."

CHAPTER SEVEN

SHADOW MAN'S TWIN

W e stood and faced the door as Dom buzzed them in. Two druids filed in first, both of whom I recognized. They wore severe white ceremonial robes covered in embroidered druidic runes, which always meant serious magic.

I nodded politely at Collin. He nodded back with a small but friendly smile. He immediately moved to take a seat near his Arch, bowing his head to Dom in deference as he passed.

Sloan filed in next. I couldn't help an outright grin at the sight of her. I was still so relieved that I hadn't gotten her killed. Though I was surprised she had been assigned to *this*.

"I volunteered," she said, as if she'd read my thoughts. She even gave me a tiny, bloodthirsty smile. "I have a score to settle with those Viking bastards."

A thought struck me. "Does Cam know?"

She held up a hand, rolling her eyes as she went to the chair nearest to Dom. Of course, she bowed her head to her Arch before she sat. "Don't even go there."

She caught sight of my Caleb twin. She shot him a disgusted look. "You really love being Jillian, don't you, you sick bastard?"

Caleb gave her a chilling little smile out of my face. It was a downright fond look, coming from him.

After a beat, two more white-robed druids I didn't recognize came in and went to the chairs beside Collin. One was a tall man with the same coloring as Sloan. He had long black hair that fell down his back in a smooth cascade. He also shared Sloan's beautiful, mixed heritage features. A mix of Asian and European features, if I had to guess. Like Sloan, he'd somehow managed to get the best of both. They could have been siblings with their tall, lean figures. They even had the same impeccable posture and steely silver eyes. I assumed they were relatives of some sort and made a note to ask her about it later.

This man bowed lower to his Arch than the two lieutenants had. A rank thing. The druids had a lot of respect for rank. And Dom had declared me the dragon leader. I could call myself the dragon queen.

Hmm, it had possibilities.

The other was a tall, slender man with dark red hair and alabaster skin. His eyes were a pale gold. His hair fanned to his shoulders in a way you usually only saw in anime. He bowed low to his Arch, his face solemn.

The next to walk in was a grinning Corbin, a vampire slayer that we'd met briefly but memorably. He took a seat on our side of the table, next to Christian.

I made a note to tell him later that he had horrible political instincts. He'd stepped onto the wrong side of the line on the sand. The crazy people on *this* side of the table only seemed to know how to make enemies.

"Barbie," he said quietly, sending me an affable grin.

"Buffy." I grinned back, nodding to him.

Three more filed in together, taking the seats on the other side of Dom, next to Helen. I couldn't tell what they were right away, which meant that whatever their powers were, they weren't animalistic in nature. Which meant they could *all* be slayers. It was likely. From what Dom had said, at least two of them were.

I studied them. The one closest to Helen was a large, bald, black man. He was handsome, with dark skin and even features, and he looked at absolute ease in the tense setting. That alone meant he was someone formidable. His eyes were so dark they shone black. He had the ageless look that many other supernaturals had. He was wearing a simple white dress shirt with tan slacks. He was dressed down compared to the druids, but his confidence made up for it. He inclined his head respectfully to Dom as he stood behind his chair.

The next man was yet another tall, Nordic blond. He, Helen, Christian, and I could have all been siblings. On closer inspection of his dark blue eyes, I thought it a good possibility that he and Helen actually were. I wondered if all the British slayers were related in some way to Christian. It sure looked like at least some of them were. His nod to Dom was particularly stiff. Some hostility there, perhaps? He being Helen's brother might explain that.

Everyone that entered cast strange looks between Caleb and me, but no one else mentioned it.

The last man to sit made my body go stiff; my blood felt like it was freezing in my veins.

My heart skipped a beat.

"Sit," Dom commanded the room.

We all sat.

A long ago memory of a man standing in the shadows, a threat in the dark, always waiting to punish, surfaced in my mind. Countless punishments ordered by my father that the shadow-man had administered. The shadow man in my memories had a relic much like Christian's around his neck. It had been the weapon used in 'The Purging.' He would run it down my cheek sometimes, smiling.

He had long unkempt black hair that trailed down the sides of his face to his thick chest, and swarthy dark skin, his jaw shadowed. His eyes were pale green and direct. He wore a well-used, dark gray leather trench coat, buttoned to his throat. Hiding weapons, I thought. Hiding that terrible relic?

He didn't even look at the others in the room. His enigmatic gaze zeroed in on me and stayed there. "You recognize me?" he asked directly. His voice was gravelly and mean and accent-less, just how I remembered.

I nodded slightly, my hands reaching instinctively for a weapon at my back. There was none. Weapons were not allowed here, and I had assumed I would be safe at a meeting where Dom was presiding. I sent him an accusing look. He looked confused, but I could tell from his eyes that the *beast-call* was moving through him. He knew that I felt threatened, even if he didn't know why.

"You must have met my twin," the man said distinctly. "He was captured by your clan centuries ago. That is why I've asked to join this endeavor, actually. I would like to finally get my brother back. And the family relic. It was stolen with him."

The relief that I felt worried me. Was I that afraid of the shadow-man? It was a child's horror, from my memories. But that didn't lessen it. And why should I believe that it was his twin?

But this man did have a different feel... He didn't stink of the brain sickness like the shadow-man. This was no thrall.

Something that he said bothered me. I addressed it first. "We won't be rescuing that one." My tone was emotionless and steady as a rock. "If I see that man again, I will kill him. He was instrumental in 'The Purging.' And he beat me regularly as a child, tortured me and my sister relentlessly. So I repeat, if I see your twin, I will *kill* him."

The man looked furious. He turned to address Dom. "Arch—" he started but Dom's expression stopped him.

We all looked at the Arch, who had a look on his face that I couldn't read, but something about it made my chest ache.

He was frozen for an endless moment, something haunting him, lighting up his lovely, discordant eyes.

"Dom," I prompted him. He's distraught, I realized, and wondered if anyone else knew him well enough to notice.

My anger at him fled for a moment, and I felt a flood of concern.

He blinked, running a hand over his face to regain his composure. "Harvey, your brother has been a captive for centuries. His mind has been enthralled for far too long to ever make a recovery. You need to be prepared to confront your twin as an enemy."

Harvey's mouth tightened. "All I ask for is a *chance* to try to recover him."

Dom and I stared at each other for a pregnant moment. *What was he thinking?* His mask had come back down, but he was obviously struggling with something.

"That kind of hesitation could get somebody killed in the middle of battle. If he's fighting with the enemy when we engage, he is a target. I'll kill him myself," Dom said, finality in his voice, "and I will make it quick. I'm sorry for your loss, but that's all I can give you. If this decision doesn't sit well with you, I'll understand if you can't help with the hunt."

Harvey's eyes shut tightly for a moment in pain. When he opened them, they were full of resignation. "I trust your judgement, Arch."

It was a testament to the absolute authority Dom wielded that Harvey could concede such a thing without a fight. Druids were the law, and the law was not questioned. And Dom was their King. There was nothing to do but submit. "If you feel this is the way it has to be, I will accept your decision. Perhaps I have been hanging on to false hope for too long. It is hard to let go of a twin bond. But I still want in. Even if it takes death to free him, I want him free of those monsters." His eyes shifted to me, and I was surprised to find no animosity there. Was this what the shadow-man was like without my father's taint? "No offense," he said.

I raised my brows, surprised. "None taken. I know firsthand how monstrous they are. And I've called my clan far worse. I ran away when I was very young. There is no pull of kinship for me there."

"What is 'The Purging?'" Harvey asked.

I tried to keep the story short and to the point, and my emotions out of it. "It was before I was born, but I know that your twin was the executioner. The elders loved to tell me the story when I was disobedient. The females of the clan were too rebellious. The men betrayed them, chained them all and had your brother execute them, one by one, while the men watched. The only one left alive was my mother, since she was considered young enough to still be malleable. That left all of the burden of breeding on that one woman. She went mad by the fifth child, they said. That fifth child was me. So they gave her the 'Sleep of Eternity.' By then they had Lynn and me to replace her. It didn't work out quite how they'd planned." I smiled without humor. "I freed Lynn and we ran before we could be made to breed." The memories were too old to hurt me anymore. Mercifully, the years almost made it feel like it had all happened to someone else.

No one spoke for a long time. What can you say to a story like that? Not much, apparently. They all just stared at me in varying degrees of horror and disbelief.

Eventually Dom made introductions. The black man was Hamish, and he was a slayer. He wasn't friendly, but he wasn't hostile, either. The one that looked like Helen's brother was, in fact, her twin, James. Twins were apparently very common in slayer families. The male druid who looked like Sloan was Calum, the red-head Jasper.

"Jillian will be leading you when I am not there myself," Dom briefed us. "Your goals are as follows. Finding and rescuing Jillian's sister, Lynn. Also locating and eliminating any rogue dragons or those assisting them. I want in on any dragon kills. You are not to make any moves without reporting to me. In fact, I expect to be updated daily. I want no unnecessary risks here."

I sighed. I shouldn't have been surprised. He never looked away from me as he gave his orders. I inclined my head in agreement. He looked relieved that I wasn't throwing a fit about it. What choice did I have? I clearly couldn't do this alone.

Dom rose, and his entire side of the table rose with him. "Now for the geases," he said.

Everyone but Sloan seemed confused by that. I was watching her, and she seemed to be the only one on Dom's side that knew it was coming. Interesting.

Several of the slayers shook their wrists. "We all already have them, Dom," Helen said pointedly.

He smiled amiably enough but his eyes were cold. "You do, but I've created a spell of my own to add reinforcement to it. I needed you all together to cast it."

I made a note of the ones that protested the loudest and the ones that didn't have a problem with it. A list with two columns marked ENEMIES and NOT ENEMIES. . . YET. Optimism had never been my thing.

"If you insist," Hamish's voice split cleanly through the vocal melee.

"I do," Dom said implacably. "A room has been readied for the ritual just down the hall. Sloan will lead the way. Thank you all for your cooperation."

"Let's get it over with then," said Hamish. He was quickly

going to the top of my favorite new people list, though admittedly that wasn't hard considering how much I distrusted new people.

They filed out. Helen sent me a venomous look as she left the room, but I didn't like her either, so I wasn't bothered by it. It was no fun to hate alone. Two was a number for lovers *and* haters as far as I was concerned.

Dom was the last to leave, and I almost put a crick in my neck watching him go. He drove me crazy, but damn it was nice to watch him leave.

"Can we go?" Christian asked quietly. "Was that a dismissal? I'm bored to tears. Let's get outta here."

I blinked. I really had no idea. "Best to wait," Caleb and I said in sync.

I pointed at him. "Stop that. It's creepy."

He smiled, and that was creepy too.

They were in the ritual room for less than thirty minutes. We were waiting back in the lobby when they came out. The geases on their wrists had all changed from white bones to black. I'd never seen such a thing, but I found it encouraging. Helen looked particularly pissed, and I found that even more encouraging.

Dom came out last, the tallest in a room of extremely tall men. When was he not? Only when his cousin Cam was around, I supposed. Cam might have had an inch or so on him. But Cam wasn't here. I guessed that he was in a rage somewhere on account of Sloan's involvement in this whole mess.

Helen stepped close to Dom, speaking quietly. I couldn't hear what she said, but Dom was looking at me. He didn't look away once. His face was closed, but I thought his eyes were asking me a question.

He wants forgiveness, I thought. For not warning me about Helen and the other slayers.

Pointedly, I turned away, in no mood to forgive. My temper needed to cool down first. For a few hours or a few decades.

I remembered right as Caleb spoke to me quietly. "You need to get us in to see the captive dragon."

I gave him a narrow-eyed glare, because he'd just spoken my thoughts aloud. "Creepy," I muttered, then moved to approach Dom.

"I need to talk to you," I told him, my jaw set hard. "Alone."

I caught Helen staring daggers into me at the edge of my vision.

Dom just pointed back to the conference room, waiting for me to precede him.

I walked stiffly ahead of him, stepping just inside the door. I stood there, arms folded across my chest as he followed behind me and shut the door.

"Jillian," he began, his voice pitched low and *soft*, something so conciliatory, so tender in his deep voice uttering my name that I ached with it.

Perhaps this was why I'd stayed away so long. The real reason. He had too strong an effect on me. One minute I wanted to throttle him, the next I wanted to melt into a puddle at his feet.

Unfortunately, I was still mad enough to spit, and my temper and making peace had never gone hand in hand.

"*Don't*," I told him, my tone set. I felt betrayed, and I would be giving no quarter to my betrayer. "You said you had a dragon in custody, and I want to see him."

Dom moved in front of me, his arms folded across his chest in his own standoffish way. "I'm sure you do. I'll make you a deal. If you can go one day without slipping away, without running, without raising hell *just because you can*, I'll bring you to see him."

"Me, Caleb, and Christian. All of us to see him or no deal."

He sighed, and I saw his face turn away to gaze out the window. I'd very deliberately avoided glancing up at his face, my eyes steadfastly on his chest. The less I saw of those mismatched, unbearable eyes the more I kept my resolve to stay furious at him.

Some anger was best to hold onto even if only long enough to teach you a lesson.

"Tell me about this captive," I said, my voice hoarse with a simmering anger. "What does he look like? How does he act? I might be able to tell you more about who he is than you've learned from him."

"He's blond."

I snorted out a laugh. We were *all* blond Vikings, for fuck's sake.

"Tall, with eyes like yours. I don't suppose you were referring to his looks, so I'll just get to the point. He has a calm manner, and I believe he is a telepath."

My head shot up at that, and I met his gaze head on. That could only be one man. My closest brother. Or rather, the only brother I had that I didn't despise. "How do you know?"

"He knows things...things he couldn't know unless he picked them from my brain. Is this a common thing among your kind?"

"It is not. As far as I know, there is only one that had this power...before Conan, that is. You've captured my brother, and if there are any of my kind that could be swayed to our side, or to give me information, it is him. I need to see him right away."

"Tomorrow."

"Today!"

His jaw hardened, and his eyes got very cold, his expression haughty. I forgot sometimes that I was dealing with a king. Being reminded was hardly welcome.

"You forget yourself. I don't take orders from anyone, Jillian, not even you. You may see him tomorrow, if you can manage to behave yourself for this one day."

"What exactly does that mean?"

"How about just sticking to the casino property?"

"If we get a lead about Lynn—"

"If you get a lead, you can tell me and I'll arrange for you to take a detail with you."

"That's bullshit. I'm not a child."

"I'm well aware, but if you want to see your brother tomorrow this is what you'll do. Manage to stay out of trouble for one fucking day and you and your boys can see my captive tomorrow."

I turned away because I wanted to punch him. I was still furious, and he should have known better than to rile me at a time like this.

"Fine. I'll stay on the property. All fucking day."

"It's not a prison. There's plenty to do here. You have carte blanche of all of the shops and even the gambling hall. Try to relax for a day. It won't kill you."

Relax, I thought. He wants me to relax. I couldn't even wrap my mind around that idiocy, so I stayed silent, not looking at him as I waited for him to open the door, signaling that we were done.

He had the sheer gall to grip my shoulder from behind.

"Jillian…about earlier. I'm sor—"

I wrenched away. "Save it. I don't want to hear it. Your apology would mean *nothing* to me, now that I know just how little you care for my welfare."

"Jillian," he said again, his voice thick with emotion, and the beginnings of rage. "I would *never*—"

"Don't bother. I don't want to hear it right now."

I opened the door myself, not able to bear another

moment in his presence, knowing I'd do something crazy if I had to breathe the same air for even one more second.

I strode straight to the elevator, not looking at anyone as I punched the button to go down.

I could feel the power stirring behind me. The rage I'd provoked in him had the hair rising on the nape of my neck, but I kept my back to him. I wasn't sad that I'd angered him. No one wanted to feel this kind of fury alone. I supposed I'd needed company. Perversely, knowing how I'd gotten to him instantly assuaged my own temper.

The car opened, and I walked inside. I didn't turn as I felt Christian and Caleb file in behind me, and the door slid closed.

"So what's the plan?" Christian asked as we began to descend.

"We can see the dragon tomorrow. It's my brother."

"*Tomorrow*?" Caleb asked, sounding disgusted. "What are we supposed to do while we wait?"

My voice was just as disgusted. "We're supposed to *relax*."

CHAPTER EIGHT
THAT EFFING GROVE

After much debate and general confusion, we decided that the pool was where we were supposed to 'relax.'

"I'll never understand what you see in him," Christian muttered, as we rifled through swim wear at one of the casino mall's many shops. "He'd better be a bloody good shag."

I shot him a look for that one. "He is. He's out of this world amazing in bed. Did you really want to know? Feel better now?"

He made a face, grabbing a pair of swim trunks. "Touché. I did not."

"Don't bring it up then." I grabbed the first bikini that caught my eye. It was gold and sparkly. I grabbed a matching cover-up and a pair of gold aviator sunglasses at the checkout counter.

Relax. Grrrrr.

"I don't know what he could be thinking," Caleb muttered quietly as walked to the pool. "Wanting you to stay here, thinking this would keep you out of trouble. He knows better than anyone that this place houses the very *worst* kind of trouble."

I studied Caleb. "Are you talking about a *thing* that lives here that we can't directly talk about?"

He nodded. Scowled. "I fucking hate this place."

He wasn't the only one.

We spent a few hours lounging around the resort's opulent pool. I told the guys they didn't have to stay on house arrest with me, but neither of them listened. I knew why. They were half-afraid I might disappear if they didn't keep an eye on me. And the odds of running into trouble went up exponentially when they hung around with me. And they both loved trouble.

Also, though none of us would likely admit it except under direct torture—we'd missed each other.

I was sporting the tiny gold bikini I'd found, and Caleb sat beside me, mimicking me, but in an even tinier bikini. One with a thong. It was gross. I told him so, but of course he was unfazed.

Christian sat in a lounger beside me, sipping a Piña Colada. We had spent a good amount of time making fun of his girly drink, but we weren't done.

"They forgot your pink umbrella," I told him.

"And your vagina," Caleb added, deadpan.

Of course, deadpan was easy when you were dead inside. Still it did the trick.

I couldn't stifle a laugh, instead just let it out. Christian didn't care. He just smiled and toasted the air.

That was how Corbin, the vampire slayer found us, laughing and lazing about like we did this every day.

Dammit, we were kind of relaxing.

"Buffy!" I called out.

He smiled and sat on the foot of my lounger, just as though he was one of the guys. He could be. I thought he'd fit in well with our demented little group.

"Barbie," he said to me, "we need to talk."

I sat up a bit. That sounded ominous. "Sure. Shoot."

"Something is going on, something bad."

This was hardly news. You might say it was the story of my life.

"Beyond the usual bad shit," he continued. "I haven't seen a vamp in months, which *never* happens. They've gone into hiding, deep hiding, and that worries the hell out of me. The necros, as well. No sign of them anywhere. The druids want to think that our last raid was just that effective, and they may have had a point if we were just talking necros. But we're not. Vamps are different, and no one knows them like I do. If they've gone this deep into hiding, they are planning something, something that involves multiple kisses working together, and if they are thinking enough to collude, I have a fucking problem with it, and we all have a fucking problem in general."

That was a bit to process, so I just looked at him while I thought about it.

"I have a tendency to be paranoid," he continued, making me like him more by the word, "but I think they're working together. I think we should be preparing for some sort of a mass attack."

"You don't know us very well, mate," Christian said with a smile. "We're always preparing ourselves for an attack. The good news, though, is that I think you might be paranoid enough to join our little club."

"Well, that's a relief," Corbin said dryly.

"No, no, no, you're doing it wrong." Christian explained, "In the paranoid club, you're only ever supposed to get more worried."

"So this is what you guys are doing today?" Corbin asked, looking suspicious, like we were up to something.

"We were ordered to relax," Christian explained.

"None of us can figure out what that means. We were thinking about getting manis and pedis next."

"Dom thinks that this casino is where Jillian needs to stay to keep out of trouble," Caleb added, skepticism in every word.

"It seems to be working," Corbin pointed out.

I snorted, and all three of them looked at me. "Caleb is right. This place is nowhere to be if you want to stay *out* of trouble."

"Yes, it's been terribly dangerous so far, lounging at the pool," said Christian.

I shook my head. "You don't get it. There are things about the druids that no one seems to understand." I pitched my voice low, paranoid even mentioning it. "They have more secrets than we even thought. Dark secrets."

"Of course you must know that they're the Illuminati," Christian threw out like he'd been waiting for the chance.

I laughed hard. "Not what I was referring to, but I like where your head's at."

"No, they really are," he insisted.

No one could stop laughing.

"And they're taking over the music industry," he continued. "I saw it in a Rihanna music video...and a Beyoncé video...and a Katy Perry video. The bastards even got Taylor Swift."

I'd needed that, so I smiled at him. "Don't forget Jay-Z."

"Oh, I'm not." He lifted a brow and held his hands up into a triangle. "I mean, come on!"

Still laughing, I excused myself, heading to the closest restroom.

I had taken maybe five steps down the hallway that led to the women's restroom when the carpet began to squish with liquid under my gold flip-flops. I stopped, cursed, looked around, and began to run back the way I'd come.

Of course that didn't work.

I was already caught.

What should have been the pool area was a forested Grove. It tried to give me a harmless show for maybe ten seconds before it switched from a pretty atrium and into straight creepy, the trees going black, the soil red, the pools turning dark with what I knew was blood.

"What the fuck?!" I called out, pissed.

I didn't have time for this, and I was agitated that I was caught, when I knew that was supposed to be *impossible*. I had deduced that it had only caught me before because I was carrying a half-druid child at the time.

The white thing, that odd, wrong, creepy as hell presence, was out of the water and nearly to me in the strangest move. It never looked like it was moving fast, but it covered ground between one blink and the next.

I really, really hated that.

"You aren't supposed to be able to do this," I told the thing. "You're going to get yourself into trouble, and I know why you were able to trap me before, but that should *not* be a possibility anymore."

Its mouth opened, showing me its disturbing teeth that looked more like tusks. "I got you before because you carried a powerful druid child inside of you," it hissed in its dissonant screech of a voice, its words reaffirming my suspicions. "That connection never ends, you know. You're mother to a half-druid. That has bonded you here as though you were born to it."

I cursed. "You think that explanation will save you from your guardian when he finds out?"

It threw back its head and began to make a noise out of nightmares that I suspected was supposed to be a really fucked up laugh. "I do not. He will punish me. That is why I have a deal for you."

"Fuck your deal," I said with no hesitation. There was no way in hell I would bargain with this thing.

"Blood for knowledge," it continued.

"Fuck your knowledge," I said.

I tried to walk, to move, but I was caught fast. "I say no to whatever you're offering, now let me go."

It was in touching distance with a breath. "It's not so simple as that. I can give you a taste before you refuse me. You see, I have knowledge that you want, not for its value to me, no, but for your own sentiment, which may be very valuable to you."

I opened my mouth to speak when it touched one long, bone white finger to my forehead.

The world dropped away.

The first time I saw her I thought she was an angel. I'd never seen one before, but I knew they were ethereal creatures with a golden glow that surrounded their bodies. The way the sun was shining cast a perfect halo over her chin length, pale golden hair.

I didn't know much about angels. Few did. They rarely graced this realm with their presence. But I had heard that one glance at their perfect faces would strike your heart with pure love. I knew at once that I was struck. I began to follow the golden apparition as she glided slowly and smoothly down the street.

I felt no qualms about jumping the fence from the elite private school I attended, ditching class. I rarely missed school, and the ones who taught me and my kind didn't reprimand us without a better reason than disappearing for an hour or two. But even fear of getting in trouble wouldn't have stopped me.

I trailed behind her for several blocks as she strolled leisurely. She wore all black, with a high necked lace blouse, and one of the plain pencil skirts that were in fashion. Her silky hair fell in perfect waves against her jaw. She wore flat-soled, sensible shoes that seemed out of place with the fashionable outfit. At a glance it looked like she was in mourning.

She walked with a large picnic basket hooked on her elbow until she reached the lake. She found a nice spot on the grass, spread out a blanket, sat down with her basket and opened it. She pulled a book out and started reading.

I watched her for hours as she read and ate a few bites of food absently, moving as close as I dared without being detected.

Her pace was much brisker after she packed up and started walking again, but I had no trouble keeping up. I followed her for over a mile, watching her back intently, picking up every nuance of her walk. My goal at that point was only to hear her speak and have her look at me. I wanted to hear her voice, to see her eyes.

Finally she stopped at a small café, going quickly inside. I tried to wait five minutes to follow, but didn't last more than two.

As I entered the the café I noticed right away that it's simple, elegant decor was at direct odds with the rowdy shouting coming from some room off to the left of the main dining area.

"Can I help you?" a quiet voice asked from my right.

I knew immediately that it was her and visibly started. Her voice was soft and feminine but husky, the cadence low in pitch, and exactly what I'd imagined. I turned, swallowing hard at my first close up view of her.

She wore a white waist apron now, and I realized that she worked at the café. But my eyes were glued to her face. Her skin was perfect alabaster, her lips a soft pink that I suspected was untouched by makeup, a rare occurrence among the women I'd known. Her features were even and perfect, dominated by pale aquamarine eyes, framed by thick dark lashes. They were the color of the ocean. She stared back at me without blinking. I'd been staring at her for a very long time before she finally spoke, smiling slightly, "Why don't you have a seat? Do you prefer the main dining room or the kids' room?"

I blinked. "Kids' room?" I felt hot color spread on my cheeks. She was obviously in her twenties, and I was only fourteen, but I often got mistaken for older, and I'd hoped she wouldn't see me as a kid.

"Yeah, I'm sure you can hear it. It's a large room to the left we've reserved as an after school hangout. We don't have any of the kids from your school as regulars, but there's plenty of room in there."

I shook my head, trying to pretend I wasn't blushing like a little kid. "The main dining room would be fine."

She nodded. "Have a seat anywhere you want. What can I get you?"

I bit my lip, sitting in the nearest chair. "A cola, and whatever your special is for lunch." I wasn't even a little bit hungry, which was unusual for me, but I knew the more I ordered, the longer I could sit and watch her.

"Burger and chips sound okay?"

I nodded, still staring at her, drinking her in.

She smiled, but it was sad. I wondered if she always smiled like that. "I'll whip that up myself. The cook's on lunch. Just give me a minute."

She came back several minutes later, carrying a tray with my food and drink.

"How did you know what school I attend?" I asked her as she set it in front of me. I'd been stewing about it almost since she'd left.

She surprised me by taking a seat directly across from me. "Your uniform gives you away. Only a few of the schools around here require suits and ties."

"Oh, that."

She smiled that sad smile again. "Also, I recognized you. I've seen you hanging around that private school with your friends."

I almost coughed up the soda I'd been sipping. "Oh?' I asked in a strangled voice. I couldn't imagine how she'd noticed me but not I her.

"Yes, you, those two dark-haired boys, and that redhead. I'm guessing your brothers and your girlfriend?"

I looked at her, mortified that she thought Siobhan was my girlfriend. She was two years younger than me, and mostly a nuisance.

I shook my head vehemently. "My cousins, and their friend. I don't have a girlfriend."

She smiled deeper, almost making that sadness disappear. "My mistake. You aren't eating." I started eating the chips mechanically, trying desperately to think of something to talk about to keep her sitting there.

"You followed me from the lake," she said quietly, and I started choking on a chip.

"Why?" she asked after I'd stopped.

I shrugged, blushing. "I was bored," I mumbled. "School's a drag."

"What's your name?" she asked, studying me intently.

I couldn't look away from her eyes.

"Domhnall. Everyone calls me Dom."

She held out her hand as though to shake, something I'd never seen a woman do before.

I wiped my hand carefully on my napkin before clasping hers. I gripped it tight, prolonging the touch. "Well, I'm Jillian. Can we be friends, Dom?"

I nodded immediately, still gripping her hand. She let me, but looked at our clasped hands with a furrowed brow. "Yes, of course." I tried to sound polite, but nowhere near as eager as I felt.

She smiled warmly, flashing perfect teeth. "Good. Now that we're friends, Dom, can I ask a favor of you?"

I nodded. "Anything," slipped out, and I cringed at how desperate I sounded.

She bit her bottom lip, a nervous habit maybe, and my eyes were glued.

I felt bereft as she finally took her hand away.

"Can you keep this place a secret from your classmates? I've noticed that the kids from that school are a lot...rowdier than the other kids that hang out here. I wouldn't want any fights to break out. Not to say that you're rowdy, of course. From what I've observed, you seem to be on the best of behavior, but I've seen too many of the kids at that school fighting. It's strange, they all seem to look up to you, but they don't follow your example of stoicism. They're a bit too wild, as I'm sure you know."

I started blushing again. The youths of my kind had a hard time learning control. The more powerful ones learned it early, like I had. But for the first time I felt shame at how the other ones must appear to the outside world. "I won't tell a soul," I promised her.

She rewarded me with a warm smile.

She pointed to my plate. "If you don't eat that, you'll hurt my feelings. I don't cook for just anyone."

I ate my burger so fast she started laughing. "What a darling boy you are," she said as she stood.

I wanted to erase the boy part from her sentence, but was happy nonetheless to get a compliment from her.

I lingered for as long as I could without embarrassing myself. She wouldn't let me pay as I prepared to leave. She walked me out, touching my elbow lightly. "This time is my treat. It was a pleasure to meet you, Dom. Don't be a stranger."

I turned back and thanked her.

She eyed me up. "My god, you're a tall one," she suddenly noted.

I was already over six feet tall, above eye level with her. I hadn't realized until that moment how unusually tall she was for a woman, taller than most men. "How old are you?"

"Seventeen. Almost eighteen," I tried the lie out on her.

She gave me a dubious look. "You are not. How old are you

really?"

"Almost fifteen," I told her the truth hesitantly, disappointed that she hadn't bought the lie.

Her eyes widened. "My god, you're going to grow into a brute."

I must have looked as crushed as I felt at her comment, because she patted my shoulder comfortingly. "It was a compliment. There's nothing more attractive to women than a physically imposing man who knows what to do with himself. I bet the girls at your school go crazy for you. That redhead already looks more than half in love with you."

I shrugged, looking down at my shoes.

She touched my cheek softly, and I looked back up.

"It really was a compliment. Believe me, that height and those shoulders are going to get you more female attention than you'll even want." I knew that she was speaking abstractly, not putting herself in the category of interested females, and again I felt crushed.

I left on leaden feet after that, looking back at the café every few feet, but Jillian had walked inside and never looked back.

I came back into my own body swinging. I knew whose memories I'd been privy to. I had known it right away. I had my own memories of that first fateful meeting.

The thing dodged me easily, not even needing to step away to avoid my swing.

"There's more. There's so much more. You may walk away now, but if you want more of his memories, you'll offer me blood. Just a bit. You won't even miss it."

"You bastard," I said, feeling ripped open. The thing didn't have an ounce of humanity inside of it as far as I could tell, and yet it could read needs inside of me that I hadn't even known I possessed.

More than his memories, I'd felt what he felt, and it was addictive at first taste.

I knew it was wrong. It was dangerous, and masochistic,

and out-and-out crazy, but I held out my arm for it to feed.

"This must be our secret," it hissed, its monstrous mouth giving some semblance of a smile. "You must tell no one. That is our deal."

I nodded, hating myself for it. This was the stupidest thing I'd done in a while, hands down, but I couldn't seem to resist…

"Yes," I whispered. "I want more."

It cackled, and struck. I took that as its agreement.

I was back at the café the next day after school. It was easier than it normally would have been to slip away from my friends. I'd been moody for the last few months, spending more and more time on my own, and they were getting used to it.

My parents had been called away to fight two months ago, an unprecedented order from my uncle, the European Arch. No other kid I knew of had two parents away fighting, and I'd felt more than a little slighted, even when the Arch himself explained to me why he'd needed them both to fight. They were both exceptionally strong warriors, two of his best, and he'd felt both of their skills were needed for the battles. They worked better together, he'd explained. Talking to him hadn't lessened my angst, and most of my friends were smart enough to let me be while I worked through it.

Jillian wasn't in the main room when I entered. A tiny, dark-haired woman was waiting tables. "Kids' room?" she asked me.

I shrugged. "Sure," I said, mostly hoping that Jillian was in there.

"What can I get you to eat?" the woman asked as she led me down the hallway to the left.

"Whatever's on special and a glass of water, please."

"Sure thing, sugar."

The kids' room was bigger than I'd expected. And emptier. Only one corner of the room was occupied by about a dozen kids ranging from a few years younger than me, to a few years older. They were grouped around a large corner booth, where they were all intent on some sort of card game. Jillian was at the center of it all, cards clutched loosely in one hand, while she laughed as loud as any of the kids.

It was a heart-stopping sight.

She glanced up briefly at my entrance, spoke softly to the table, then set down her cards, and made her way to me.

She sat across from me.

"And how are you today, Dom?" she asked, giving me a small smile.

I shrugged, looking down.

"Did you come just to visit me?" she asked. Her voice was soft and careful, but she sounded almost pleased.

I nodded, looking up into her beautiful eyes. She sucked in a breath. "I'm sure you hear this all the time, Dom, but you have the most amazing eyes I've ever seen. They are quite exceptional."

I stared at her, feeling a sense of power there. I knew she saw me as a child, but my eyes held some hold over her. She couldn't seem to look away, as though mesmerized. I thought that was fair, since she completely captivated me. "They are a legacy from my mother's family. She and I are the last alive to carry them."

She looked a little sad at that. "Well, I'm sure when you grow up and have children, you'll pass them down to the next generation. It would be a real pity for something like that to die out."

I wanted to reassure her that they wouldn't, because I wouldn't die out. My kind didn't age, and we didn't die of old age, but our deaths were all too common. We could be beheaded, and we fought often and furiously. There were those of us that were thousands of years old, thanks to some dark magic that our ancestors had performed, but most of my kind didn't live for more than two centuries. A warrior's life was often cut short.

I suddenly processed what she'd said about children, and my gaze ran over her greedily, drinking in her perfect figure. She had spoken of my children, and I suddenly had an unbidden vision of her bearing them. I wanted that, I realized. It didn't take me long to decide. I wanted her, wanted everything about her. We were nearly strangers, but every instinct I had told me that she was my mate. Obviously, with our age difference and her seeing me as a child, it would take me some time and work to convince her of that, but I knew I was up to the challenge.

Something in my gaze, hunger I'm sure, made her uncomfortable, and she glanced away suddenly. She took a deep breath. When she was finally able to meet my gaze again, hers was smiling, her expression a little too bright. "Will you play cards with me?"

We played for nearly two hours, and she had me laughing as I watched her. When she was in the room, it was nearly impossible for me to look away from her. She seemed to have a similar problem, and we found ourselves looking into each other's eyes often. I could tell this made her uncomfortable, but she tried to shrug it off. I went out of my way to give her the best of my charm, surprising carefree laughs out of her that I could tell caught her off guard.

I visited her often after that, slipping away to see her whenever I could. She always found a few precious minutes to spend with me, sitting to laugh and joke with me. I found myself opening up to her about everything that I was allowed to speak about in my life, my parents' absence, my frustration with time spent in a school that had little to teach me. I picked things up very quickly, and had little patience for relearning things that I had learned the first time. The growing alienation I felt with kids my own age, who could never seem to understand that life was about more than the everyday anecdotes of being a teenager. She always listened, and I was always soothed by her calming presence, and her sensible advice. She would often walk me out of her restaurant. She owned it with her sister, so she could usually do as she pleased. She would touch my hand with a smile, saying things like, "I value our friendship, Dom," or, "you are a dear boy, Dom," and I was putty in her hands. I would have done or said anything to get her approval, her smile, *her laugh, her regard.*

She was very close-mouthed when talking about herself, but over time, I was able to uncover some precious gems. She seemed kind and genteel, not the kind of person I was used to dealing with, but she would often refer to the fact that she was no saint.

I had made some reference to her kind benevolence once, and she had smiled sadly. "I wish I was as you see me, Dom, but I have a rather...violent and colorful past. I've done things that you would never associate with kindness. I've had to do many dark and horrible things to survive. And there is a rage inside of me that is hard to contain. You and I are more alike than you could ever realize."

Rather than be put off or alarmed, her words had been like a balm to me. I hadn't wanted her to be a perfect and pacifist spirit. I was a warrior, it was my legacy. And the women I was used to dealing with were just as vicious and fierce as the men. That she knew about the leashed beast inside of me, even a little, and still wanted my friendship, was a relief. But that she could understand it, perhaps even had a similar disposition herself, well, that was a marvel. I didn't question the things she said. I just accepted them and relished them.

I began to embrace her when I saw her, and when we parted, light hugs that made her stiffen at first, but over time she began to accept them with ease. I could be patient. Someday she would return my love.

I overheard her and her sister talking about me once. She hadn't made an appearance since I'd arrived, and I'd gone snooping, intent on finding out if she was even there, if it was even worth waiting for her that day.

"He's going to rat us out," I heard her sister's voice on the other side of a door at the back of the restaurant. I froze and listened intently. "I don't care how wide, innocent, and bedazzled those insane eyes of his are as they follow you around, he can't be

trusted."

"Don't worry about him," responded Jillian calmly.   "He's harmless."

Lynn was laughing as she said, "Harmless? Harmless as a loose tiger with a headache. Tread carefully. Jesus, are you even serious? Harmless!   He's young, but I'd wager that's the most powerful druid we've ever seen.   That eye. . . that wolf eye is something—I don't even know what—but it's not just there to enhance his looks. He's so dangerous. I know you see what I see."

"I'll grant you, he is dangerous. What I'm telling you is he's not dangerous to us. You don't have to trust him, just trust me. That boy will never betray us."

"You trust him?" said Lynn.   She paused.   "You don't trust anyone but me. Not even yourself usually," she added dryly.

There was a long pause, and I could hear my heartbeat so loud I thought they might hear it through the door.

"I do," Jillian said. "I don't think we can stay here much longer either way, but it won't be because of betrayal from him. He's loyal to a fault. I'm certain of it."

"I'm not doubting that. But you think that loyalty is for you? Druids only care about their own, as we both well know."

Unfortunately she didn't answer that directly.

My hands were trembling I wanted so badly to hear her response to that.

"He's going through a rough time, and he finds it peaceful here. Let him be," said Jillian.

"Fine.   Your call, but if it all goes to hell I get to say I told you so."

"You certainly do," Jillian agreed.

They were silent for a spell, and I went back to my table swiftly, not wanting to be caught.

I'd gleaned one important thing from that conversation.   Even though it went against her very nature, Jillian trusted me.

CHAPTER NINE
ZEN AF

I was shaky when I rejoined the guys by the pool.

The huge bite marks had healed almost instantly, all evidence of my strange encounter erased. Well, on the outside at least. Inside, I was pretty messed up about it for all kinds of reasons.

Christian was chatting with Corbin about his Illuminati theories rather enthusiastically as I sat down, and they barely glanced at me as I rejoined them.

Caleb was another matter. He was in his default form again. Nondescript male. Until you looked at his eyes. Then he was nondescript scary guy. He looked at me, did a double take, then sat straight up, his intense gaze boring into mine.

"What on earth would make you bargain with it?" he asked, his voice quiet, intense and accusatory all at once.

It was a minute before my mind caught onto the implication. I looked at him. Stared his psychotic alien ass down.

"What did you just say?" I asked softly. How could he know?

"I know. Not the why, but the what. How about you tell me the why?"

"I don't have a clue what you're talking about."

Christian had overheard and his curiosity was piqued by then. "What in bloody hell is he going on about, Jillian?"

Caleb kept staring at me coldly. "Don't bother lying to me about it. Save the lies for your lover. He can't know it's gotten ahold of you. He'd never allow it."

"Tell me what you know," I said quietly, a bit scared to even speak about it openly.

"I know that look," he replied just as quietly, "You look like you've seen a ghost. Actually something much, much worse than a ghost. I know about the thing."

"The thing?" Christian spoke loudly and we both shushed him.

"The thing in The Grove," Caleb stated softly. "A fucked up monstrosity, a cosmic horror born from nightmares."

"How do *you* know about it?" I was honestly shocked. "You're no kin to the druids."

"I am not," he agreed. "But I felt a strange presence the first time I entered this building, and I spent a considerable amount of time trying to figure out what it was. Enough to rile the thing out of hiding. Enough to make it show itself and scare me off. It worked."

"*You're* scared of this thing?" Christian asked, sounding impressed. "This I've got to see. Where is it?"

"Trust me, you don't want to rattle that tiger's cage," Caleb said softly and convincingly.

"Have you met me?" Christian asked, utterly undeterred.

"What did it offer you?" Caleb asked me, already tired of talking sense to the senseless.

"What did it offer *you*?" I shot back.

He grimaced and it wasn't a show. It was a genuine expression of regret, which was horrifying in itself. "All it did was scare me off. I have nothing that it wants. But I'm assuming that you, being the love of the druid Arch's life, had much more that it coveted. A better bargain all around. Do not go in too deep with this thing, Jillian. You do not want to be at its mercy."

"All it wanted was my blood."

He stared. "You can't possibly be naive enough to believe that. And what did it offer you?"

I closed my eyes, my mind going back against itself. To the past. To the clean feel of Dom's mind. The pure love of it. "Memories," I said softly.

"Tell Dom," Caleb said decisively. "Before it gets its hooks in you. Before you make a bargain that you can't be free of."

He was right. No question. But the thing was, I really, really didn't wanna. So I put it off. At least, the telling Dom part of it. Just for a bit. "We'll stick together in this place. I don't think it can catch me unless I'm alone."

"I think you're right about that, but it worries me that it caught you between here and the bathroom. That's what, a hundred feet? That means it's focused on you. It wants you bad. Dom's quarters are warded and so are most of the places that the druids do their business in here. It's the free space, the civilian play areas, I think, where it's found a way to roam free. And I don't think the druids realize it."

I didn't ask him how he knew all of that. Caleb didn't do anything in half-measures. If he said he'd spent a considerable amount of time looking into it, I knew he'd been thorough.

"So we don't go anywhere alone around here," Caleb said.

"Agreed," Christian said with a sad sigh. "What now? I'm booored. And I need to pee, and I don't particularly want a buddy holding my hand while I do it."

Caleb stood abruptly. "I'll go with you."

When they came back I was trying and failing to take a nap

under my sunglasses.

"She's doing it!" Christian said cheerfully. "She's relaxing. Look at her. She's zen af."

Corbin had left to check out another empty vampire nest before dark but promised he'd contact us if he figured anything new out.

I lifted my shades at him. "Af?"

He smirked in a very British way. "Oh that's right, you've been gone for a minute. Af means as fuck. As in, you're zen as fuck."

"Something tells me you're going to start adding an af to the end of everything you say."

"Correct af."

"Great."

"Great af."

"Enough."

"Okay. I won't do anymore. I'm done. . . as fuck."

"Have you ever been separated from her for so long before?" Christian asked.

It was some time later and we were lounging in the pool. We'd been people watching, aka giving nicknames to strangers.

I was startled by the unexpectedly serious question out of the least serious guy I knew. "Oh Gods, yes. We've been apart for years. Once for decades. Near the end of that, I thought I'd never see her again. Those were dark times, and the way we found each other again is. . . unprecedented. You'll have to find a really good bribe to get me to tell you *that* story."

He looked like he was thinking about it. "Noted."

"I mean really good."

"You know how I love a challenge."

"You are underestimating how much I don't want to tell

that story."

"You're just getting me more excited."

"Barf."

His grin died suddenly. "Seriously, though, Jillian, how are you holding up? I know this is killing you."

I shut my eyes, bringing a hand up to rub at my tired temples. Anything to distract from the tears that suddenly wanted to burn into my lids.

"I'm fine. Or I'll be fine. We just need to find her, Christian. We'll deal with whatever they've done to her after." My voice broke just a bit on the last sentence, and I felt one of his big hands squeezing my shoulder reassuringly. They'd had her for a long time, and I had no idea just what they were capable of. Every second that I'd been away, out of my senses as I gave birth, may have been a precious second for Lynn. Even now a clock was ticking away in my head, trying to do the math for all of the potential damage.

"We'll kill them *all*, Jillian. Everyone that helped to take her. Everyone that's hurt her. They're *all* gonna die. I promise you that."

It was so like Christian to deal with his pain with a body count, but I found it reassuring even if I knew that we couldn't have vengeance when my only concern was getting her back alive.

Still, there was something inside of me that had grown, was growing, something harsh and ugly, filthy, and it would only be washed clean with more pain.

I knew myself well enough to know that I'd get there when the time came.

I would have someone's blood for this.

Rivers of it.

So much for zen af.

CHAPTER TEN

THE OTHER BIG EX

I 'm not ready to talk to you," I told Dom as he approached our group alone. Several of his henchmen waited a ways behind watching him nervously. They were all in suits now, looking more like mob goons than druids while they were amongst the gen pop.

"I understand your anger, but you have to know I'd never put you in danger."

"I *used* to think that."

"Don't say a thing like that to me. It's uncalled for."

"Why didn't you tell me?"

"I needed to know if you could sense a slayer without being told. That seemed like the only safe way to do it. In my presence, under my protection, and with a geas. You were *never* in danger. Can you understand now?"

"I don't appreciate being kept in the dark, even if you have a reason for it. If we're going to work together, you don't get to do that. It's my last warning. I'll walk, Dom, I swear to the gods."

"Understood. Again, I apologize. I didn't think you'd take

it that way."

"What way did you think I'd take it?"

"More. . . reasonably. As I say it I see it's a ridiculous assumption. But can we do this another time? You can rage at me to your heart's content later but I actually didn't come here for this," he said.

"What for then?" I tossed it out like a challenge.

His nostrils flared as though finding a scent. "I didn't come here for *that* either."

I'd just been messing with him, but now I felt challenged myself. "You'd turn it down, then?" I asked. I just couldn't help myself.

His eyes shuttered, and he looked vulnerable for a moment before he composed himself. "Of course not," he said quietly, straightening his tie, a nervous motion. "What are you offering?"

"I'd hate to interrupt your schedule," I said slowly. "What was the urgent issue that brought you here?"

He looked torn but finally settled on the business at hand. "There's someone else I need you to meet. A latecomer for your team. His flight was delayed."

"Oh."

"Can you cover up for this?" He waved a hand at my body to illustrate his point.

I would have automatically thrown on a cover-up if he hadn't asked and in just *that* tone. A tone that practically begged me to meet this stranger in my tiny gold bikini.

"I'm fine like this," I said testily. "Let's go meet the new guy."

I spotted him before he caught sight of me, as little good as that would do me.

This was bad, and I had barely any time to brace for the impact.

This car wreck was going to hit me full force either way, I just knew it.

"Oh, shit," I said succinctly.

"Oh shit what?" Christian asked, sounding vaguely alarmed for his typically carefree self.

"Shit shit shit," was my only answer.

"Shit shit shit what?" It was Caleb's turn to sound more alarmed than was customary. Apparently I wasn't hiding my own personal freak out as well as I could have.

"I know this guy," I said with resignation. In my head I was taking bets against myself on who would react worse to this little reunion—me, Dom, or the new guy who was actually quite old. Both to me and to the planet earth. "Shit shit shit," I said. "I should have worn the cover-up."

Dom shot me an I-told-you-so look, but he didn't even know the first thing about it. He was about to, though.

The new/old guy spotted me right around the time Dom realized something was up. He was eyeing me with suspicion even as I heard an accented, familiar voice boom out in bewilderment edging toward outrage. "Amarante?"

"Shit shit shit," I just kept muttering. I was so not ready for this.

Dom glanced back at the man, who was almost on us. "Henri, what's wrong? What is Amarante?"

Henri didn't seem to hear him, his eyes locked on me. He was quite tall, with kind brown eyes, the hands of an absolute artist, curly brown hair, and a full beard that hipsters the world over would give their left nut for. He was ahead of that trend by a few neat centuries. He hadn't changed a bit. He still looked like a hot, French Jesus. He stopped abruptly within reach of me, his eyes wide with horror and wonder. "*Amarante.* Mon chéri, are you a ghost? Are you haunting me at last? Why now? After all this time." His hands reached out to grip my shoulders as though to test if I was real.

I winced. Amarante had some 'splaining to do. Where to start?

"Amarante?" Christian asked, looking instantly cheerful again now that he saw that the alarm was only my own personal discomfort looming ahead. "That's a new one."

I glared at him, then winced again. "An old one, as a matter of fact."

Henri seemed to realize that the shoulders he was gripping were not ghostly at all and moved his artist's hands up to cup my face. "But I saw you die. I watched your head roll to the ground during the bloodiest sunrise of my life. *Putain.* It has haunted me in dreams ever since. I was but moments too late to save you. *You can't be real.*"

The strange interaction had rendered Dom temporarily mute, but it didn't last long. "Get your hands off her." His voice came from behind me and his own clenched teeth.

Henri's hands dropped away instantly. He hadn't lived this long without recognizing murder in the air when he heard it.

"Introduce us, love," Christian chimed in like this was a great treat for him, the bastard. "It's passing rare to meet an ex of yours. Tell us about this lovesick chap."

I took a bracing step back, eyes flying to Dom. He was fuming, but I still knew how to deal with fuming Dom. How to deal with lovesick Henri was a trick I'd forgotten long ago.

"Guys, meet Henri. French painter by day and a quite talented necromancer by night. We knew each other a very long time ago."

"How long ago, exactly?" Dom asked. His teeth were still clenched. Not a good sign.

I chewed on my lip, trying to look thoughtful. "My memory's a little fuzzy, but sometime around one of those pesky French revolutions."

"And those bastards beheaded you!" Henri spat out as though it had actually happened and quite recently at that. His brows drew together as he tried to reconcile the impossible in his head. "I don't understand. I saw you die. *I saw it.*"

"That wasn't me.   An unfortunate and completely accidental lookalike just happened to get the guillotine on the same morning I took off. You know how it was. They were killing every wealthy looking person they could get their hands on. I heard about it later and never came back to tell you otherwise. You weren't supposed to think I was dead, just that I'd taken off. Sorry." It was an inadequate but more or less accurate explanation of events.

The shock was wearing off, anger rising up to take its place. "I *mourned* you. I couldn't paint for years after the death of my muse. I do not understand."

"She ran away without a trace," Dom said bitterly. "It's what she's best at."

That might have been a bit harsh, but I could hardly argue. "It was time to move on, and I could have handled it better. I have commitment issues. We've established this. My bad."

"Your bad?" Henri and Dom repeated back at the same time. They looked at each other, Dom glaring, Henri looking dazed.

"Jinx," Christian added, helpful as always.

"The French Revolution, huh," Caleb spoke up. "I'm intrigued. What would it take to hear that story?"

"Not happening," I said flatly.

"Buy me a beer, and I'll tell you anything you want to know," Henri said, shooting me a newly antagonistic glance. His emotions had been bouncing around but seemed to have found a steady place to land which was squarely on bitter anger toward me. Fair enough. Maybe he and Dom could start a club. Or a support group.

I shrugged. "As long as I don't have to hear it. Not my favorite time period."

"Ouch," Henri said with a flinch.

"No offense," I said, meaning it. I hadn't even been thinking of him when I'd said it.

"Insult to injury was always your specialty," Henri said, not quite under his breath.

I didn't argue with him. The man had a point.

"So, uh, how've you been?" I asked him. "What brings you to Sin City?"

"Not sin, unfortunately. I was asked to help with a pesky dragon problem."

"I'm not sure I follow. How would a necromancer help with a dragon?"

Dom spoke, "Tracking is half our battle. I figured anyone that's actively killing things would leave fresh bodies behind. They're like homing beacons for a necromancer."

"Smart," Christian pointed out the obvious.

"And what's in it for you?" I asked Henri.

He shrugged in a very French way. "I've always wanted to see a dragon. We used to think they were only a legend."

Caleb was staring at Dom in an odd way. "He doesn't know?" he asked.

"He hasn't been briefed as of yet," Dom said flatly.

"Know what?" Henri seemed to be directing the question at me.

I sighed. "I'm not actually a sorceress," I told him.

He stared. "Is there no end to your secrets?"

"Don't feel bad, mate," Christian told him. "We've all been digging for years and have yet to see the bottom of *that* well."

I glared at my unhelpful friend.

Henri was going off on a tangent in French. It was colorful and unflattering to me in a very personal way.

I let it go on for a bit.

"If you don't have anything nice to say," Christian began in a chipper voice.

"Say something mean," Caleb finished unhelpfully.

Christian blinked. "Well, yes."

I glared at them both. Their joking just seemed to be egging Henri on.

Henri resumed cursing me, mostly in French.

I would have let him go on longer just to get it out of his system, but Dom lost his patience first. "Enough!" he clipped out. "That was your one free pass. You'll watch how you speak to her. I don't care what happened between you two in the past. It's over now."

Henri was panting, but he stopped spouting obscenities. "All of my paintings of you have been locked away since the day I thought I saw you die, but no more. I'm going to unearth every single of them and sell them to the highest bidder!" He looked triumphant.

I sighed. This just got better and better. "Any chance I get first bid on them?"

He laughed theatrically. "I don't think so, Ma Colombe."

"Don't call her that," Dom snapped. "Enough. Henri, with me. I need a word."

The two men strode off together, causing me all kinds of anxiety.

"This can't be fun for you," Christian said in a tone that let me know it was, in fact, quite fun for *him*.

"There's no way they won't be talking about you," Caleb added as unhelpfully as possible.

"You can't even make a run for it," Christian continued as though I'd asked. "We have to stay put so we can go see your brother tomorrow. What kind of dirt does Henri have on you, other than the art? Wait. Is it nudes?"

I grimaced. "No comment," I said, referring to the nudes. "And he has the average amount of dirt any ex might have.

More than I care to dive into."

Caleb shrugged like that was the end of it. "Back to the pool?"

"Ma Colombe?" Christian asked as though he hadn't spoken. He wasn't going to drop this subject for a while.

"An old endearment he used to have for me. Again, this was all a very long time ago."

"Well it's new to us," said Christian, "so you know we won't just be dropping the subject."

And they didn't. There seemed no end to the questions Christian had about Henri, and I answered about one in ten just to get past it.

It was sometime later, Dom and Henri had not reappeared and Christian had somehow talked us into a lazy game of truth or dare by the pool.

"Truth," I chose, for some insane reason. Mostly because I didn't want to get up from my lounger.

"You have to answer anything I ask," Christian told me.

"Have to is a strong phrase," I returned.

"How old was Dom the first time you guys, ya know?" He made his hands into fists and did a thrusting motion with his hips.

I rolled my eyes. "Oh Lord. Why are you so *obsessed* with this topic?" This was possibly the thousandth time the question had come up. Everyone *always* wanted to know. Over many years it'd remained a topic of much debate.

"Because the only reason you'd be this close-lipped about it is because he was jailbait when it happened, you scandalous old *lech*, you."

"That isn't the only reason," Caleb added quietly, which was about the only thing that saved Christian from getting decked just then.

We both looked at him.

"There are plenty of reasons she wouldn't answer that, the least of which being she never wants to talk about *anything* that concerns her and Dom. Everyone has one touchy, taboo thing in their life, something too tender to speak about."

That was fascinating indeed, not just because it was absolutely the truth, but also, it implied that Caleb himself had such a topic. A weakness.

"Who knew Caleb was a sensitive bloke?" Christian's tone was sing-song, mocking, but in that charming way he had that somehow made the offensive less so.

"Me telling you doesn't mean you can pass the information around," I warned him.

"You mean I can't sell it? I wouldn't sell it cheap."

I curled my lip at him in a less than mature way and ignored what he'd said.

"He was legal," I finally answered the question of the century. Mostly just so he'd never ask it again. "Modern day legal, not old school legal."

Christian looked crestfallen. He'd *really* been hoping for a more scandalous answer.

"What even made you think about it, by the way? With all of the things going on, how did *that* even come up?"

He ignored both questions. "So he was at least eighteen, is what you're saying? Wait, no, legal means sixteen in certain states, right? Why aren't you directly answering the question? Which state were you in? What year was it? You do know that legal refers to the actual laws, don't you? Not just the ones in your head? So he was older than eighteen, is what you're saying?"

Stubborn, curious bastard. "He was eighteen exactly."

He made a loud whooping noise, like I'd made his day. "Still pretty scandalous. More than I was hoping for. And how old was he when you met him? You knew him for a long time first, right?"

"I'm done. No more questions."

"Was he fifteen? *Younger*? Fourteen? I bet he fell for you the second he saw you and never got over it. Obviously. And you *never* put a spell on him?"

"Unless it was by accident, no."

"Quit playing dumb, Christian. You already knew that." Caleb's voice was quiet, and I thought, highly annoyed.

"It's someone else's turn to get tortured here," I said sourly. The conversation brought up old memories, old regrets.

"Fair enough. You do the honors, then."

I thought about it for a while. "Caleb," I said. "Truth or dare."

"Truth," he said. Christian looked as surprised as I felt. This was apparently our lucky day.

"Are there more of you?"

He didn't like the question, it was clear. "Not anymore," he finally answered.

"Care to elaborate?"

"I don't."

"What happened to the others?" I tried a different tact.

"There was only one that I know of, and I killed it. There wasn't enough room for two of us in this world. That's all I'll say."

That was a lot to take in. Christian and I just stared at each other for a while with wide eyes.

"Someone say something," Caleb said gruffly, sounding as ill-at-ease as I'd ever heard him. "It's Jillian's turn. Christian, ask her something uncomfortable."

Christian recovered.   "So when you were gone for six months giving birth, were you like in labor the whole time?" he asked me.

I studied him. His tone was light, teasing, but I could tell he very much wanted to know the answer.

"I've answered more questions than anyone else," I told him. "If this was just an excuse to grill me, you're going to need to pay up. You know how this little song and dance goes."

I was a dragon. Everyone knew it now. We were stubborn, we hoarded treasure, and we did not give out our secrets for free.

He pursed his lips. "I'll find something you want. Something shiny and irresistible to you. You know I'm good for it. Now give me the goods."

He was right. He'd proven himself, and so I figured why not tell him. "I don't know how long I was in labor, but it wasn't for six months. It was for a few days, but afterward I went into a sleep."

"A sleep?"

"A trancelike sleep. We do it every so often, after time or trauma wears on us too much. When we wake up we feel. . . much better. It's not just for our bodies, but for our minds. It helps us cope with the burden of being immortal."

He grinned, and it was bloodthirsty. My favorite flavor of Christian. "Some of your kind are about to be a whole lot less immortal."

I nodded grimly. "Hear, hear."

CHAPTER ELEVEN
NO MORE HOES

When Dom came back he was alone and carrying a white hotel robe.

"Did you kill Henri?" Christian asked, only half-joking.

"He's settling in. And I've convinced him to rein in his temper around you, Jillian. He won't step out of line again. He's given his word."

As he spoke he tossed the robe at me. I caught it. "Dom," I said slowly, wondering how to ask for this favor. "Those paintings he mentioned—"

"I'm handling it," he cut in but didn't elaborate. I took him at his word and dropped it.

"I'm taking the afternoon off," he shocked me by adding. I didn't even know he could do that. An Arch's job was never done and all that stuff.

"Jillian, come with me. You two, stay out of trouble."

I stood and he took the robe from me, threw it around my shoulders, and stuffed my arms in it one at a time before tying it tightly.

I rolled my eyes but let him do it.

He took my hand and started walking. I followed and we were halfway across the property when I asked, "Where are we going?"

"To bed," he said, and it was enough.

We passed by a dozen druids, and they all saw us holding hands, me barely dressed, and heading up to his rooms in the middle of the day.

"The rumor mill is going to lose it over this," I said.

"I don't care and I never have. Did you want to rage at me some more before we. . ." he trailed off, just looking at me, waiting to see if I had something to say.

"Before we what?" I asked, bemused.

His eyes were too much. Just ruinous. I looked down. "You can always get the rage out of your system another way," he told me softly. The timbre of his voice sent shivers down my spine.

"You'd like that, wouldn't you?" I muttered.

"I would," he said instantly.

"Has anyone ever told you you're moody?"

"Look who's talking."

He had a point. It was a fact that he drove me out of my mind.

"Want to see something?" he asked me as he opened the door to his quarters, handing me in with his warm palm on the small of my back, leading me back to his bedroom.

"I've heard that before," I said.

"Not that. Want to see something you haven't seen before?"

"Absolutely."

"Eyes on me. Now. Watch."

He said it in a count, like he was hypnotizing me.

I couldn't take my gaze away from him. I was enthralled.

I blinked one time, and suddenly the room was changed. Rearranged in some subtle way my mind couldn't catch. Also, my robe was gone, and I stood there in nothing but my gold bikini.

Dom was in the same spot, but I knew somehow he had moved.

"What did you do?"

"I'll try again. See if you can catch it this time."

"Wait," I said but I'd already missed it again.

Again, he was in the same spot, my bikini top in his hands. My nipples were sensitive and wet like he'd been sucking on them. I watched him watching me as things low in my stomach clenched. "How?"

"You don't want to guess?" He smiled, his discordant eyes wicked. "Shall I show you again?"

I licked my lips. "Do your worst," I told him.

This time *I* had moved. I was naked in bed, legs spread. Dom was standing over me. He wore white druid robes now, open down the middle and showing a delicious strip of flesh. I followed it down with my eyes, from his collar, to his chest, down his abs, and then stopped. "What is happening?" I asked, a little dazed.

"I'll show you. It's better this way, trust me. Have you guessed what I'm doing?"

"I haven't, but if it was anyone else doing this, I'd be terrified."

"Watch me," he said.

He did it again and this time he was kneeling between my legs, still in his robes, and he had what looked like a delicate paintbrush. He was etching runes into my belly, his face intent.

"What's happening?" I asked him, feeling disoriented.

"How are you doing this?"

"I slowed time."

"What? You can do that?"

"I can and I did."

"How? That's not a druid power."

"The runes, the spells, the beast-call, the chants, the rituals, the geases. That's only part of it. The superficial rituals that hide the true potential. When I became Arch, I learned that there was . . . much more. So much more if you have enough power to seize it and enough will to pay the price."

And he did. "That's. . .unexpected," I said, understatement of the century. "What are the runes for?"

"Protection spells, mostly."

"Mostly?"

He painted the brush down, a cool trace of sensation following and I gasped. He drew a complicated rune just above my sex, lingering at it. The sensation went deeper until I felt what he did with the brush on the inside as well as out.

"This one is for pleasure," he murmured.

I remembered something. "You did this once before. Soon after we reunited, almost twenty years ago. It's not just for pleasure, right?"

His gaze bore into mine, and there was a promise in it. "That's right. It's a very powerful spell, more powerful now than it was then. I've been preparing for it since you flew away seven months ago. Do you remember the rest?"

"Something about ownership."

"Yes. That's right. Any objections? Speak now."

"Do your worst," I told him.

He pulled back for a moment, looking at me, a world of intensity in his mercurial eyes. A lifetime's worth of our tempestuous history was there as well. How not? "Lie still," he ordered me. "I need to do something important."

He splayed me out on the bed, arranged my arms at my sides, pointed straight outward, even arranging my hands and fingers just so. My legs were placed a foot apart, my feet placed straight, pointing up. He tilted my chin up. He even arranged my hair evenly around my body. "Don't speak until I'm done," he whispered and began to chant.

He worked on me for at least an hour. It was torture. It was ecstasy. I couldn't move. Each rune was precise, and he covered nearly every inch of me with them.

I had to stay quiet so he could concentrate.

His white robes lit up with dark runes as he began to place light kisses all over my body, chanting in Druidic as he moved. It was not a language I had ever learned, but it sounded like some form of Gaelic.

Slowly, his magic worked its way all over me, and it became hard not to cry out in pleasure. It was running in my very blood, that cool, irresistible force. It infiltrated all of my senses with a feeling of comfort and security. He had placed this spell on me before, or something similar. It was a strong protection spell. I did not know what it would cost him, and I knew he would never tell me. But all druid power had a price of some kind.

I had given him a protection spell of my own, unbeknownst to him. I had placed drops of my blood in his drinks many times back when we were together. Dragon blood had many beneficial effects, not the least of which was making the drinker more powerful and harder to injure. It was one of the reasons it was so dangerous for anyone to know what we were. If any slayer could get the jump on us, we would be weakened, chained, and harvested for parts at the first opportunity. Every part of our bodies had magical benefits, if consumed. Eyes, blood, teeth. It was a gory business, being dragon kin.

Bright white runes began to flash across my skin as he

chanted faster and faster. It was ecstasy, the sweetest sensations running through my veins. His hands and lips and voice were reverent as he moved over my heart. He stayed there the longest, his lovely deep voice almost singing, his lilting accent bringing me to tears.

"The runes are similar, but each one means something slightly different," he explained. "Put together it is a tapestry of power and an added layer of protection."

"Protection from what?"

"Anything that seeks to harm you."

He was looming over me, his attentions on my nipple. He was painting it lightly. My back arched involuntarily.

"Stay still."

"When you said you were taking me to bed, I pictured something else."

"Shh. Give me time." He did something subtle with the brush, and suddenly I was gasping, coming between one breath and the next.

The smile he gave me then would stay burned in my memory, a shadow of it haunting every fantasy I had from that moment forward.

"Your pleasure points get something extra," he said, still working at my nipple, working the brush over it delicately, relentlessly. "These runes mean I own your pleasure. With a thought I can make you come. Your body will dance to my tune."

I was pretty sure it already did.

His hand reached down, cupping my sex. "Mine." His fingers barely moved, but he did something with the runes that had me gasping out his name, vision fuzzy as I came again.

His eyes were intense now, angry. "Say it."

"Yours."

I knew he was done when he whispered my name and

began to suck on my breasts, all semblance of the ritual overtaken by stark, powerful intention.

He was naked, robe gone, straddling one of my thighs while pushing the other high over his shoulder. He'd stopped time again.

We needed to set up some ground rules for this little trick of his. Later.

He came into me like he was splitting me open, claiming me in one heavy thrust. It was too intense, the cool sensation of the runes and his huge, hot girth overwhelming, and I screamed. And came.

He was just getting started.

I awoke to near darkness. All that kept the room from being pitch black was the golden glow still emitting from me.

I was naked, lying on a warm chest with a familiar steady heartbeat.

His hand pulling out of my hair was the only proof I had that he'd been stroking it while I slept.

I sat up, straddling his stomach, my hands on his chest.

This hostility, this never ending standoff, had to end. And tonight I was feeling brave enough to try.

"Dom," I said softly, stroking his cheek.

"What?" he said gruffly, his voice showing no hint of sleep, because clearly he hadn't been sleeping.

"I'm waiting," I paused.

"For what? I'm pretty sure I've given you all I've got for at least another hour."

I was pretty sure he was selling himself short there, but I tried to stay on topic. "Not that. I'm waiting for the blowup."

"Which blowup would that be?"

I sighed. I didn't want to say his name, in case that set

Dom off in and of itself. "Henri."

"What about Henri?"

"You're not going to kill him in a jealous rage?"

"I might kill him if he doesn't learn some manners fast, but I'm not jealous of Henri."

I studied him. His tone had been firm, convincing. "Really?" I asked.

"Henri is not a threat. What you had was a long time ago, and the spark is clearly gone from your end. You left him without looking back. I hate that anyone but me has ever touched you, but that's never been the thing that sets me off."

"You sound so reasonable for someone who's been jealous of *Christian* on more than one occasion."

"You don't see it? The way you champion him? Of course I'm jealous of a man you keep close to you even when you push me away. Imagine if the shoe were on the other foot."

I saw his point then with crystal clarity. When we were together, there was nothing and no one he'd choose to keep close over me. It had been worrisome, that devotion. I was not a suitable mate for someone higher up in the druid hierarchy, and someone with his power had to either rise or die in such a society. Messed up as it had been, I'd left him in part to help him rise. "Touché. If it's any consolation I didn't want to leave you. I'm still not sure how I found the will to do it. I thought it was what was necessary for both of us to survive."

His voice was low and harsh, "Don't you know I would've *happily* died for you?"

It hurt like only an old wound could to hear him say that in the past tense.

"I do know it. That's always been my biggest fear. Don't you know I'd choose your survival over my own happiness, my own life?"

His eyes were glinting at me, positively glowing from

within. "And you're saying that's really the only reason you left me? To save me."

"I would have done a lot worse to protect you."

"You weren't getting bored and restless in one place? Can you really say you weren't starting to feel trapped? Will you swear that there wasn't some part of you that *wanted* to leave?"

"I swear it! It's been hell for me without you. Every minute was against my wishes, even if I believed it was necessary."

In a move too quick for me to anticipate, he grabbed me, pulling me close against his warm chest. He was squeezing to the point of pain. I didn't protest. Nothing could ever compare to being wrapped in him. I wanted to stay that way forever.

"I'm not sure I ever told you," I began after a long spell of silence. "I'd gone a bit numb before I met you. I didn't feel much at all. And then I saw you and poof the world was in color again. That's why you always scared me a bit. Feelings are scary when you've allowed yourself to grow anesthetized to the world."

I pushed my hand between us and felt along his body until I had my palm over his heart. I pushed there meaningfully. "When are we going to talk about this?"

"I don't know. When are you going to stop running and destroying everything you leave behind?" His voice was stark with pain, with bitterness.

He couldn't forgive what I'd done, which I could well understand; I'd never so much as tried forgiving myself.

"I'm self-destructive," I told him quietly, my voice shaking.

That surprised a bark of a laugh out of him. "You think?" Sarcasm dripped from the words.

"Yes. I never learned how to build. All the talents in my life have been honed toward deconstruction, and because of that, I am better at destroying than I have *ever* been at building, and in spite of everything I've always known it. I know it's no surprise to you. It wasn't easy for me to do what I did. I hated leaving you. It hurt me too. I hope someday you can believe that. You can't lead a life like mine without killing important parts of yourself. To make the things that make you weak die. I killed a part of myself when I left you. I thought I'd killed it forever. I realize now I didn't do a good job."

"For once in your life, can you speak fucking plainly?"

I couldn't say it. I just couldn't get the words out.

It would destroy me to learn for a certainty that I'd lost his heart forever.

"How can we fix this?" I finally asked him. "I want a truce. I don't want you to hate me anymore. I don't want to hate myself."

He gripped my hair in both hands and dragged my face to his to kiss me, growling, "Does this feel like hate to you? Are you so blind?"

I nodded, tears falling from my face onto his. "Completely. I've never trusted my heart. Everything it tells me feels like a lie. I do think it makes me blind. But this hostility, this never-ending rage of yours. . . I can't stand it. Tell me how to make it go away."

The fury, that overwhelming resentment of his was finally stripped from his voice when he said quietly and emotionally, "Stay. Don't leave again."

"Keeping me here with you indefinitely will ruin your political career. They will unseat you."

"They can try. None of that is your concern. Your job is to stay. Just stay."

It was much easier to reply to that than it had ever been before. Our child had changed everything.

I would go to war with him.

I would reshape my whole purpose, my whole existence to keep him now and to protect our son.

"I will stay here for as long as I'm welcome. I promise."

"Please, don't promise. I can't stomach the sound of that yet. Time is all that can prove the truth to me."

"Fair enough. So are we like, together now?"

He pushed my head down to his chest, ear to his steady, pounding heart. He said something softly but vehemently in *Druidic*.

"Care to translate?"

"It is hard to translate precisely to English, but I said that we are bound until the stars fall from the sky, until all life ends."

He was quiet for a time, stroking my hair with his perfect, healing hands. "I know how you are. If you start to feel the prison doors closing, you run. Whether you want to or not, you always just run. Your biggest fear is a cage. Do you know what my prison is?"

"What?"

He spoke in *Druidic* again but translated before I asked. "Every step you take away from me is a prison. That's where you left me. I've been in purgatory. I've spent most of my life there, knowing you were somewhere in this world, apart from me. I'm asking you to change your very nature to set me free from that, and I'd like to know if you can do that for me, for our family, but it has to be of your own free will. I can't be your jailor."

"You were never that. I would love to stay with you, there's nothing I want more. I just don't see how it can work. As Arch you can't—"

"Just do your part. Leave the politics to me."

"On one condition," I said, shifting my tone.

He watched me like I was fascinating, like he had no idea what I'd say next, and he didn't.

I was a song he'd heard a thousand times, and he still never knew how to guess the next verse.

"Anything," he said softly.

"No more hoes," I said with a straight face.

He smiled at me, and it was like the sun rising, brilliant and beautiful and a reason to love life.

"Well?" I pressed when he just laughed.

"No more hoes," he said, kissing the palm of my hand.

"Are we really crazy enough to give this thing another go?" I asked him, hugging him bare chest to bare chest, our hearts beating together.

"Finally, you're getting it," said Dom succinctly. "Good to see that you're paying attention at last. And you didn't ask, but I haven't touched another woman since you strode back into my life seven months ago. I swear it."

I processed that, his chin rubbing against the top of my head. I remembered clearly that another woman was walking in even as I left his bedroom right after our reunion seven months ago.

"I sent her home the second you stepped out of sight."

"You aren't allowed to start reading my mind."

I could hear the smile in his voice. "I wasn't. It isn't one of my powers. I just know you that well. Parts of you will always be a mystery, but other parts of you I know better than you yourself do."

CHAPTER TWELVE
THE GOOD BROTHER

D om, are you going to show us the set where you guys staged the moon landing?" asked Christian cheekily.

"No," Dom said casually. "That sets been taken apart and turned into an alien habitat."

The ride to the hidden desert bunker was accompanied by countless Area 51 jokes from Christian, which was expected. What wasn't expected was Dom throwing out a few of his own.

He smiled at the look on my face. "What?" he said into my ear. "You forgot I have a sense of humor? You cast me as a villain in your little drama and forgot I was more nuanced than that."

"You were never the villain. I cast myself in that role."

"Another poor choice for the part. How about this? Stick around longer, and you'll see more from me than rage and lust."

He had a point, and I stayed quiet and stewed about it for a time.

We were in the back of a large military transport vehicle with no windows. Dom was sitting with us for some reason, instead of in the front with the grown-ups where he obviously belonged.

It occurred to me that he was making nice with my friends. And in spite of all the sour history between them, my friends seemed to be returning the sentiment.

A new and interesting development, to be sure.

Dom was sprawling next to me on a bench seat directly across from Caleb and Christian. His arm was slung casually along my seat back, and he was in a rare mellow mood.

Our evening together could probably account for that. He'd worked a lot of aggression out over and through the long hours of the night.

I touched his thigh, drawing his attention to me. I smiled at him tentatively. "This is nice," I told him quietly.

He smiled back, his devastating eyes melting me a bit.

"Yeah, just a nice ride into the desert to an underground druid dungeon to torture one of your brothers," Christian couldn't help but to add. "We should have a picnic while we're at it."

Dom just kept smiling at me.

"You should tell him our plan," Caleb said, ruining the spell. "We need his help."

"What plan?" Dom asked, smile dying. He knew he wouldn't like it and he was right, as usual.

I sighed, but Caleb was right. Our deadline was fast approaching, and we needed Dom's cooperation for all kinds of reasons. "I'm supposed to meet with Tianlong for dinner or something. It would be nice if you could come along."

"Dinner or something?" he asked, focusing on just the thing I didn't want him to, of course.

"I made a deal with him for some information before I left. . . like a meetup sort of thing. I'm going to schedule it with him in a few days and I think it would. . . go better if you joined us."

"A meetup sort of thing," Dom repeated back, reading between the lines just how I didn't want him to. I wondered what Sloan had told him. Everything, probably, about my last meeting with the scary, seductive dragon.

"A date," Caleb said flatly. "She owes him a date. Can you get to the point already, Jillian?"

I glared at him.

I could feel Dom staring at me and I met his eyes. "Not a real date, of course. And there's no rule I can't bring you along. But, anyway," I tried my best to breeze past that part in spite of the look of death in his eyes, "Drake's due in town in a few days, and we were going to try to arrange the meeting then, so when we have Tianlong's attention, Caleb and Christian can grab Drake and see what he knows about Lynn. It's a chance we can't afford to ignore. Will you help?"

"If you're asking me if I'd rather you go on a date with a dragon king who wants to mate with you with or without me I think the answer is obvious."

We just stared at each other. He broke first. "I wouldn't miss it for the world."

His gaze shot to Caleb. "Be careful capturing Drake. Don't cross the wrong line. The druids aren't at war with those dragons. You break that peace treaty, you're on your own."

Caleb didn't strike me as worried about it. "We usually are."

We reached the compound and took an elevator down, down, down. It was a hell of a dungeon, a cavernous space that would fit a full-grown dragon, which made sense, though at the moment it held what at first glance looked like a normal man. He was tall, blond, and slender. He had beautiful, clean, even features and perfect skin. Ocean eyes smiled at me.

It was as I'd suspected. They had the good brother.

"Sven," I called my favorite brother by his nickname as I drew close to the bars of his cage.

"Svenga," he replied with a smile I remembered well. It had been a rare and shining light during my dark childhood.

We kept staring at each other, taking it in. We could have been twins. There was a bond here that the years apart had not diminished. It hurt to think how we could break it today.

"Sveinhild," he said, this time softer, more heartfelt.

"Bropir," I said. My accent was all wrong, it had been too long, and it made his smile grow bigger, warmer.

"Lillasyster," he responded.

"Not so little now."

He was saying something to me in the old language when Dom snapped, "English, please."

How he managed to turn a please into an order was a talent all his own.

"How'd they capture you and keep you here?" I asked curiously. Both were feats on their own, but achieving them together was downright impressive.

"I let them. I wanted to get away from our family, and I wanted to talk to you." His accent wasn't strong, but he'd clearly spent more time in Europe than the States. "I just didn't think it would take this long for them to let me see you."

"I've been a bit busy," I said vaguely. "Do you know who has Lynn?"

"I was taken not long after she was, if you'll recall."

"Yes, but you had to know something about what they were planning. I was taken by our family to a location close by. Where was she supposed to end up? You have to know *something*."

"Not as much as you'd think, considering my *talents*. If it's any consolation, I don't believe she's in any real danger, though I don't have a clue *where* she is. All I know is that the one called Drake has her, and he wouldn't harm her."

Caleb, Christian, and I shared a look.

"Last time I saw her someone had taken her eyes," I told my brother.

"That wasn't Drake, it was Villi, and he was acting on his own. He was settling an old score. Those were *not* his orders."

I'd guessed as much. "When did Villi ever take orders?"

"A fair point, but one our father was determined to learn the hard way. Villi won't be ignoring any more of his orders any time soon now, will he?"

My brother seemed as pleased by that as anyone. If it was a trick, it worked, because I was reassured. "Our family let the Chinese dragons take Lynn. Why?"

"It was a deal I wasn't privy to. Father's learned to block me from his mind, so I only have bits and pieces. I do think the deal went sour after they took her, though. Our family is at war with the Chinese dragons as well as the druids now, if you didn't know."

I hadn't. Even Dom had a thoughtful look on his face as though he was putting pieces of a puzzle together as Sven spoke.

"How do we know if he's telling the truth?" Christian asked.

"We don't," I said. "I can't read his mind. I've never had that talent."

"Some druids were working with you," I said to my brother, memories coming back to me even as I said it. "Who were they?"

He grimaced. "There were druids working with our relatives. At least two. I don't know who. They went to some trouble to hide that from me, too. And for my part, I was just brought in to try to take you peaceably."

"How'd that work out for you?"

"Worse than I'd hoped.

"You don't say.

"Considerably worse. I don't think Father understood that the full force of the druids was behind you. He didn't imagine taking you could start a war."

"I wouldn't put it that way," I said carefully.

"I would," Dom cut in. "And he knows it now. I'll have his head for trying."

Sven just smiled and shook his head. "Very druid of you, Arch. I wish you luck. Let me loose and I'll help."

Dom looked half-tempted. "If only we could trust you."

"I can help her," my brother told him, his tone coaxing. "I can teach her all the things she needs to know, all the things she never learned because she and Lynn escaped so young and have been alone in the world without anyone of our kind to teach them."

"We've done alright," I said defensively.

"Not as well as you could be doing," he spoke to me, then returned to Dom. "She'll be safer with this knowledge. It could be the difference between her living or dying, I promise you this."

He was clever. No one could sniff out a weakness in others quite like a telepath.

Sven looked my way and waved in Dom's direction. "You're with that one, right? The druid Arch? You're on his mind constantly."

It took me a moment to recover from my shock. I hadn't expected him to start talking about my love life. Also the 'on his mind constantly' part was a bit distracting.

I was almost blushing. I took a calming breath.

"Yes," Dom said when it took me too long to answer.

My brother just kept looking at me. "Well, say you end up

together. Say it works out, and you need to go into a sleep for a few months, years, hell, decades. I can teach you how to bring him with you. There are benefits to our trances, not the least of which that you wouldn't have to leave him every time you needed a recovery phase."

It was times like these that I realized my lack of knowledge about myself and my kind was vast. There were big, gaping holes that left me ignorant. I hadn't even known that we could choose when to go into one of the deep sleeps.

I hadn't thought Dom was still listening. He was turned away, talking to one of his people, but he turned suddenly, striding right up like he'd been part of the conversation all along. "How?" he asked my brother, voice cold and determined.

I blinked at Dom. What was even going through his head? He could never leave for long periods of time. He had too much responsibility to even consider a short-term leave.

Sven smiled at him. "Let me loose and I'll tell you. I'll work with you, and with her, on whatever you want in exchange for my freedom. Give me a geas. Make it airtight. I know you've been plotting it out in your head. *Just do it* so we can get to work."

And just like that, I knew he had Dom convinced.

Sven looked at me. "Your son is a telepath."

Fucking mind-reader. I glared at him.

"It's a challenging gift to master, but he doesn't have to do it alone. It doesn't need to be a curse for him as it has for me. It took centuries but I've mastered it, and I can teach him, guide him as no one else can. Let me help you. *Let me help your son.*"

And just like that, he had me too.

We were traveling back to town, errant brother in tow, when he said casually, "I'll join the guys getting to Drake. If we can get past his guards, I think I can make him talk without bloodshed."

"It's rude to read the minds of your allies," Christian told him with a very British sniff.

Sven shrugged. "It's hard to stop it, and you project your thoughts like you're blowing them out of a cannon. That's as much your fault as mine." He pointed at Caleb. "He doesn't project at all, but his mind is very scary so I plan to stay clear."

Caleb looked fascinated. "What did you see?"

"I don't even know. No one here is human, strictly speaking, but you're. . . something else entirely. Not like a human at all. Like looking inside of a spider's brain."

Caleb smiled and it was not at all pleasant. "Staying clear is a good plan for you. Wander around in my mind again, and I just might trap you there."

I looked at him. I didn't think he was joking. "You can do that?"

He stared.

I changed the subject. "Anyone have Tianlong's number? Let's set this thing up. The sooner the better."

"I'll set it up myself," Dom said firmly.

"I'm not sure he'll like that," I said.

"All the better. I'll take care of the details."

Of course he would. Telling Dom about a plan was as good as setting him in charge of it.

CHAPTER THIRTEEN
DEAL WITH THE DRUID DEVIL

I t was the day of the meeting with Tianlong, and I took a quick trip to the shops downstairs to find something appropriate to wear.

Dom's rooms were protected with an Arch's power. I could sleep easy there, if I could just ignore the world of baggage and lust between me and the room's other inhabitant. Those protected rooms were a short trip away from the elevators that led down to the shops. A very short window of opportunity, but one I still saw clearly.

I wouldn't say I sought it out, but no one could say I avoided it, which even I knew amounted to the same thing at this point.

Perhaps I was just in the mood to make a deal with the druid devil.

I was walking alone from the protected quarters to the bank of elevators that led to the first floor of the mall.

I pushed the down button, my attention caught by a mirror

against the wall. It hung above an ornate desk, heavy and thick with a strangely shaped frame that gave the impression it was expensive but very old.

It did not fit. In this sparse, contemporary space, it was garish, outlandish. Old-fashioned.

Ancient.

I wasn't sure why I thought that last word. It had felt like it was put into my brain.

I took a step closer to it, then another, eyes glued to the mirror, though my instincts told me to do the opposite.

They were yelling at me, and what they were saying was very clear.

Run. Run like hell and don't look back.

But I did not do that. I stepped closer.

It wasn't that it was blank. Oh no. There was a reflection. I was there, and I seemed to be myself, normal, the same. But behind me was not the room I'd entered. Behind me was not a room at all.

It was The Grove. One as familiar as it was terrifying.

Such a very bad idea. I shouldn't let it catch me, not again.

Well, perhaps, maybe just a taste. Just one more little memory to feed on.

I won't gorge myself this time, I promised myself.

I held the secret of her like a precious, hidden gift for as long as I could. For years, in fact, I led that double life.

It always took a bit of maneuvering for me to sneak away from my school and friends without getting questioned, but I was managing quite often by this point.

I'd been in strong denial about it for months, but she was obviously seeing someone. Some guy named Tom.

I was sick about it even as I studied him at every opportunity. He was human. Nothing supernatural about him that I could detect. He was in the restaurant at least as often as I was, waiting for her to make an appearance, no matter how brief, just so I could bask in her presence.

I caught them sharing a certain kind of smile once. She'd leaned down and touched his shoulder as she said something to him, and it wrenched some beastly thing open inside of me that I didn't recognize.

I wanted to murder him, and I even considered it. I could kill him so easily, and she would never smile at him again. It was frightening how tempted I was.

I couldn't bring myself to ask her about it for a long time, but it consumed me.

One afternoon he was absent, and she had a little extra time for me. We played cards, and when it was time for me to leave I embraced her, and she let me, patting my back lightly. I lingered at it, pressing against her until she pushed me away.

"Are you dating that man that's in here all the time?"

She looked uncomfortable, but she answered. "Yes, we're seeing each other."

I wanted to howl in pain but made myself speak as calmly as I could manage. "Is it serious?"

She smirked. The question was funny to her, and I found some relief in that. "No. I've only known him for a few months. Why? Did he say something to you?"

"No. I just noticed he's here a lot. Are you sleeping together?"

She was shocked and displeased at my nerve, I could tell. "That is none of your business, young man."

I wanted to beg her to tell me, but only if it was the answer I wanted.

Once he and I were both in the café, seated a few tables apart, and we were there for the same reason. Some sight of her, however brief. She was particularly elusive on that day.

I watched Tom wait so long for an appearance from her that he got up and went into her back office, a place so private I'd never even gotten to step foot inside of it.

I lasted five minutes before I followed him. I couldn't help it.

I found him crowding her, his arms on either side of her, not letting her pass though it looked like she wanted to.

They were arguing as he trapped her against the wall. He bumped her chest with his aggressively.

I saw red and lost my mind.

I only came back into myself when I realized I was now being pinned to the wall.

Tom was gone, though I could remember the feel of his neck between my hands.

All that was forgotten by the feel of her hands against my chest, pushing, holding me against the wall by force. She was strong, impossibly so, and I was now in the position Tom had had her in when I'd lost my mind.

"You're not human. What are you?" I asked her. It wasn't the first time.

"I told you not to ask me that or you won't see me again. I'll have to leave. You understand?"

I nodded, relaxing as I studied her. "I almost killed him," I said even as I was realizing it myself. I would have snapped his neck if she hadn't stopped me by force.

She looked as agitated as I'd never seen her. Worry was written across her face as she studied mine intently.

She didn't take her hands away, and I didn't bring it up. It was rare to get that kind of contact from her.

She fisted my shirt in both hands, an attempt to shake me though I wasn't budging now. She looked deep into my eyes and spoke softly, "You can't do things like that. You have to control it. You can't come back from taking a human life, do you understand? And you should never take one for something so trivial.

"He was manhandling you."

"And you thought that should have a death sentence?"

"I'm sorry. Are you mad at me?"

She let go of me, taking a deep trembling breath as she ran a hand over her face. "No, Dom. I'm worried about you. You can't get mixed up in my business like this. I think you should steer clear of this place for a while, and while you're gone you should work on your control, especially how it's triggered by your protective instinct."

I was crushed, but I did what she said faithfully because I wanted to be able to see her again.

A few months later I was back at her place, and she didn't send me away so I kept returning in my usual pattern.

Tom was still hanging around, his eyes following her and more lovesick by the day. She was barely looking at him by this point, and I started to have hope that it was over.

I was controlling my temper constantly, I had improved, but eventually Tom followed her back to her office again, and I followed him because I simply had to.

He was holding her against the wall again, and she was turning her face away passively. She looked bored more than anything.

"At least tell me why," he was saying to her.

"I already did," she said and she was calm as could be.

He punched the wall near her face and I started to shake.

"Get away from her," I told him in a voice I didn't recognize. The beast-call was a heartbeat away from taking over.

She wasn't bored anymore. She was frantic, pushing him aside to reach me. She grabbed my hands and looked deep into my eyes. "Fight it, Dom. Don't let it take over. You're stronger than that."

It was working. Having her close was enough. At some point Tom left, she forced him out, and I was sitting at her desk and she was hovering near me.

"Are you back? Are you under control?" she asked me.

She was holding my face in her hands, and all I could see were her pale ocean eyes. I was caught in their waves wholly, more than happy to drown.

All I could feel was her presence, close and caring and all-consuming.

126

"Is he gone for good?" I finally asked.

She sighed, shaking her head at me, and let go of my face.

She tried to step away, but I pulled her between my legs and hugged her to me, her standing, me sitting, and lay my head against her soft chest.

She sighed again, stroking a reluctant hand over my hair. "Look, I don't need you to protect me from a guy like Tom. I know that you're capable, but you can't and you don't need to. I've got him handled with both hands tied behind my back. Trust me. I'm only in danger of being annoyed by him. And if there's ever something I can't protect myself from I want you to run the other way. Fast."

"That's not how this is going to work," I said, hugging her tighter. "I'd never leave you behind to fight by yourself."

She tried to push away but there wasn't much strength in it. "You need to be more pragmatic than that. Survival at all costs. Look out for yourself first. No use in both of us going down."

I finally pulled back to look up into her eyes. "That's not how this is going to work. You go down, I go down. We go down together. I'd never leave you."

She looked bewildered and agitated. But there was something else there. She didn't want me to see it, but I could feel it. And it felt like the smallest spark of pleasure. She was at least flattered by my devotion to her. It was a start. "You're too young to understand this," she said, "but life doesn't work like that. Eventually everyone has to leave."

"Do you know some things are written in the stars?" I stood, towering over her, and now it was me backing her against the wall, though I didn't touch her, just held her with my eyes. They were my mother's eyes, and they were said to have mysterious powers. "And some druids are able to read it. If a love is strong enough it paints a pattern in the cosmos that cannot be denied. Such is fate. Did you know that?"

She shook her head at me, white blond hair just the length of her perfect jaw, falling over one eye as she did so. I brushed it back

behind her ear, taking the opportunity to step closer as I did so. She
was very tall for a woman, but I was much taller now. She had to
look up at me, and I had to tilt my head down. I smiled at her, and
she wrinkled up her nose at me, trying to glare, trying to be stern
with me, but I knew her heart wasn't in it.

"You have to be the most incorrigible sixteen-year-old on the
planet."

I smiled wider. "Almost seventeen."

I came back propped against the wall, the elevator door open
and dinging at me. The Grove had just disappeared and sort
of spit me out. A new trick for it, at least for me.

I studied myself in the mirror on the way down. My
clothing was dark enough that the blood just looked like
slightly damp spots on my shirt. I looked normal enough
after I wiped the blood off my skin, my bite wounds healed.

I needed to tell Dom. And I promised myself I would.
After we got Lynn back. Probably.

CHAPTER FOURTEEN
THE BLOODY KIND

I was slipping into my dress, hair and makeup already done, when Dom arrived at his suite to escort me. He was good to go in his usual impeccable suit and tie.

I showed him my back, and he fastened the delicate buttons at my neck in a few neat motions.

I turned back around and he studied the dress like he wasn't sure if he loved it or hated it. It was gold, just the tone to set off my skin, and made up of a series of straps that more or less covered the essentials. It had a halter that rigged my breasts up high, showing a few inches of teasing under-boob instead of the usual cleavage. From the ribs down it was a series of thick bands of material that played peekaboo with my skin and ended well above my knees.

I turned around so he could see the back at his leisure. It was tight enough that all the straps weren't in danger of shifting and uncovering anything important. Revealing but overall pretty comfortable.

Unlike the shoes. Those were spiked torture devices— Loubi Kates in vamp, mirrored red. I hadn't been able to resist them with carte blanche store credit at my disposal. Just another form of treasure hoarding.

I slipped into them as I looked back at him over my shoulder.

My hair was loose down my back, and he brushed it aside as he stepped close behind me.

"You've outdone yourself," he said roughly into my ear. "All of this to go on a date with *another man*?"

I shivered at his tone. "It's not a date. And the point is to distract him, right?"

"Mission accomplished," he said and bit my neck hard enough to leave a mark. "Later I'm going to take it off you with my teeth. Let's go." He grabbed my hand and tugged me along.

"Why did I need to be ready so early? The meeting's not for hours. What's going on?"

"I have some last minute druid business to attend to. My presence is required, and I'd like you to accompany me. Everyone needs to get used to seeing you on my arm again."

"This should be fun."

He slowed down to kiss my hand, his gaze holding me so deeply that I had to look away or we wouldn't make it even one step farther from his bed.

"What kind of business is it?"

"The bloody kind."

"Sounds fun."

"It's not. It's quite unexpected and unwelcome. Collin surprised us all by challenging Patrick this morning. I had no idea he had such ambitions."

I remembered Patrick, though I hadn't known him well. I could've guessed he'd be one of Dom's lieutenants. He was part of Dom's childhood pack of friends. "Patrick is higher up than Collin?" I asked, surprised.

"He's number four. He took it a while ago, and Collin

didn't even fight him for it. This move now is both poorly timed and a shock to everyone. It couldn't have come at a worse moment, and I still haven't gotten a good reason why. Nonetheless, it is his right."

"Will he win?"

"Patrick is the more vicious fighter, and he's always had an edge over Collin. Besides that, he's very angry about the challenge. I think he'll prevail. I just can't figure out what's going on in Collin's head."

"Are you worried about him?"

"I'm worried about them both. A challenge always carries risk, and I thought all of their ranks were settled. My lieutenants fighting is the last thing I ever want or need."

I held his arm as we strode through the casino floor and to its attached coliseum.

Security was tight, it wouldn't due to have any humans slipping in and witnessing some druids tearing each other apart, but we were waved past it all easily, and I could feel every druid eye we passed staring at us. Dom was making quite a statement today.

We were escorted into an owner's box that led out to a balcony with a clear view of the arena. It held twenty thousand, at least, that I recalled, and it looked to be filled to a seat.

"You really did mean everyone," I said softly, eyes scanning the huge crowd.

"I did."

"Quite a showing on short notice," I observed.

"It's a rare event, and seats are coveted," Sloan said as she joined us near the balcony. "Some drove from hours away, some even booked last minute flights to see this. These don't happen often. There's a waiting list a mile long."

"Where are the rest?" Dom asked her, referring to the other lieutenants, I assumed.

"All except Cam are down by the arena floor, in view and on display for the crowd.   Unless you'd like me to call them up here?"

"No, that's good. Where is Cam?"

"I'm here," a deep voice growled from behind us.   I glanced back at him. He glared at me, then at Sloan, then even at Dom.

"I'm going to *kill him* for this," Cam told Dom.

"Get in line," Dom told him.

I was shocked when Sloan moved to Cam, touching his chest and saying something to him in a quiet, soothing voice. Cam didn't shove her away, in fact seemed to huddle her closer, his head bending down to her until his mouth was at her ear.

"What's up with them?" I asked Dom quietly. "Don't they hate each other?"

"They're. . . complicated. But it's not really hate between them. It never was. Cam's overbearing nature has always been at its strongest when it was directed at Sloan, but it was only ever born from concern. Sometimes the person you love the most is the one you fight the hardest."

Whoa. Holy shit. I couldn't wait to tell Christian.

I'd known there was chemistry and complications there but love? No one knew them better than Dom, and for him to say a thing like that. . . I kept stealing glances back at them until Dom put his arm around me, blocking them from my sight.

"Behave yourself," he told me, a twinkle in his eye.

"Have you met me?" I asked him, but I was effectively distracted from trying and failing to eavesdrop on the strange pair when he pulled me into his chest for a warm hug.

"I missed this," I said, voice muffled as I nuzzled against him.

The crowd went suddenly silent, and with a heavy sigh,

Dom kissed the top of my head and moved toward the balcony.

"Give me a moment," he told me politely, and Cam was suddenly there, placing a crown of massive antlers on his head that would have bent a lesser man. As he did this, Sloan hooked a mic up to his lapel.

Without pausing, he strode out to the balcony to greet his people like royalty.

And he was that. Their perfect druid king, out of this world beautiful and more powerful than the ones that came before him. I wasn't alone in my enthrallment of his devastating presence.

The crowd went wild. I wasn't sure how long they would have gone on, but when he raised his hand the enormous crowd bowed to him as if on cue, a silence that lasted until he spoke.

"I've been called here to oversee an ancient rite of our people," he began, his deep voice captivating. I wondered how much of that was magic and how much was just the man himself. I honestly couldn't tell at this point what all of his powers entailed.

"My fifth lieutenant, Collin, has challenged my fourth lieutenant, Patrick," he continued, clear disapproval in every syllable. "The timing is less than ideal, but it's brought an issue to the fore that I've long been planning to address."

I had no idea where he was going with this, and by the looks on Cam's face he didn't either. Sloan's expression, however, was stone-faced to a point that made me think she was in the know. Interesting.

"The challenge has been issued and accepted. So be it. But I forbid any more deaths in the arena from this point forward. You will fight to victory alone."

There were murmurs in the crowd, the volume growing until Dom roared, "Silence," and they went deathly quiet again. "I am your Arch and this is my right. We need to stop throwing druid lives away with these petty games. Anyone who does not agree is welcome to challenge me." By the continued silence, I was guessing that wasn't going to happen.

"Contenders!" he spoke to the two men in the center of the ring. "Prepare yourselves! When I give the word you may begin."

The crowd went wild.

He turned and motioned for the three of us to join him.

I went with dread, but my head was held high.

The mood of the crowd shifted, but I think they were too excited to let even my presence get in the way of the spectacle to come.

Dom turned off his mic, took my hand, and placed it on his arm deferentially. Sloan and Cam flanked us on each side.

The contenders were still getting ready, stretching, undressing, and conferring with their seconds.

"Your people love you," I told him quietly.

He didn't respond, staring ahead, looking like a beautiful, exotic king in his crown of antlers.

"Look at them," I told him quietly. The crowd was looking at him more than even the fighters in the ring. "And look at you. You were born for this."

He was silent for a time, just watching his lieutenants prepare, and I thought he wouldn't respond. And when he did I almost wished he hadn't. "I never wanted any of this. I was maneuvered into it by you, if you'll recall."

"It was always going to end up here," I defended. "I've known it since I set eyes on you. It was inevitable."

"You're so convincing I almost believe it myself. But it's not true, you know. It was never what I wanted." He said it all quietly but with absolute conviction.

It hit me like a devastating blow then.

He had said as much before. I'd never believed it. I'd convinced myself he was only saying it to soothe me, to assure me that he'd never leave me, that he couldn't have this thing he wanted out of a sacrifice at the altar of our love. Because a king of druids could never have a non-druid mate. It was impossible.

But hearing him say that he did not want it now at the pinnacle of his power, I realized I'd convinced myself of a lie.

"I don't understand," I said, but even that was a bit of a lie. I was beginning to understand very well and breaking my own heart all over again in the process. "You're the one that believes in destiny."

"I don't want this," he waved at the mass of his people in the stands. "I never did. I don't know how to tell you more clearly. *This was not my destiny.*"

I shook my head, blinking away useless tears. "I thought it was the only way. And now you're trapped." *What had I done?*

"As I've said, leave the politics to me," he said scathingly. "Your track record isn't exactly stellar where these things are concerned."

I said, my heart aching with the utter hopelessness of it, "I'm so sorry. You can't quit, and they'll never accept me by your side. Can't you see it?"

His jaw was hardened, his face unreadable, his eyes faraway, but still somehow clearly focused on something I couldn't fathom. "I've always seen more than you give me credit for, Jillian. You're the one that's blind."

I leaned into him, getting worked up in a hurry. "What don't I see? Enlighten me."

He turned to me, and that far-sighted, focused gaze of his bore into me. It was intense.

"As I've said, power was never the most important thing, not for me."

I swallowed, bracing myself for what was coming.

"You know what is even if you won't admit it."

I shook my head, but I knew. He'd already made it clear, and now it felt like he was just twisting the knife.

"This was never my destiny. *You* are. All I've ever wanted is to walk through the ages with you. You can throw me away as many times as you want, Jillian, but I'll never throw *you* away, and I'd never put my rank above our *family*. Especially not now." His voice was raw, as though a protective layer had been stripped from it, his vulnerability bared.

The problem with Dom was what that exposed was not weakness but a core of steel. He was so steady in his convictions that even the softest part of them was *indestructible*.

It was as incredible to me as it had always been.

"But won't you be in danger if they depose you? Your predecessor won't let you live. You're too strong. Any new Arch will see you as a ticking time bomb, a problem to be solved, and there's only one solution. It'll be Declan all over again. You won't be challenged; they'll just make it easy on themselves and assassinate you."

"It won't be the same situation as before. I've already solved that problem. And I won't be deposed. I'll abdicate and maneuver a peaceful shift of power."

It was as if the whole world moved and reformed itself to his perception with a few words that would have made no sense coming out of anyone else. "How?"

"I've groomed a successor from the start. Someone I trust implicitly. It may take a few more years, but when they're ready, when the people are ready, I'll support the claim, and help to defend it. It won't be an easy transition, but that won't stop me."

"Cam," I guessed. He was a natural leader. A bit mean and overzealous but well respected and a true powerhouse.

No sane druid would challenge him.

"No, he doesn't have the temperament for it, though he will help to defend it, hopefully as consort if they ever come to their senses. It will be Sloan."

I wasn't expecting that at all, though I liked it. On paper you might overlook her. She was only half-druid and a woman, which was uncommon for the role though there were no explicit rules against that. But she had the temperament for it. She was cool-headed, clever, and just. A lot like Dom when he wasn't dealing with me, which was a large reason why they'd always been the strongest of allies and friends. She would make radical changes, but they would all be improvements, I had no doubt.

"It won't be easy," I remarked, though I wasn't discouraging the idea. They'd just have a fight on their hands to get it done.

"Nothing worth doing is ever easy. She'll make Cam and I lieutenants, and anyone that wants to have a shot at her will have to go through both of us. That alone will prevent most of the bloodshed that's usually involved in a power shift."

His head turned suddenly back to the arena, and I knew he'd been given some signal that I couldn't detect. He straightened, stepping close to the balcony rail and pulling me with him with an arm around my waist.

He turned his mic back on and without further ado said, "Contenders, you may commence."

I'd forgotten Cam was there until he spoke from my right, "One of them should have gone feline for maneuvering. What arrogance." He sounded disgusted but also very worried. I looked over and was surprised to find Sloan clutching his hand and rubbing his back. Curiouser and curiouser.

The two lieutenants in the arena were about twenty feet apart. Both had shifted into bears, so there would be no weapons aside from what grew out of their flesh with magic. At his word, one of them roared loud enough to shake the stands and rushed at the other. The other, clearly a beat behind, started moving a few seconds too late, and it cost him. The other was on him with momentum before he'd effectively picked up enough speed to counter.

"Which one is which?" I asked Dom quietly as they tore into each other.

"Collin is the one that's winning," Dom said with no expression.

The fight was gory, claws ripping into flesh, blood and fur flying, their movements almost too fast to follow once they got within grappling range.

"Are you sure Patrick is the stronger fighter?"

"At this moment, no, though I would have had a different answer an hour ago."

The noises they were making were horrible, like two wild animals being tortured and screaming in rage.

"It's more straightforward than I would have guessed," I noted. The fighters didn't seem to be using any actual technique other than to try to rip the other one open.

"It's unusual, what they're doing," Sloan said. "It should be more of a dance, as much skill as strength. It's like they both went berserker right away."

One of the bears looked bigger than the other, I noted just as it started to glow green. "What is *that*?" I asked.

Dom was cursing and turning his mic back on. "Watch it, Collin. You break the rules, you'll answer to me!"

"What is he doing?"

"Crossing a line. It's a spell that's been banned from the arena. It would make it very hard for Patrick to pierce his flesh."

Collin must've been in control enough to hear Dom because he stopped glowing but kept ripping into the other bear. He had him on his back now, his muzzle in the other druid's neck. It went on for a while, one mauling the other and making horrible noises even when the other looked to be limp on the ground.

He didn't stop even then, digging his claws deep into the other druid with abandon but when he started to slash at the slack druid's neck with his claws the crowd went wild, yelling and pounding their chests.

"Enough," Dom roared. "It is finished! You have your victory, Collin, now walk away. Healers, to Patrick!" At his words a furious flurry of activity ensued on the sand below us. Collin was dragged off Patrick by several druids. He didn't go easy. The healers had already descended on Patrick and were working frantically as a growing crowd was still forcing Collin away one stubborn foot at a time.

"What's he doing?" Cam kept repeating. "What's wrong with him?"

Siobhan was on the sand now in human form in a slinky golden dress. Great, we matched. She was pushing at Collin's bear chest and shouting into his face.

"He's gone full berserker," Dom said quietly, "It's common enough, we've just never seen Collin succumb to it before."

"It'll wear off eventually," Sloan said, rubbing Cam's chest now. He had an arm around her, and it looked natural, like he'd held her many times before. "And he'll regret trying to kill his friend," Sloan continued, "Look, he's calming even now. I think Siobhan is getting through to him."

"I'm going down there," Cam said, but Sloan stopped him with a touch.

"You shouldn't," Dom said. It wasn't an order, but a suggestion. "Five of my lieutenants are on the sand right now. It should be enough, and if it's not it will make you all look weak, and you know what that will mean."

"What will that mean?" I asked.

"New challengers will come forward to test them," Dom told me.

I thought as much. We all watched the arena for a time and I tried to pick out who was who. I'd been too removed from druid politics for too long to know all the major players that weren't on my radar. "Who are your other two lieutenants?" I asked him. I had a notion but there were a lot of people in the fray below.

"Kaska is sixth," he told me. I was a little surprised. I hadn't known the dark-haired, ochre-skinned native woman was so deep in his inner circle, but she certainly had the power for such a high position. She was one of their most ferocious fighters. "And Oisin is seventh." That I could have guessed. He was another childhood friend of Dom's, a small man for a druid but still strong enough to hold the most defensive role as the most challenged lieutenant. Any contenders would have to start with him.

We watched the flurry of activity for a time before I asked, "What now?"

Dom grimaced, a look of barely disguised distaste crossing over his face like a strobing light, there and gone. "We celebrate."

CHAPTER FIFTEEN
GETTING OVER IT

E ventually they got things under control and the whole thing turned into almost a cocktail party in the owner's box. It was surreal and perverse and oh so very druid.

The contenders were missing, both being tended to and healed and brought back into their right minds. Still, there was a good chance one or both of them would show up later to mingle like they hadn't just tried to rip each other to shreds.

Everyone else with high rank was there, as well as most of the foreign dignitaries on my task force.

Christian and Caleb were conspicuously absent. They were already getting into position with Sven for our plan.

Dom held court next to what looked suspiciously like a throne. He'd placed his crown of antlers there. Who could blame him? It couldn't have been easy to wear.

He was charming and suave, but there was an edge to his grace that left no doubt he could turn razor sharp on a dime. There was ever a warning there: Tread carefully. No matter how pleasant he behaved, you were still dealing with a deadly king.

He smoothly hosted the event with a proprietary hand on me, greeting everyone, fielding questions, conducting business like two of his closest friends hadn't just clawed each other bloody.

He didn't have to tell me to keep close to him. He was making a point by bringing me to this on his arm, and the point was better made if I stayed at his side.

The statement was further illustrated by his inability to keep his hands off me. He stroked my skin between the straps of my dress like he couldn't stop, stroked my hair, brought my hand to his lips repeatedly, each touch a statement to everyone there and the message was direct: She is mine, and if you have a problem with her you'll have to go through me.

I laid on some PDA too, and I told myself it was for the audience but the truth was touching him had always been a rare slice of heaven for me. The where and the when had never changed that, and the years apart had only heightened it.

Helen and Siobhan were in a corner of the room and talking closely with each other. It made my Spidey senses tingle, but who wouldn't be paranoid to see two of your man's exes getting along so well with each other meanwhile knowing they both despised you?

As though they heard my thoughts they both looked my way and then bent closer, talking and glancing at me rather obviously. I was clearly their hot topic of conversation.

Dom gripped my nape bringing my attention back to the task at hand, which was greeting more people and playing nice.

I murmured something polite to the druids I'd just been introduced to and tried my best not to look in the direction of Dom's fan club.

Eventually that didn't work as the two women approached us. Everyone had to greet the king eventually at a thing like this.

It didn't go well.

"What is *she* doing here, Arch?" was how Siobhan had the nerve to begin.

"That's a rude question, Siobhan," Dom said in a chiding tone. He had a certain tone he only ever used with her, like she was a particularly exasperating younger relative. "Where are your manners?" The set-down made her fingertips tremble, and I knew she was close to snapping.

His hand was at my stomach, pressing me to him, my back into his side, his fingers threading through the straps of my dress to feel my skin. "Jillian and I have finally reconciled," he continued. "It is well known that I have long wished for this." His voice was soft, succinct and matter-of-fact but not unkind.

It was not Siobhan's night. She looked like he'd slapped her. Helen looked like she'd just tasted something particularly bitter.

I didn't feel sorry for either of them, and I kept my chin raised, staring them down.

He was mine again, and he'd *always* liked me best, neener neener.

I managed to keep most of my less productive thoughts in. In fact I stayed uncharacteristically quiet. Dom seemed to have things under control, and he'd always been better at diplomacy than I.

"What am I supposed to say to that?" Siobhan asked, heartbreak in her voice. How many decades would it take this bitch to get a clue? Dom was not the type to lead anyone on, and I knew he'd always been particularly clear with her. "You know how I feel about her," she added as though any of this had *anything* to do with her.

"And you know how *I* feel about her." His voice was louder now, less kind. "I've never made a secret of it. And if you'd like to say something, that's simple enough. Congratulations are in order."

She took a few calming breaths looking straight at me, murder in her eyes. My own met hers and raised her one. As I've said, two is a number for love and hate, and there's no point in doing any of it alone.

I smiled blandly, but my eyes weren't bland. They were as cold and sharp as a knife.

She stormed away.

Helen was more cool-headed and probably less affected in general. She managed a stilted congratulations before she left in what wasn't quite a storm but more of a very contained raincloud.

Dom gave a signal and no one else approached us, the line to pay homage to him halted for the moment, and we had a bit of privacy at last.

"That went better than I was expecting," Dom said quietly, stroking a hand over my hair.

"How did you think it would go?"

"More violently. Thank you, by the way, for handling it well. She was provoking you, and you didn't rise to the bait."

"I can't believe you fucked *her*, of all people." It just sort of slipped out.

Like any violent urge, it showed itself in due time.

My restraint had its limits, and while it had been exercised when dealing with Siobhan, Dom was apparently going to get the sharp end of it.

"You heard about that," he said like we were talking about

Sunday brunch.

"Of course I did."

"It was a mistake," he said, giving me an unfriendly look like it was all my fault. I was always willing to take responsibility for my fuck-ups, but *this*? Not fucking likely.

"You think?" I asked unpleasantly.

"Would you like me to explain myself to you? Would that help or hurt you getting over it?"

I was grinding my teeth, I suddenly wanted to deck him so bad. "As though you're so good at *getting over* things yourself?"

"You can take exception to my wording or you can answer the question. I'll leave it to you how you'd like to play this.

It was a surprisingly raw wound, but I'd always rather know than stay in the dark. "Go ahead, then. Explain yourself, if you can."

"You asked for it. I did it to hurt you. That's the simple truth of it."

"Good job, then. It hurt. It still hurts."

"Her more than the others, huh?"

"Yes, that one hurt more than the others."

"It's not pretty, but that was whole point. I was still being heavily sedated, with spells *and* drugs, it was not long after I butchered Declan and his lieutenants, and about the fifth time she slipped into my bed, I didn't turn her down. I was still in enough denial that I thought something so blasphemous would bring you back even if only out of pure wrath. It was once, I barely remember it, but she took it too seriously, and I regretted it as soon as I was in my right mind. If it's any consolation, I think it hurt her more than it hurt you."

"It's not," I said. "And you don't get to decide who was hurt more. You can't imagine how it felt for me."

"Can't I?"

Touché. I took a few deep breaths, trying to be calm and

mature when I wanted to punch him and rip her hair out. "And yet you're the only one of us that truly betrayed our oath to each other. I was never actually unfaithful to you while *you* fucked your way through half of North America."

It was such a mean, low blow that I instantly regretted it.

Sometimes my vicious tongue had a mind of its own.

He was stone-faced, jaw clenched, looking straight ahead as he tried to absorb the blow.

"I'm sorry," I said quickly, touching his cheek. "That was unfair. I just lost my temper."

He grabbed my other hand and pressed it firmly over his pounding heart, eyes still aimed sightlessly forward.

"Did you know she poisoned me?" I said to distract him. I'd been meaning to tell him anyway and not just out of spite for Siobhan. There were more important things to worry about now.

He was still as a grave and just his eyes moved to meet mine. They were filled with dawning horror, his savage wolf eye flashing like a warning. "Excuse me?"

"She poisoned me. Nasty stuff. Enough to kill several humans and make me quite sick. She had no idea what I am so she was certainly trying to kill me, and she gloated about it, *wanted* me to know it was her. That's why I threw her out of a window."

"Why didn't you tell me?" He was reacting even worse than I was expecting, and I rubbed his chest comfortingly as I answered. "I was being stubborn. I wanted the fight all to myself. But you should know that about her. She'll break your rules if it means hurting me. And you should think about what that might mean for Conan. He won't be safe from her. She can't be allowed near him, *ever*."

"She needs to be punished," he said quietly, vehemently.

"That wasn't really the point of me telling you. It was years ago, and I already punished her. It took her weeks to heal from that fall."

"It wasn't enough." He looked like a wrathful fallen angel set to go on a holy rampage.

Alright then. I changed the subject again if only to shift his attention away from murder. "I also heard you two were seeing each other again right before I came back."

It worked. His mouth twisted and he looked annoyed, though not at me for once. "Siobhan started that rumor. She thought that the positive public reaction to it would prove some point to me about her suitability as a mate. I corrected the notion quite vehemently as soon as I heard of it. And then everyone drew their own conclusions. They always do, as you well know. Druids love gossip. Anything else?"

"I guess not. It's in the past. Thank you for explaining yourself. I know I have no right to question the things you did after I left you."

"You don't need to put limits on your rights where I'm concerned." He touched my cheek and caught my eye. "You have them all. You always did."

That earned him a rare public kiss from me. Both hands gripped into his hair, and I really let him have it. It always floored me that he never hesitated to show vulnerability. He'd always been like that, giving me the world before I even thought to ask for it.

"I'd like to say something." The loud statement came out of nowhere and the room turned its attention to the speaker.

I pulled back from a reluctant Dom. We'd both forgotten ourselves for a rare moment there.

It was Siobhan. She looked like she'd been crying. She was in the middle of the room, and she strode up to Sloan as she said it, not stopping until they were face to face, less than a foot apart.

"I challenge you," Siobhan told Sloan.

Sloan just eyed her like she was a particularly pesky insect.

She was only a few inches taller than the other woman, but managed to look down at her like it was a full mile. "Really? Now?" she asked, but she didn't refuse.

"Yes, now. Right this minute."

I felt Dom tense, about to intercede, but someone beat him to it.

"Not a chance!" Cam growled at Siobhan, getting between them and right in her face. There was venom in his tone, contempt in his demeanor when I'd never heard him so much as say a harsh word to Siobhan before. No one looked more taken aback by that than Siobhan herself.

"Did you forget how to count?" he asked her in a snarl, "You know how this works. You want a shot at her you go through me first. I'm third. You wanna go? We'll go." Relish hugged every word.

"She never even fought you!" Siobhan yelled at him. She looked baffled and hurt, but even with tears pouring down her face she wasn't backing down. "Why are you standing in my way but not *hers*?"

"I don't answer to you, but I'll tell you this: You challenge her again, and I'll put you down so hard into the dirt you won't be getting back up."

I glanced at Dom's face. He had his hand at the small of my back and was watching them gimlet-eyed, but he was still not interfering.

"Why do you defend her like this?" Siobhan asked him. She was crying openly now.

I almost told her myself to get a clue, but I kept my mouth shut. I didn't want to get in the middle of this mess. I had plenty of my own. For once I hadn't made the mess myself. Mostly.

Though I admitted to myself that her misdirected rage was probably fueled in large part by hatred of me and Dom's reconciliation.

"You've had plenty of time to adjust to this," Cam told her. "I won't coddle you anymore. All you need to know is that I will *never* challenge Sloan, and she will *always* outrank you. Grow up and fucking deal with it."

She just stared at him like she didn't believe it.

If it was anyone else I'd have felt bad for her.

"Unless you're challenging me?" he said like he was looking forward to it. "If so, I'll go right now. Otherwise, leave now and compose yourself. You've caused enough scenes tonight."

She left in a furious rush, but I doubted that would be the end of it. Siobhan had never been a fast learner.

CHAPTER SIXTEEN
NOT A DATE

The meeting with Tianlong was set for eight o'clock, but we didn't have to go far. Dom had arranged it on home territory, booking a private room in one of the casino's ritzy restaurants.

We showed up early, another home court advantage.

"I'm surprised he agreed to have the meeting here, dead center of your kingdom," I told Dom as we entered the private room. We were alone for the moment, his usual entourage outside waiting to show our guest in.

He moved so we were standing face to face. "I doubt he's happy about it, but I didn't give him a choice," he said, smoothing my hair. "He can't try any of his tricks here. I heard how your last meeting with him went."

Oh that. I'd nearly forgotten. He'd enthralled me effortlessly, even stolen a kiss though I'd bitten his tongue hard enough to make him bleed for it. And that wasn't even the worst of it. The weirdo had suggested that I'd be bearing his sons. "He's a scary motherfucker," I remarked. "What are you doing?" I asked. He was fussing with my dress.

"Helping you prepare for your date," he said, a hint of temper in it.

"It's not a date."

He cupped my face with his hand, rubbing his thumb softly over my lower lip. His discordant eyes captured me. "Your formal meeting with a dragon king that wants to mate with you, then," he returned. "Is that better?"

"Not really. You know I don't like this any more than you do, right? I just want my sister back. Can you chill with the jealousy and think about that for a minute?"

He closed his eyes, opened them, said, "You're right," and started kissing me like our very lives depended on it.

We pulled back sometime later at a throat being pointedly cleared.

Tianlong had arrived, and he was just inside the room, staring back and forth between the two of us like we were being particularly offensive, and I didn't think it was just the PDA. I recalled that he had a real issue with my choice to be with a druid instead of a dragon.

He moved forward in a blur and Dom was suddenly in front of me, blocking me from even seeing the other man.

He'd tried something, I couldn't tell what, and Dom had beaten him to the punch.

"Tsk tsk, druid," Tianlong said, sounding amused. "You're a better diplomat than this. Won't you even honor the most basic of niceties? I was simply attempting to give her a formal greeting, as is customary among our kind."

"You won't touch her. Find another way to be polite. Now, be seated."

Tianlong actually did it. By sheer force of his arrogance, Dom had made the other man submit.

It was impressive, almost instructive.

Dom and I took our seats on the opposite side of the table from him.

Tianlong just studied me for a long time. It got to the point of being insulting. I stared right back.

He was a beautiful man, tall and elegant with perfect porcelain skin and long, silky black hair. He was exotic, almost delicate and lovely enough to make your teeth ache, but inside that head of his I knew he was a big ol' basket of crazy.

"It is a true mating between you then," he addressed me as though we were alone. "You've tied yourself to this druid. *What a waste.* You had so much promise." He was different than at our last meeting, not so cool and unflappable this time. He was clearly riled at Dom's presence and not being able to use/abuse his powers on me.

He'd lost his edge this time.

Or so I thought.

"Such a pity, but forever is a very long time and I am patient." He smiled at me and it was seduction personified.

I felt Dom simmering beside me and reached out to take his hand.

Tianlong stared at our intertwined fingers, disgust and indignation twisting his pretty features into something ugly.

"Aren't you going to ask me about your sister?" he asked. "Isn't that the real reason behind this sudden meeting? Divide and conquer."

I just stared at him. "What are you talking about?"

"Oh, nothing, just your friends and some silly little scheme where they thought they would catch my nephew unawares while you had me distracted. Foolhardy is the word for it though that feels like an understatement."

Shit. The guys. They'd been discovered. "What have you done with them?" I asked him through my teeth.

He smiled at me, his eyes on mine soft, intimate.

Dom's hand clutching mine was bordering on pain. I stroked a thumb against him to calm him, and he relaxed his hold a bit.

"Me?" Tianlong asked, enjoying himself. "I've done nothing to them. I'm here with you. Drake on the other hand. . . I can't speak for him."

I stood and both men stood with me. "Where are they?"

"Why should I tell you? What will you give me?"

"Watch it," Dom growled at him.

"How about this?" Tianlong asked, and it was practically a purr. "I'll tell you for another kiss. I still remember the taste of you. This time we'll see if I lose myself enough to let you draw blood again."

I was clutching Dom, holding him back and hoping he didn't really lose his temper because I knew I couldn't t hold him back then.

"Enough!" Dom finally snapped. "I don't know who you think you're dealing with," Dom continued, voice filling the room so heavily that it felt like we were swimming in it. "You're in my territory, speaking to my mate. Did you think I'd come here unprepared for you? You're not that special, and certainly not as clever as you seem to think. There are four slayers outside the door right now. Their weapons are primed and ready for you, and they've been waiting their whole lives for this rare chance."

It was a casual lesson thrown out—pay attention.

Something crossed Tianlong's face, and I didn't know him well, but I thought it might have been a rare showing of fear.

"You're powerful," Dom continued, magic crawling out of him with every word, "and very old. But do you think even you could leave this room let alone this building without my permission? This is my kingdom. My will alone rules here. I could end you now with one word."

"You play a dirty game, druid."

"Arch to you, and yes, always. I play to win. Now what'll it be? Will you give us Jillian's sister and our men back or will your long forever end tonight?

"You're willing to start a war over this?" Tianlong asked like he couldn't quite believe it.

Dom had truly shocked him.

Me, too. Though I should have been prepared for the extra tricks up his sleeve, as ever.

"Are *you*?" Dom asked without hesitation. "It doesn't matter if you are, you won't be around to see it. But yes, you've just insulted my mate. For that alone I'm willing and ready. Now again, what'll it be? I'm losing patience."

Tianlong took a long time to answer, just glared at Dom like hatred alone could solve the mess he was in. Finally he pulled out his cell and said, "I'll arrange it."

He had a long conversation over the phone as we watched, but we didn't know the language so we didn't catch what was said other than to notice that he was becoming more agitated the longer he spoke.

He hung up and stared at me, taking his time to speak again. "I've arranged for the men to be dropped off here, but your sister is another matter. That issue is out of my hands. Drake refuses to let her go, but he's agreed to meet with you," at this he glared at Dom, "though not in druid territory."

Dom protested that, but I didn't bother. "When and where?"

"It would be nice if you told me the real plan instead of leaving me in the dark," I said to Dom sometime later.

We were waiting at the hotel valet for the guys to be delivered. My meeting with Drake was in two days at a remote location in the desert. Tianlong had tried to negotiate for me to go alone, but much as I would have done it, Dom refused and negotiations had taken hours. We'd finally settled on meeting Drake with only Dom and Sven as my backup.

Afterward, Dom had shown the other man he wasn't bluffing by having his four dragon slayers escort him off the premises.

"That was *not* the real plan," Dom told me. "That was plan B. To tell you the truth I had hoped that your brother and your cohorts would do a better job and it wouldn't come to that."

"I guess Drake is even more of a scary motherfucker than we thought."

"Indeed." It was only one word, but he said it like he was actively planning the other man's demise.

"Were you really ready to kill Tianlong and go to war?"

He didn't hesitate. "I'm always ready for my tap on the shoulder."

That sounded familiar. "You quoting Churchill to me?"

He smiled and it was beautiful. God, I'd missed him. "Maybe," he said.

"If you're going through hell, keep going," I returned.

His smile grew. "That's the perfect quote for *you*."

"And what's a good one for you?"

"My tastes are simple: I am easily satisfied with the *very* best." As he said it he touched my face, and we shared a moment that only lovers with a lot of history between them could.

The spell was broken as a silver van skidded to a stop in front of valet.

The doors opened and an unconscious Caleb and Christian were set on the ground in front of us by a few of the Chinese dragons' henchmen. Sven was bound but awake and when they set him free he didn't so much as look at his captors. He looked completely unfazed by the whole thing.

I had an ugly thought.

Sven, predictably, read my mind before I could speak. "I didn't betray you; I just let them take me peaceably. I didn't see the point in bloodshed when Lynn wasn't even there. Caleb and Christian had a different approach. They're bespelled, but it'll wear off in a few hours."

"What exactly happened?" Dom asked him.

"Drake was ready for us, I suppose. Caleb and Christian wanted to fight, but I just wanted information. He bespelled them before any of us could react, he's a very scary creature, and he and I had a chat. He has Lynn but she wasn't there tonight. He hasn't harmed her. In fact, he's infatuated with her but their relationship seems to be. . . complicated."

"He told you all that?" I asked him, my mind going over all the information he'd spewed out, but mostly I'd just felt a flooring relief since he'd said the words *he hasn't harmed her.*

"Of course not," Sven said cheerfully. "He told me some of it and I picked the rest out of his brain. Telepaths are rather handy, aren't they?"

Caleb and Christian were sent to the infirmary while they slept it off, and we finished debriefing Sven until we were satisfied and let him loose for the rest of the night. Kind of. I was sure Dom had set a tail on him, but I wasn't going to ruin the surprise.

It had been a strange, long day, and we wrapped it up by visiting Conan.

I lay on the ground beside our egg and wrapped myself into a ball around him.

Dom wasn't hesitant this time, joining me, wrapping himself around both of us, his hand covering mine and squeezing. He was speaking softly into my hair in Druidic, and I didn't have to ask to know that it was something terribly romantic.

Conan was quiet, which wasn't unusual. He spent most of his time asleep, incubating until he was ready to join us.

Our hands were touching on the glowing golden surface. "I hope he looks like you," I said into the quiet.

I felt his whole body tense then release, his breath expelling roughly into the back of my head. He'd liked that. I fed him a bit more. It was only the truth. "I didn't let myself ever think much about having children, but when it entered my mind in the years since I've known you I always saw a gorgeous black-haired boy with mismatched eyes. If I'd ever let myself wish for something, it would have been that."

A furious, impassioned stream of Druidic was his response. I didn't make him tell me what it meant. I got the gist of it, and everything was more beautiful in druidic anyway.

"I bet you didn't picture anything like this when you thought about having children," I said. I was fishing. This had to be so odd to him. It was odd to me, and I was a dragon.

He kissed the back of my head. "I didn't. But I'm not complaining. I've longed for this, a child with you, whatever the means of delivery."

Something occurred to me. "Do you have any other children?" I had been gone seven years, and he had been by all accounts promiscuous.

He stiffened. "Of course not." He sounded deeply offended. "I would never have children with anyone but you."

I felt myself flush, the thought warming me. But what I said was, "Accidents happen."

"I've always been doubly careful. You are the only exception. I've known I would have children with you or no one since I was fourteen."

"I don't know why you always have to throw in the fourteen bit. Everyone gets it, you were young. And I didn't think we could create a child together so protection never even occurred to me."

"Do you believe in fate yet?" he asked, a warm smile in his voice.

I just shook my head.

I fell asleep like that, my head on Dom's bicep, his lips pressed to the back of my head.

CHAPTER SEVENTEEN
FATE

My own throaty moan woke me up. Dom was on top of me, inside of me, thrusting in and out tirelessly.

We were naked in his bed. I didn't recall how we'd gotten there, but I didn't give it much thought. I didn't have many thoughts at all at that moment as they were being drilled right out of me with vigor.

I clutched him to me, legs wrapping tight around his hips, nails digging into his back.

He paused mid-stroke, pushing up to make brief eye contact. He didn't say a word. No good morning.

I didn't say much either aside from, "Don't stop," and he was at it again, burying his face in my neck as he plowed me rigorously.

It was a hell of a way to wake up. I'd take it over just about anything.

Okay, if I was honest, I'd take it over anything at all. There was no hope for me. This was my bliss.

Dom was kissing my throat as he stroked in and out of me when suddenly I felt a sharp pain where my shoulder met my neck.

"Fuck," I said. It was more of a surprised yelp. Had he bit me? If so, it was a harder than the usual love bite.

A hint of pain mixed with the pleasure, like spice adding a flare of heat to a dish.

He didn't respond, didn't pause, just kept sucking on my neck and fucking like a machine.

The pain was quickly forgotten, lost in other, more urgent sensations.

Afterward I rubbed my neck, half convinced I'd find a puncture wound.

He'd bitten me *hard*.

He caught what I was doing and kissed me deeply. "I got carried away," he said by way of an apology as he pulled back. He moved my hair aside and studied the spot he'd bitten. "Here," he said, leaned forward, and I felt his cool magic running across my skin where his lips touched.

He grabbed my hips, holding me flush against him as he rolled and sat up. He was still inside of me, still hard, as he reached for something on the bedside table. He held a chalice to my lips and I drank.

It wasn't a casual sip, he held it until I swallowed every drop.

That was when I noticed how his room had changed. Candles were lit everywhere and his bedspread was covered in runes like the ones on his ceremonial robes.

Also herbs, flowers, and sticks were scattered everywhere. We had our own little indoor forest scene going in here.

"I forgot about this," I told him as I recalled. "You've done it before. It's some kind of a fertility spell, right?"

"It is the ritual of oak and mistletoe. And yes, we've done it before. Clearly it worked."

"I never imagined it could, but point for you. One kid at a time not enough for you?" I was highly amused.

"If it takes twelve years, I wanted to put my next order in. Now if you're done," as he spoke he moved his hips and his thickness nudged me deep inside. He was ready to go again, and I shouldn't have been surprised. He'd always been a demanding and tireless lover. Literally magical. "It takes months to prepare that potion, and I'd like to come inside of you as many times as possible while it's active."

"You sweet-talker, you."

He just smiled and started moving me with his hands on my hips. I rode him like that, our eyes locked.

It was some time later and he was taking me from behind, holding both of my wrists while he pumped into me without holding back when there was a persistent knock on the door.

I didn't hear what was said other than to know Dom was not happy about it, but he didn't stop, didn't so much as pause. It went on like that for long minutes until he finished us both.

"What was the knock?" I asked him after. He was pinning me to the bed facedown, both of us exhausted, or so I thought.

He was up again, turning me on my side, straddling one thigh, the other thrown over his shoulder as he shoved into me again, bottoming out and hitting the spot that made my toes curl with every stroke.

"I don't think we'll be able to have more kids if you fuck us both to death," I remarked later.

He was sitting back against the headboard of his bed, my cheek on his chest as he stroked my hair. "It's never enough with you. I could go again, to be honest. This was me holding back."

He was affectively distracting me again, but I managed to ask, "What was the knock? It must have been important for them to knock on your bedroom door."

I looked up at him and his face was an annoyed grimace. "Your boys are conscious and raising hell to see you. My phone is in the next room because I didn't want to be interrupted, but they were obnoxious enough that my people thought I should be made aware. You should probably go talk to them. I have them in holding until they can be debriefed."

I sat up, moving off the bed, but he stopped me with a hand, pulling me back for a long kiss before he let me go with a light pat on the ass.

Dom joined me in the shower and lathered up my body without a word. I thought that was the end of it, but he could in fact go another round. He had me up against the shower wall, my breasts in his hands as he took me from behind.

He gave me directions to the infirmary turned holding cell as we both got dressed. "I have some business to attend to, but I'll join you there as soon as I can."

I knew it was a risk, traveling through the druid property alone, but I did it anyway.

I'd always been a little too comfortable playing with fire.

Just ask anyone.

The bloody grove caught me only one turn away from my destination.

My uncle was talking but I couldn't hear him anymore, still trying to process what he'd already told me.

He was a loving uncle, we'd always been close, but he was not the type to coddle. He gave me every gory detail in as quick a deluge as he could. He knew I would find out one way or another, the rumor mill was too strong, and he knew it would hurt less coming from someone like him, who was suffering as he must have been at the loss of his beloved brother.

He was the Arch for all of Europe and had the countless responsibilities that entailed and still he'd flown to the States just to tell me in person.

The bullet points were stark but simple. The conflict was over but my parents were dead, the last casualties in decades' worth of conflict. The last blood druid keep had been stormed and cleansed, but my parents' heads were already mounted on spikes on the gates. They had died mere hours before we won the war.

The grief was impossible to bear, too much to hold on my own.

I fled as soon as I could, and my kin let me, knowing me well enough to give me space.

I was at the restaurant without even thinking, at my usual table waiting for her.

I must have been a sight because her sister saw me first, took one long look at me, and left. Jillian came in soon after, studied me, and just knew with a glance that something was wrong.

I looked at her like I was drowning as she took my hand without a word and led me back to her office. She sat us both on a couch side by side, and I let her lead me around with no resistance.

"What's wrong?" she asked, patting my hand.

"It's my parents," was all I got out.

The look in her eyes, the sympathy, was my undoing.

She held me in her arms as I sobbed my great grief out against her.

It took hours of her comfort for me to get the whole story out, every bloody detail of it.

Fat tears were rolling down her cheeks, and I cupped her flawless face, using my thumbs to gently wipe them from her perfect alabaster skin.

I didn't mean to take advantage of her kindness or her pity, but eventually I was kissing her neck, touching all over her body without conscious thought. It was more of an instinct than a choice. It felt natural. Wanting her was written into my DNA.

What was the point of that kind of beauty if it couldn't be touched?

I kissed her tears, worked my way to her lips for one deep kiss before she wrenched away, turning her back on me. I hugged her back to my chest, kissing the top of her head, my hands on her taut stomach, pressing her firmly back against me. "I love you."

"This is wrong, Domhnall. You need to stop."

I kissed her neck, running my hands over her, pressing my body firmly against her. "How can it be wrong when it feels like this? You can't tell me you're indifferent. I'm not so blind."

"You're grieving. You're looking for a distraction from the pain, I get it. You need comfort, but this is not the way."

"What if I were old enough?"

"You'll never be old enough for me."

"What if I were an adult?"

"You're not, so we're not discussing it."

I wasn't discouraged. It was only a few more months until I came of age. And we both knew that when I did, I was coming for her.

I came back into my own body on the damp ground of The Grove. The horrifying creature was standing over me, leering.

"More?" it asked me.

I didn't answer, but it had me too much under its spell to need permission now.

It struck again.

I went to see her at the restaurant on my eighteenth birthday. I wore my best suit, hair slicked back. I didn't try to hide my intentions from her. That's not the way it would be between us.

She saw me and stopped in her tracks. "It's your birthday," she said almost absently, smiling warmly.

I grinned. I was huge now and confident sexually. I knew precisely all the things I wanted to do to her. From our prior dealings I knew I'd be the aggressor, and I'd learned enough that I knew if I pushed the right buttons, I could take her how I'd been longing to. "Will you celebrate with me?" I asked.

She ignored the innuendo in my tone completely, running her hands through her hair. She looked as perfect as ever, but she fussed at her clothes like she wished she'd dressed better. "I didn't notice the date. Happy Birthday."

"Can you leave early today?" I asked her.

She gave me a certain look, like she didn't trust me, but she was charmed nonetheless. She didn't know the half of it.

"Sure I can. I'll bake you a cake if you promise to behave."

I grinned. "Only part of that is happening. It's my birthday." I said it like I was reminding her of a pact. "You know how old I am now."

She watched me like she had no idea what I was about to do. It was almost innocent, though I knew she wasn't that. She was unvarnished sin, worldly and untouched, a perfect balance between all things light and dark. Demure carnality. Seduction incarnate. She was Eve and Lilith both. Designed to inspire devotion as well as debasement.

I took her arm as we walked, and she gave me an arch look but otherwise allowed it. Her place was a few blocks away from the café.

I knew where she lived, but I'd never been inside before. It was a small but nice apartment. I explored from room to room without asking and she didn't say anything, just trailed me slowly and watched.

I knew which room was hers without having to ask, but as soon as I sat on her bed she turned and headed in the opposite direction.

I found her in the kitchen setting up to bake. I sat at a small table by the window and watched her. "I like your place," I told her. "Do you live with your sister?"

"She has an apartment above this one."

"So you're alone?"

She didn't look at me, busy measuring some flour into a bowl. "Usually. Right now you're here."

She was wearing a fitted black skirt that went to her knees with a tidy white shirt tucked into it. She'd kicked off her shoes when we walked in the door and put on a short white apron before she started cooking.

I stood up, crowding her against the counter, my front to her back. I towered over her barefoot. It was a heady experience, being alone with her and knowing that nothing was standing in my way.

I pressed against her, hands at her hips, and kissed her neck.

She was frozen. She hadn't moved a muscle since I'd touched her, and I wished I could see her face.

I fondled her and bit her ear. There was some movement now, her ragged breath in and out. "What are you doing?" she asked unsteadily.

"Did you think we came here for cake?" I asked her, pinching her nipples and biting tendon between her neck and shoulder.

"Domhnall," she said sternly, though her breath was unsteady. "We can't—"

"Why not? No more excuses. If you don't want me, say it now, but no more bullshit about my age."

She moved her body to turn around, and I dropped my hands to my sides. She pushed me back far enough to look up at me with her hands on my chest.

Our eyes met and she tilted her head sideways at me. I could read her movements, I'd been studying her closely, but I couldn't read her eyes just then other than to capture them with mine. She touched my cheek. "Your eyes. . ." she trailed off.

"Do they disturb you?"

"Not at all. I love them too much. They're captivating. Right now they're glowing, especially the wolf eye. Domhnall, are you sure you know what you're doing?"

In answer I bent down and kissed her like I'd been waiting my whole life to do it. The world stopped. I'd found her too young, but she was my eternity. Every cell in my body knew it. I held nothing back.

She trembled, shudders that racked her body as though her walls were coming down, one barrier crumbling after another with tremor after tremor.

And at last she kissed me back, hands digging into my hair, a little noise of surrender sounding in her throat.

She pulled back eventually and looked deep into my eyes. She touched my cheek, traced an elegant finger under my wolf's eye. "Just don't fall in love with me, Dom. I'm a lost cause. Even if we built something together, in the end, I only know how to destroy."

"We're well past that," I said, picked her up, and carried her to bed.

CHAPTER EIGHTEEN
IT GETS WORSE

I hadn't lost much time in real life from The Grove, which was lucky because Caleb and Christian were close to escaping and leaving a trail of lackey druid bodies in their wake.

I arrived just in time to talk them both down from murder. They liked cages about as much as I did.

"What the fuck happened?" Caleb asked me.

"Why are the druids holding us prisoner?" Christian asked.

I tried to be diplomatic, but everyone in the room knew it wasn't one of my strong points. "You guys failed. You were both bespelled by Drake and brought here. They were just holding you until you could be debriefed."

"You sound like one of them," Caleb said flatly. Like a druid, he meant, and it was an insult.

"Bespelled?" Christian asked indignantly. "When? I don't remember being bespelled!"

"I think that's kind of the point of the whole thing." I almost laughed and Christian seemed to see the humor in it too going by his grin.

"Why'd Drake let us go? And where's Sven?" Caleb asked, as usual getting to the point.

"Sven wasn't incapacitated as you were because apparently Drake was able to speak with him while you guys were just trying to, ya know. . ."

"Stabby stab and pew pew," Christian finished, making shooting and stabbing motions with his hands.

Good to see he was unfazed by the whole thing.

"Yes, that," I agreed. "Do you guys remember anything at all?"

Caleb shook his head. He looked *very* fazed by the whole thing. "Nothing after we got to the location. I don't like it."

"I don't like it either, but luckily Dom was able to negotiate your release using Tianlong as leverage. He set four slayers up outside of our meeting and basically held him hostage until we got what we wanted."

"That's *so* Dom," Christian remarked. "He's always been a thorough wanker."

Caleb stayed on task. "What else did Sven learn from talking to Drake?"

"He thinks Lynn is unharmed, and I'm meeting with Drake in a day and a half to ask about her and hopefully find a path to getting her back."

"I'm coming," Caleb said.

"I want to come!" Christian said at the same time.

I felt bad for some reason. "Only Dom and Sven get to come. It was part of the negotiations."

"We'll wait close by," Caleb said. "If it goes sour, maybe we can kill Drake."

I didn't point out that he seemed to be too much for them to handle going by their last meeting. I was uncomfortable with the notion of someone that powerful, especially when that something was holding my sister prisoner, harmed or not.

The day of the meeting, Caleb and Christian tailed us to within a few miles of the location and parked on the side of the road to wait impatiently.

There'd been no stipulations about what weapons we could bring, and I found that unsettling. It implied that Drake wasn't even worried about it, like there was nothing we could bring that would faze him.

I brought a still quiet Torst and a small arsenal of whatever I could strap to my body. Everyone else was similarly armed. We were ready for a fight.

Drake was already there when we arrived. He was dressed all in black, the top half of his gorgeous black hair pulled up into a bun, the lower half moving with the breeze. He was set against a stark desert background, no means of transportation in sight. He was standing straight and tall and just watched us approach with a serene expression.

The whole thing felt like a scene from a movie.

He had a flair for the dramatic. It was no wonder he was infatuated with Lynn.

I didn't beat around the bush. "Where's my sister?" I asked him with a glare.

He just smiled. "Would you like to see her?"

I was pissed off, assuming he was toying with me. "Of course I would. What have you done with her?"

He did something quick and strange with his hands that had me reaching for Torst, but everything went hazy for a heartbeat, the air around us turning bright red until I couldn't see an inch in front of me.

I felt Dom's hand on my shoulder as though he'd grabbed for me as soon as things went strange, but that seemed to be the end of it.

The red cloud dissipated like a switch had controlled it, and Lynn appeared out of nowhere standing in a graceful martial arts stance as though performing. She was wearing a blindfold but was clearly unbound.

Her hair was still black, shoulder length now, half of it pulled back into a little bun. It was the short twin to Drake's hairstyle. Even their clothes were nearly identical.

"Twinning, huh?" I asked her. There was barely a quaver to my voice, and if my hands were shaking I assumed there was too much going on for anyone else to notice.

Sheer relief is a powerful thing.

Lynn grinned like she didn't have a care in the world.

I glared at them both, but blind kung-fu Lynn couldn't see it, of course.

"Where have you been?" I asked her.

"Where have I been?" she asked incredulously, her smile dying. She was standing up straight and waving her arms around wildly. "Where have I been? Miss *leaves this plain of existence* for *months* without a word is asking where *I've* been?

This plain of existence? I'd known I was somewhere far away. Somewhere strange. But a different dimension? That bat-shit crazy thought hadn't crossed my mind.

"Hello, sister," Sven said into the awkward silence.

Lynn's head swiveled in his direction. "Who is that? Is that Sven?"

"Yes. Nice to see you after all these years."

"I'd say it's mutual, but I can't see anything. Nice to hear you."

"I've defected to your side," Sven said simply.

She nodded, looking impressed. "Nice. That should be handy."

"Can Jillian and I speak alone?" she asked everyone politely. She waved at who knows what. "Go over that way.

Just far enough to give us a bit of privacy."

They did it, though none of them liked it.

"What the hell is going on?" I asked her when we were alone.

She sighed. "Drake wants me to marry him. I explained my commitment issues, and he didn't really get it. He says I have to marry him, and he's made some convincing arguments about it. I said I'd have to think about it. He says he'll help me get my eyes back when I've given him a straight answer.

"You have the worst taste in men. Literally the worst."

"Erg. I know. It's well documented. You know, Drake's actually kind of nice when he's not being completely evil, but that's neither here nor there. And hey! Like you're one to talk. Oh I'm sorry miss finds a guy who worships her and leaves, never giving him the slightest explanation as to why. How's that worked out for you?"

I scowled. "That's not what happened."

"Tell that to Dom. And literally everyone you've ever been involved with. Dom just affected you more than the others because you became attached. You never realized that worshipping thing could go both ways and how much it sucks from the wrong end."

I scowled harder, realized she couldn't see it, and shushed her loudly. "Uncle. No more talk about our love lives, please."

"Truce accepted and reciprocated," she said easily and instantly.

We rarely fought. Hadn't had a real row in centuries. This was as close as it got, in fact. We were always quick to wave the white flag.

When you have as much ammo against each other as we do and you're both too good at war as we are, a real fight is the equivalent of launching nukes from both sides.

Peace or total destruction were our only options. So peace it was, always. True sisterhood was a law unto itself.

"Now listen," said Lynn. "I've been thinking."

"Uh-oh."

"It gets worse. I've been planning."

"Yikes."

"I can't give Drake an answer. If I say yes, it's permanent, and I need a few decades to process that, and if I say no, it's not going to be pretty. We do not want war with the Chinese dragons. I cannot stress this enough. His family scares the *shit* out of me. I need to hang on to my maybe as long as possible, but I do kind of want my eyes back."

"That's fair."

"I do pretty well without them though, you've gotta admit. I've developed some extra . . . perks out of the deal." She performed a few precise moves.

"If you could see my face, you'd know I was suitably impressed by your blind kung-fu."

"I knew you'd appreciate that. But back to the plan."

"Again. Fucking yikes."

"Yes. Fucking yikes. You need to steal my eyes back."

"Seems reasonable. Where are they?"

"Well, that's the problem. Drake doesn't actually have them. Our daddy dearest—"

"Ew, don't call him that," I had to interrupt.

"Fair enough. Our evil father has them. It's a whole thing. But I think I know where he is, kind of."

"Kind of?"

"I'm working on it, okay? He's on the move, but I'm spying and using my other senses and shit, and now that I have contact with you again, I'll pin it down and tell you and you, Caleb, and Christian can go, ya know, slay him and get my eyes back."

"We've actually got a whole druid task force ready for

slaying rogue Viking dragons," I told her. "So your half-assed plan might be doable if we get a location."

"It's like three-quarters assed, okay?"

"Fair enough. So you're actually going to stay with this guy?" I asked her since that seemed to be how the spying part would go down.

"For now. Aside from the blackmail thing we get along."

"That's good to hear," I said sarcastically.

She shrugged. "That's all I've got. Now tell me where you flew off to for so long."

"What made you say it was another plain of existence?"

"Drake said so, and he seems to know a lot more dragon shit than we do. By the way, do you know how worried I was?"

"Ditto, sis. Ditto. And I was. . . giving birth."

Her confused, disgusted expression was gratifying. "What in the ever-loving fuck did I just hear?"

I laughed. "I laid an egg."

She twisted her fingers in her ears as though to clear them out. "I'm sorry. I think I've lost my mind. Say that again?"

"I have a son now. His name is Conan, but he still hasn't hatched."

Her mouth just kept opening and closing like she couldn't find words.

I laughed harder.

"Are you fucking with me?" she finally managed to ask.

"I swear it's all true."

She was quiet for a time. "I'll bet Dom is ecstatic. Holy shit. When could you even have gotten pregnant?"

"Twelve-ish years ago, we think. Did you know we had that long of a gestation period?"

"Nope. I didn't know we laid eggs either, though it makes enough sense. They kept us as in the dark as possible back in the clan. So you gave birth in dragon form?"

"Yes, and then slept it off. I was gone for months, but to me it felt like days."

"How big is the egg?"

"He's like a big watermelon now, but when I laid him I think he was like a small watermelon."

"Well I suppose childbirth is easier as a dragon and a small egg than with a big baby and a human body, so there's that."

"You make a good point," I said, amused.

"So I'm an aunt now, huh? I wasn't expecting it, but it makes me happy. Congratulations. Can't wait to meet him."

"Thanks. I can't wait for you to meet him either. He's still in an egg but already making waves." I switched gears. "Are you sure you want to go back with Drake? We can fight our way out. Dom and Sven are here with me and Caleb and Christian are only a few miles out. We got this."

"Not necessary. I can handle him."

"It doesn't feel right, leaving here without you."

"I know, but trust me, this is the way. For now. About that task force. Is it big?"

"Big enough. We have several slayers."

"Good. When I give you dad's location, he might not be the only draak you need to slay to get to the eyes."

"Will there be more than two?"

"I don't think so, but there's no way to know for certain.

"Good to know. I'll brief the team. We should be able to split up and get the job done if we're prepared for it. Where is he keeping you?"

"It's not clear. He travels in an. . . odd way."

"How will I get your eyes to you once I have them?"

"We'll burn that bridge when we get to it."

"I think you're mixing up sayings there."

"Maybe, but it's still accurate."

"Do you have a number I can call or anything?"

"Not right now, but I'll have our people work it out."

"Our people as in Dom and Drake?"

"Probably."

"I really don't want to let you go with him."

"I know," said Lynn. "But you have to trust me."

"That I can do."

CHAPTER NINETEEN
INTERESTED, INTERESTED

On the way back I got a call from Corbin. I wasn't even sure how he'd gotten my number, but I recognized who was calling with the first thing out of his mouth.

"Did you know they brought me a necromancer?" his excited voice asked over the line.

"Henri?" My tone was sardonic. "They brought him just for you, huh?"

"A necromancer is a rare treat for a vampire slayer, as I'm sure you're well aware. I'm planning to coax him into staying and partnering with me long-term. He says he used to date you. Will you tell me some of his weaknesses so I can use them against him?" He paused. "That sounded bad. I just want to know what tempts him."

"Did he explain how long ago it was that we dated?"

I felt Dom's attention, already on me in the limited confines of the car, gain laser focus.

"No. But some things transcend time. You must have some clue about what he likes, about his character. I'm clearly not pretty enough for him if *you're* his type, so I need some tricks here. Help me out and I'll owe you."

That surprised me, I don't know why. I hadn't realized he was interested, interested. I'd thought he was just trying for a working partnership. For some reason it made me more inclined to help him.

I thought about it for a moment while Corbin waited patiently on the other end. "Try working together with him toward a common goal, something that utilizes both of your skills," I instructed. "If he sees how useful he can be with your powers to complement his, he'll like that. He likes to be useful. Also, let him paint you. Offer, at least."

"I doubt he wants to paint *me*."

"You have an interesting, expressive face. That's what draws his inspiration out more than anything, and if you're his muse, he won't want to be far from your side. In fact, once you're his muse it will be hard to shake him."

"So hard you have to fake your own death," Dom said ruefully.

I shot him a look. It wasn't friendly. He just smiled warmly at me. I immediately warmed. That was his power over me.

"What's he mean by that?" Corbin asked, clearly having heard the other man.

"Nothing important."

"Did he say you faked your own death? To get away from Henri?"

"That's a gross exaggeration," I said and even I thought it sounded unconvincing."

Corbin had the nerve to laugh richly. "Oh, now some of the unflattering things he's said about you are starting to make sense."

Dom took the phone from my hand and put it to his ear. "Tell Henri to keep Jillian's name out of his mouth or he'll answer to me. This is his last warning."

He handed the phone back.

Oookaaay.

"Did you have anything else to ask me?" I asked impatiently. "I'm not going to stay on the line for this."

"No, I think I'm good," he said, laughter still in his voice, "I think you gave me enough. Thanks. I owe you." Without further ado, he hung up.

Huh.

It felt as I had said the words to Corbin that I was setting something in motion, and less than a day later I was proven right in my own hunch. He'd followed my advice with Henri. The two men had worked together and found an abandoned casino full of multiple vampire kisses.

It was at the edge of town, a property scheduled for implosion, though not soon enough.

Necromancers are quite useful, and Henri is a very talented one. I've yet to see his equal in the craft. He'd managed to find an area with mass dead bodies, new ones, and from there Corbin had found one of the vampire familiars and used whatever scary vampire hunter skills he had to make the creature talk.

They really did make a good team.

The bodies Henri had sensed weren't buried or hidden, just strewn about wherever they'd been drained of blood, above ground and inside of the property.

This was particularly fortunate for us as that made the order for execution easy and instant. We could take action that very day, preferably well before sunset.

It was also fortunate because with Henri on hand, those bodies became both weapon and shield as we stormed the bloodsuckers.

We met in the parking lot, as large of a force as the druids could muster on short notice, which was an impressive size indeed. The entire dragon task force was there, as well as a small army of druids and various other supernaturals that could be scrounged up on short notice.

I was surprised to even see a rare dark elf.

The fae are seldom seen on this side of the veil, let alone here and doing something useful. He was shorter than an average human, though with how thin he was he looked taller. He had sharp teeth and red eyes and didn't speak to anyone. The fae are notoriously wary of outsiders and impossible to trust, but they are very good fighters. I wondered how he'd been talked into joining the battle. They rarely did something for nothing, or for the good of anyone but themselves.

Corbin saw me staring and commented, "Waylen's half-vampire. He hates them more than anyone, something about avenging his mother, and I always call him when there are vampires to be killed."

Fair enough.

Dom was a hands-on type of general, so he was striding through the crowd, checking with lieutenants and captains alike to make sure everyone was on the same page.

He'd placed all of the non-druid others in his unit, under his direct command, and I knew that was because of me. He wanted to keep me close, and he wasn't even trying to hide it anymore—one of the downsides/perks of dating a king, depending on how you wanted to look at it.

Caleb and Christian were flanking me, ready to roll and itching for a fight, as usual.

Sven was close, battle axe in hand. I'd never fought with him before, but we'd both been amused when we saw that we favored the same weapon. I tried to trick him into trading with me, but even with a still quiet Torst, Sven seemed to understand that there was something wrong with my weapon and politely but instantly declined.

Oh well, it was worth a shot.

Very few of the druids were using beast-call as they found it less efficient for fighting vamps. The way they needed to be killed was better suited to blades and pointy things.

The plan of attack was simple, though vampires never cooperated with plans.

Henri was the first wave, an entire dedicated platoon protecting him. He would raise a large army of the dead and use it as the frontline while we swarmed the place and killed the masters. There were likely twelve by Corbin's calculations.

We were in the second wave, Corbin in front. We'd go in and wreak havoc, incapacitating as many as possible as quickly as we could as we carved our way to the masters.

It was the riskiest position, reserved for the stronger druids and supernaturals that could withstand a lot of damage, and we were sure to get the most action. And the most bites.

Sven and I had suggested using dragon fire, but druids hated fire as a rule, and it was decided that to target and stake the master vampires, we'd need more precision and manpower.

A raging, uncontrollable inferno didn't exactly go hand in hand with precision.

And those masters needed to die today. They were responsible for several hundred recent human deaths that we knew of, and we were here to make them pay.

Wave three was for the more delicate others, and the druids that couldn't use beastcall. They would follow us, a few careful minutes behind, to stake any vamps we downed. Tedious work, but necessary with the bloodsuckers.

Wave four was kind of overkill. They were positioned in a large, loose circle around the building just in case anything escaped, though it was hours from sunset so that was unlikely.

Between having Henri and the sun high in the sky for this battle, I was feeling downright optimistic.

Now let's see how the universe could prove me wrong.

After we were lined up and ready, just before the charge, Dom halted everything to move in front of me.

I watched him, a little shocked, as he touched one of my battle-braided buns and brought our foreheads together. "Be careful, my love," he said, his voice not at all quiet, not at all pitched low for my ears alone.

With Dom, I honestly didn't know if he was just declaring his intention toward me or doing it to countermand his own rule, or both.

Either way, the results were the same.

He was planting the seeds of his abdication, far away as it was, likely years in the future.

Everyone who saw him would believe he was under my spell, a strange other with way too much influence over their throne.

After that he did something to further my suspicions, nodding to Sloan at the last, letting her make the stirring battle speech and command the charge.

He's really going to do it, I thought in wonder. He's going to hand the throne to Sloan. I could scarcely believe it—which was foolish.

He'd said as much, and I'd believed him from the start. He wasn't the liar. That was me.

I was distracted from my musings by Henri. He was up to bat.

He was surrounded by a druid shield, or rather a shield of druids. His skin had gone white, his eyes black, dark veins popping up all along his skin, a black mist surrounding him. Oh yeah and he was floating about two feet off the ground.

He looked less like a hot Jesus now and more like a

terrifying Satan.

He began to chant in Latin and some horrifying noises started to seep from the building and to our ears, screeches of pain, mournful cries of sorrow. And fighting, but not with weapons. It was the sound of flesh on flesh combat as the hoard of dead bodies reanimated and became, for the moment, Henri's pets.

It went on for some time and windows began to break, doors opening as desperate newborn vamps beat the hoard back, so far somewhat ineffectively, since nothing was making it out.

Corbin was vamped out, dripping fangs protruding, face scary. He looked at Dom for his cue.

Finally Dom called it. "Wave two, charge!"

And we were off, running straight into hell.

And it was that. It stank of death in there, old and new, rotting and rich. That alone was enough to give pause, and then there was the noise, overwhelming, blood-curdling screeching.

Fucking vampires.

Henri was more than holding up his end of the bargain ,and a good chunk of the wave two dodged past the newborn nasties pretty easily.

I had my axe out, eyes trained on Corbin. He knew where the masters were. He was the man to follow.

I vaguely noted Caleb, Christian, and Sven keeping pace with me, though I'd expected that so it barely registered.

Dom was close too, I felt him like a hot breath on my neck, possibly close to literally.

We were past the first floor of carnage and on a stairwell without even wetting our weapons. Things were going much smoother than we were used to.

I no more had the thought when things went weird in a hurry.

The masters weren't asleep, which was expected as Henri had been murdering all their babies for a good fifteen minutes.

What wasn't expected was the protective circle the masters stood in, all twelve of them, a pile of torn up body parts at the center. They were all gaunt and pale, slimy, ugly, and tall. They all wore long black robes that looked suspiciously druid-like.

"That's a blood druid circle!" Sloan shouted.

"Fall back into formation!" Dom shouted nearly on top of that.

We listened without questioning, druids knew best what to do with master vampires using *blood* druid circles—what in the ever-loving fuck?

With efficient coordination the druids were setting up their own circle, the rest of us pushed back.

Corbin was the only one that hadn't backed off. He was right outside of the rogue circle, pacing, eyes on the vamp masters like a predator stalking prey.

"What can they do with that circle?" I asked no one in particular.

"I don't think anyone knows, but it can't be something good," Caleb remarked calmly.

I glanced at Sven. He was looking at the circle like it was a particularly interesting puzzle.

"We've broken one before," I told him, "Christian and I, working together. Though even I'm not sure just *why* it worked."

"That circle was more invisible than fortified," Christian remarked, though by the way he was jumping from foot to foot, I could tell he wanted to try again.

I shrugged. "Can't hurt to give it a shot," I said.

Christian grinned at me and it was as carefree and happy as it was bloodthirsty. "Let's roll."

But before we could take action the druids were ready with their own, better informed plans. They were nothing if not efficient.

A thick tree sprouted suddenly and violently into the middle of the vampire master circle, throwing the creatures in all directions and breaking their strange stolen spell.

At almost the same moment a group of newborn vampires tore up the stairs behind us. Henri's corpse army couldn't last forever. It'd had a good run.

It was a split second judgement which direction to fight in, but as I saw the newborns tear into the back of the group I shot that way, hoping there were enough strong fighters focusing on the masters for the moment.

After that it was a gore fest of a battle. Vampires lived on blood and so were in fact full of it, and each one I caught with my spinning axe effectively exploded blood into the air on contact. It was grisly.

I had to piece it together after the fighting was done, but Sven had joined me taking out the force behind us while almost everyone else went after the masters, which was for the best.

We fought well together for siblings that had been separated for most of their long lives. We'd never even trained with each other but our styles were similar, and I gave the credit for that to our love of a good battle axe.

The newborns coming up the stairs had taken out a few of ours with the element of distraction and surprise on their side, and those bodies combined with the growing pile of undead made for some slippery footing. At one point I just planted my ass down at the top of the stairs and started bonking them on the head as they came up.

They were new and weak but still vampire fast, so I got about a half dozen gnarly bites before the stream of creatures stopped.

At that point Sven helped me up from the floor, and we turned back to the room, assessing who needed help finishing off the masters.

I rushed to help Dom with one, but he was already squeezing its head between his hands until it was flat, casually pulled a stake out of a thigh sheath and drove it through its heart, moving on to the next.

Dom wouldn't be needing my help.

Cam, who I'd barely seen in the melee seemed to be struggling with two of them on him. I came up behind one of the vamps and cleanly sliced its head off and in the same motion took the other one's head and shoulders clean off.

I was rather impressed with my own moves but Cam just glared at me, the ingrate, and moved to stake them.

When the last master was dead, Dom caught sight of me, his eyes taking inventory, top to bottom.

"None of that's yours, I hope?" he asked referring to the fact that I was covered in blood.

I waved at the room. *Everyone* was covered in blood and gore. "I look the same as everyone else."

"Just answer the question, please," he asked through his teeth.

"I was bitten a few times but am otherwise unharmed."

Cleanup was a bitch, but we got out of most of it. That was a perk of being in the mess of it, I supposed. Waves three and four had faced less carnage but got the brunt of the bitch duty at the end.

The mood was somber after all danger had passed, and I assumed it was because the druids were disturbed by the darker form of their magic being stolen, yet again.

It had happened before, at the last necro roast. Druid magic in a place it shouldn't be. And though there wasn't an exact connection between necros and vampires, it felt significant that they were both undead.

It was alarming, to say the least. And if it was making my skin crawl like this, I couldn't even imagine how crazy it was driving Dom and Sloan.

It was a perturbing development but one that the druids would be handling themselves. I wasn't even sure they'd tell any outsiders after they got to the bottom of it all, which was frustrating but typical.

CHAPTER TWENTY
YOU WOULD KNOW

I got a message from Lynn only a day later. It showed up on my phone from an unknown number, but I knew it was her by the contents and the fact that the message started with a line of black heart, black cat, and dragon emojis.

The next line was coordinates that we mapped out to a remote palace in Mexico. She also let us know there were two dragons, the shadow-man was with them (Dom *really* didn't like that part), and we had two days to get to them before they could potentially move.

It was eleven p.m. when I got the message, but time didn't matter when you had the right connections. We took a private jet to the airport nearest to the location, because druids.

There had been a slight snafu that delayed our flight a few minutes, which was when Cam had lost his ever-loving mind when he'd found out what we were doing and that Sloan was coming along. Apparently she'd managed to keep her involvement in the task force from him before then.

It had all gone down right before we headed to the airport, and Christian and I had even gotten the rare chance to witness some of it.

We'd been waiting in a private lobby for everyone to show so we could shuttle to the airport. So far it was just Christian, Sloan, and I, and we were going over some details when Cam had stormed in like Hulk on a rampage.

"What the hell is your malfunction, Sloan?" I jumped at the sound of Cam's voice, turning as he entered the room. His angry eyes were all for Sloan. He didn't look at me. He usually didn't. He was still furious at me for. . . things. Mostly the incident with Sloan getting hurt when I was captured. And I thought he was probably still livid about what I'd done to Dom. He wasn't one to let things go, and I'd done plenty for him to hold onto. "Why are you involved in this mess?" he shouted at her.

Sloan barely reacted. It was as though she'd been expecting him. "Not that it's your business, but I have a score to settle with the Viking dragons. If you'll—"

"Is it to help *her*? *Why*? Why are you always championing her? Why are you so gung-ho about her disaster of a relationship with Dom? What has she ever done to actually make his life better?" Cam's tone was venomous.

Ironically I didn't take it personally even though it very much was.

Sloan whipped her hair behind her back in agitation. Her trademark phlegmatic persona changed in a heartbeat. As always, all it took was Cam entering the room. She waved a dismissive hand at him. "It's simple. Dom loves her. She loves him. They are crazy for each other, and nothing on this earth will change the way he feels about her. Look at all the crazy shit she put him through, and he starts drooling every time she looks his way. Even after everything, he will only ever *love* her. It's not something *you* could understand."

I shot a look at Christian, who was just as curious about the always fascinating soap opera that was Sloan and Cam. He gave me wide eyes, his mouth opening in a small O.

Cam sputtered. Literally sputtered. . . I couldn't believe it, but he looked downright flabbergasted. "You—you are off your rocker!" he was shouting to take the roof off. "You think I don't understand what's it's like to love a stone-cold, heartless bitch?" He turned and punched the wall several times until he'd left a large hole in it. He turned on his heel, pointing a bloody finger at Sloan. "Fuck. You. Sloan." He charged out of the room.

Christian and I looked at each other, open-mouthed. Christian couldn't help a little smile as he mouthed at me, "Oh, no he didn't."

Sloan strode after him, cursing as she walked away. *Damn, they were gonna take it somewhere private.* But Christian and I had gotten enough of the show to be adequately distracted.

"Dammit, Cam, wait up, you Neanderthal prick!" Sloan shouted as she chased him down the hall.

Christian and I were up, heads hanging out the door to watch, in the blink of an eye.

Cam had actually stopped at her rude shout, turning to look at her. Sloan stepped close to him, speaking to him too quietly for us to hear her. He put a hand between them, as though to ward her off. "I'm only going to warn you once," he said loudly. "You know what's going to happen to you if you get that close to me again."

We could only see the back of her as she squared her shoulders and took a pointed step forward. Cam's eyes widened, and in a flash he had slung her over his shoulder, his feet eating the ground as he strode purposefully down the hall and away from us.

"Figure yourselves out!" Christian shouted after them and was soundly ignored.

Christian and I stood up straight from our undignified, spying crouches. "Holy shit." His tone was dazed. "What was that?"

"I don't know." We shared shocked looks until finally we both broke into laughter. Side-splitting laughter.

"Were they going to go fuck? Or was he going to spank her? Or were they going somewhere to beat the shit out of each other?" Christian pondered.

I shook my head, still laughing. "If I had to guess, I'd say the first one. Dom implied that they're in love, and it's a fact that they are definitely crazy for each other."

Christian grinned. "You would know the signs. I wish there was some way for us to find out what they're doing right now. I'd love to take bets on it, but the sad fact is we'll probably never know." He shook his head, running his hand through his disheveled blond locks. "I'm glad I've never found a woman to make me that batty, no offense. On the up side, I'm sure bat-shit crazy sex is amazing."

I couldn't argue with that.

The end result of the whole mess was that we had a fuming Cam on the plane with us and Collin had to stay behind so the druids weren't missing too many members of their upper management at once.

The flight was about five hours, and we prepped and briefed on the way. We'd left in a hurry so we were still gearing up as we went.

I had the still strangely quiet Torst—again that worried me —strapped to my back, and a small arsenal of other weapons that I either equipped myself or had forcibly strapped to me by either Dom or Caleb.

Christian braided my hair into neat twin buns on the sides of my head as we flew.

Dom didn't even try to kill him for it.

Helen stood too close to Dom a few times as we made our plans, and I didn't even take an axe to her.

Well, well, weren't we were all making progress toward becoming mature adults. Maybe in a few neat centuries, we'd be all grown up.

Everyone was wearing matching armored tactical gear. I really didn't know how much it could help considering we were going up against at least two dragons and one other slayer, but it was better than nothing, I supposed.

"You will stay far away from their slayer," Dom told me quietly. It had been his favorite subject since he'd found out we wouldn't be the only ones with the power to kill dragons in this fight. "Harvey and I will focus on him first, and I don't want you anywhere near him in the meantime."

I nodded. That was fine by me. Just thinking about him turned my stomach into a pit of anxiety.

The plan was simple. I'd take Caleb, Christian, Sloan, and Cam and go after my father.

Sven would lead Helen, Hamish, James, Jasper, Corbin, Henri, and Calum to take the second dragon.

Dom and Harvey would join my team directly after killing their slayer, but chances were almost 100% that my father was the more powerful dragon of the two and they would have Sven so I thought it was as even as we were going to get.

The other was likely one of Villi's sons, my cousin Ragnar, Sven was certain, and would be formidable but not at the level of my ancient father.

"Are you sure you can do this?" I asked Sven on the flight. He was quiet and spent most of his time meditating which I didn't know how to take. Was he having doubts about our new allegiance against the family?

At least he didn't hesitate to nod firmly. "I can. It won't be pleasant but it is a necessary evil. Keeping our sister's eyes in a jar on his desk is more than enough justification on its own."

I stared at him with wide eyes. "Is that really what he's doing?"

He shrugged. "It's a figure of speech but it's as likely as anything."

"Quite a figure of speech."

He smiled and it was wry. "Par for the course considering our childhood."

"Par for the course? You into golfing these days?"

He laughed and waved me off, "I've been working on my modern turns of phrase. Now I'm going back to meditating if you're quite finished making fun of me."

"Enjoy," I told him, moving to stand next to Sloan.

"How are you related?" I asked Sloan. I nodded toward Calum.

She glanced back at him, and they met eyes and they both gave a casual chin up at each other. "My brother."

"I had no clue you had a brother."

"Half-brother, and we weren't raised on the same continent so we don't know each other that well. He moved to the States recently."

That was curious. "You could be twins."

She shrugged. "My dad had a type," she said laconically.

Alright then. Change of subject time.

"Cam seems to be calming down," I observed. We were near the front of the cabin, Cam near the back talking to Dom, but at my comment he looked at me and glared. Oops, he'd heard. I looked away like nothing had happened.

"Hard to tell," Sloan said, glaring back at him. "He has a tendency to hold on to grudges beyond all sense of time or reason. Excuse me, that reminds me I need to have another word with him."

As she left Christian approached me and we watched as

Sloan said something brief to Cam, and they both disappeared into the plane's private cabin.

We looked at each other, raising our brows and covering our mouths in tandem.

"SloCam ship confirmed," Christian said with glee.

"Maybe they just went in there to talk," I said but I didn't believe it for a second.

Just then Helen approached Dom and took Cam's vacant seat across from him. She touched his hand as they started talking.

"You going to put up with that?" Christian asked me, trying to stir up shit like it was his job, as usual.

I shrugged. "I'm trying to overlook it. I'm being mature about it."

"Why?"

"I'm trying to adult now."

"Why start now? You're no spring chicken. How old are you—" He stopped mid-sentence, seeing my face, remembering how I felt about discussing my age, and re-shifted his question, "What's with the sudden maturity?"

"I'm going to be a mother, or I guess I *am* a mother. I'm turning over a new leaf."

I didn't think he believed me going by his loud laughter. I stuck my tongue out at him.

"Jillian," Caleb spoke from beside me. I almost jumped. He'd been so quiet I'd almost forgotten he was there. Dangerous habit, that.

"Yeah?" I responded because he seemed to be waiting for it.

"It seems like you might need to be a dragon to fight a dragon, no?"

I thought about it some. I'd been considering it a lot in last the few hours, and I just wasn't sure where I'd be more effective, or even if I'd be able to shift fast enough to be useful. "I might," I finally answered. "But my dad is a lot older and more powerful than me. Even the second dragon will be, no matter who he is. The power of the blood grows with age, and I'm the definitely the youngest.

The weakest.

"I have more training fighting with an axe than as a dragon," I continued, "and Torst will only be helpful if I'm my human self. Also I'm not sure how much help I'd be to the team as a draak. Some of us are flame retardant but certainly not all, whereas what we're fighting certainly is."

"I see," Caleb said. "So it's looking like you won't shift, but if you need to at any time, I'll take Torst for the fight.

"What about the hammer?"

"I can dual-wield." Christian and I shared a smirk at the gamer term. "It's not wise to do for anything but the bloodiest fight," Caleb kept talking like we weren't just immortal children, "but I'm positive this will qualify. So if at any time you need to grow scales and fly, toss Torst to me."

I nodded. It was a relief. "I will. I'm still a little freaked out that he's so quiet now, though."

Caleb looked thoughtful. "Perhaps I kept the wrong one. I've found more tricks to keep Torst quiet than you did. Any chance you'd be more suited to the hammer and me to the axe?"

The thought made me uncomfortable, but I mulled it over. "Possibly," I conceded reluctantly. I hated that fucking hammer and Caleb with the axe made me uneasy but quite frankly both options sucked.

"We'll give it more thought after we kill your father," Caleb said. It was a disturbing sentence but hardly incorrect.

About an hour out Sven roused from his meditation, took out some strange tools, and started mixing something together. He wasn't speaking but I could tell he was using magic as he worked. It was in the air and without even meaning to we began to gather around him. I was suddenly standing at his shoulder with no memory of moving.

It looked like he was playing with black tar in a little mortar and pestle.

No one was speaking, and I wondered if we were all under a spell.

He dipped his fingertips into the tar and began to paint his face. He was quick, like he'd done it a thousand times and when he finished he had a black mask painted perfectly around his eyes.

He looked up at me, eyes eerily pale and farseeing. "Your turn," he said it like we'd been in the middle of a conversation, like I was somehow in on this ritual.

"Viking war paint," I said, somewhat amused.

"Can I have some?" Christian called out, because of course he did.

Sven shifted his eyes to him with uncanny focus. "This is only for draak." He looked at me and said something in the old language that amounted to, 'for the glory of battle,' and began to paint.

I closed my eyes and when I opened them again I had a matching black mask painted across my eyes.

The group huddled up right before the plane began its descent to touch on any last minute questions or concerns.

Dom gave a stirring speech about victory then nodded at me like I should say something.

"Christian, any tips for the other slayers?" I asked, for what I thought were obvious reasons.

"We don't need any tips from *him*," Helen said disdainfully. "We've all had just as much training or more."

I opened my mouth—to correct her, I suppose, but Christian beat me to it.

He touched the relic around his neck and in a flash it was

transformed into its true form, a long blue sword that glowed and made me take a step back in caution.

"This is the only slayer weapon in this cabin full of slayers that's ever been quenched in the blood of the enemy," Christian's voice was cold and strange. I rarely saw or heard his serious side. It colored him differently. "So perhaps I do have a few things to add. It's not what you think it will be. The dragon will be faster than you trained for, and it will take much more strength to cut its scales than you imagine. One slayer will go for the head, the other the heart. You've been looking forward to this, but there will be fear, more fear than you've ever felt, and you cannot hesitate."

I stared at the weapon in his hands. I'd seen it skewer one of my kin in full dragon form. It had cut through the scales like butter, and it had ended my uncle's very long life.

It boggled the mind just what it could do to my human form.

Christian was one of my closest friends and seeing his slayer weapon bared made me tense.

The fact that I was in a room full of strangers carrying similar weapons made my molten blood run cold with dread.

Slayers were a necessary evil. I knew it logically. My kind were too powerful, too destructive if left unchecked.

I knew it. That didn't mean I liked it.

CHAPTER TWENTY-ONE
WE'RE EVERYWHERE

T he sun was just rising as we left the airport and loaded up into the back of two large armored vehicles divided up by the teams.

Dom traveled with ours.

"You have a druid presence even here?" I asked Dom. I was impressed at what they'd been able to put together with a few hours' notice. How they'd found such vehicles so quickly with two stone-faced druid drivers, to boot.

Dom looked insulted. "We're everywhere, as you well know."

Touché.

"How long is the drive?" Christian asked, looking antsy.

"Two hours, give or take," Dom said. He once again pulled up a map of the compound we were storming and we continued to plan.

Two hours felt like days with raw nerves strumming inside of me, and I knew I wasn't the only one. Everyone was on edge.

Dom touched one of my braid buns, turning my face in his direction as we drew close to the drop-off point. He leaned his head down until our foreheads touched. "You will be careful," he said to me, voice low. It was an order, and he said it like he expected to be obeyed. He said a few more lines in emotional Druidic. They sounded like either a prayer or a spell. "You will stay far away from the shadow-man while we take care of him," he added.

I pulled back far enough to meet his eyes, and his contrasting gaze bore into mine. I touched his cheek. "Trust me, I have no desire to go near him. Kill him fast so I never have to think of him again."

He kissed my forehead. "With pleasure," he murmured into my skin.

He used the last few minutes of the drive to carve a rather painful rune deep into my wrist then healed it with a kiss.

"What's that one do?" I asked.

"If somehow I lose sight of you, I will know instantly if you're hurt."

"Like forever? Or is it temporary?"

"It's not temporary though it will weaken with time."

"Wait, so you'll know if I'm hurt, but will it help you to track me?" Dom tracking me without telling me was an ongoing saga we'd beaten to *death*.

He looked like he'd swallowed something sour. "There is no rune that will let me track you permanently, unfortunately." He pulled something out of his pocket. "But indulge me with some tracking devices at least for this fight." He slipped earrings onto each of my ears that looked like pearls. "Just in case," he added.

"At least you're telling me when you're doing that now."

"We need to learn to trust each other again. It goes both ways."

He gripped my face in his hands. "Whatever happens, stay alive," he told me gruffly and gave me a hard, quick kiss. "You will survive *no matter what.*"

"You too," I replied softly. The idea that we could lose each other now, when the future held more hope for us than it ever had, hit me hard.

He said something in Druidic with such fervor that I asked him to clarify. "I said that if anything were to happen to you, I won't survive it. I won't want to. I gave you my soul a very long time ago. Where you go, it will always follow, even into the next realm."

We were dropped off as close as we could get without the large vehicles being immediately detected, which meant we had to walk the last few miles. The other group was let out on the other side of the compound with roughly the same amount of ground to cover. It wasn't ideal, but it was better than moving in as one big, obvious target.

We fanned out and headed to our destination. We had headsets on but it was radio silence unless one of us spotted a dragon or ran into trouble.

I was flanked by some distance between Dom and Caleb. We moved with quick, measured steps, eyes scanning every inch of the terrain we passed. We moved in sync as though we'd trained for it. We basically had. We were all familiar with methodically tracking prey.

I still wasn't sure it wasn't a mistake for me not to try to shift into my draak form first, but it wasn't exactly a quick or easy process for me and between forms I'd be vulnerable not to mention useless.

Sven, on other hand, was staying back to shift even now. He was confident that he could be of more use in dragon form and said he couldn't be sure but he thought it would take him about forty-five minutes to an hour.

Dense forest covered the land around the compound my dad was occupying, and we looked for traps as we moved but as far as I could tell we didn't trigger any sensors on our way. It wouldn't surprise me at all if he had little to no defenses set up. My father's arrogance and faith in his invulnerability knew no bounds. He'd been alive for a very long time, long enough to be made into a legend for the ages, which had only increased his hubris. I could not imagine a world where he would see me and a group of mixed others as a real threat to him, and I was counting on that. Being underestimated was going to work strongly in our favor.

We moved until we were in throwing distance of the sloping, manicured grounds of what looked like a palace surrounded by many smaller buildings. It looked opulent. Perhaps they'd stolen it from some local cartel.

There was literally no movement on the property that anyone could detect. It was very strange, but we advanced nonetheless.

We encountered what appeared to be a surprised gardener right as we approached the outer layer of buildings, but he didn't sound an alarm. He just stared at us until Dom caught his eyes, chanted a few words as he made a quick gesture with his hand, and caught him and laid him gently on the ground before we pushed forward again. The whole thing took all of three seconds.

There weren't any guards, I'm sure my father would be insulted by the very notion, but there were a few ordinary humans working there that had to be bespelled and set aside as we advanced deeper into the enemies' lair.

I was beginning to wonder if we were too late, if they were even there, when things turned a bit strange.

It was nothing I could even put my finger on right away, just that the very air around us seemed wrong, stale and stifling suddenly.

I paused looking to the men on either side of me. My breath was ragged, but no one else seemed affected in quite the same way.

I put my hand up to stop our advance. Something was wrong, but I didn't know what. It felt like we were walking into a trap and even one step might spring it.

I crouched, hands on my knees as I tried to catch my breath.

We were in the driveway at this point, and I was staring at the pale gray concrete as I managed my breathing when I caught it. My eyes had originally told me that the surface we were walking on was stamped asphalt, but the pattern was all wrong.

I opened my mouth to scream a warning when something caught my breath in my lungs.

I straightened, drew Torst, and whirled a beat too late. A cloud of glowing blue powder blasted into my face, and I collapsed in a fit of agony.

I had shut my eyes just in time, which was lucky because I was pretty sure I would have been blinded for the rest of the fight or longer otherwise.

By the way my body reacted, I could tell that that powder was some residue of whatever component made up the slayer weapons.

Vaguely I heard a scuffle nearby and knew it was Dom ripping into whoever had just attacked me.

The ground began to shift heavily below us and I sat up and found my voice to scream, "Fall back! We're on top of him!"

I was thrown wide as the driveway stood up and took flight.

What we'd mistaken for patterned concrete was actually dragon scales. Fucking glamour.

The dragon took flight, flying almost straight up into the sky.

I stood and took inventory of the damage even as I moved toward Dom to help him with the shadow-man.

Everyone on our team was accounted for except for two. Harvey and. . .

"Where is Christian?" I called out.

Caleb started cursing and I glanced at him. Caleb looked worried and disgusted as he pointed up. "He held onto the dragon, the reckless fool."

Fuck. It was a worrisome and potentially devastating development, but we didn't have time to linger on it.

I glanced toward the fight. The shadow-man was a bloody heap on the ground though he still had a head.

Dom and Harvey had effectively been distracted by the a larger than life blond man that stepped out of the front door of the palace, as were we all.

Where the fuck was the other team?

The man was beautiful and glowing. He smiled and nodded at me. "It's Ragnar the Spellbinder," I said loudly for everyone.

"Hello, cousin," he said in a thickly accented voice.

"Don't meet his eyes," I called out. "And don't listen to him. He can trap you with his voice!"

"So unfriendly," Ragnar chided me. "That's no greeting for a man you were betrothed to from birth."

That gave me pause. "I left when I was eleven, you sicko. I was never betrothed to anyone."

"Just because you will something doesn't make it so. We had a betrothal, written in blood, from the time of your birth. You have robbed me of many sons in the years you've been away, but we will make up for it."

He was pissing me off, but something much worse was happening to Dom.

He had transformed into some amalgam of bear, cat, and wolf that was more terrifying than any of the three. He stood almost ten feet high. He was the definition of a monster from nightmares, and he was foaming at the mouth and growling as he approached Ragnar like a hunter stalking prey.

Ragnar pointed at him, raising his brows at me. "This? This is what you chose over me? You'll both pay for that." He waved a hand at Dom and chanted something under his breath.

Dom froze in place. Everyone but me seemed frozen, in fact.

I approached Ragnar myself, picking Torst up from the ground where it'd fallen as I moved.

I thirst, the axe chanted in my head loudly.

"Your timing is impeccable," I told my axe fondly.

Without further ado, I took a heavy swing at my cousin.

He moved his hands into odd shapes as he whispered and darted out of my way.

I followed, Torst swinging with deadly intent at every step. I missed him by a hair once, twice, on and on.

His spells weren't affecting me for some reason, and I realized why only when I saw where he'd effectively maneuvered me.

I was standing nearly on top of the mangled shape that was the shadow-man when I realized the spells weren't for me. They were to keep everyone else out of the fight.

Not my cleverest moment.

That was when he cast a spell at me and as my feet seemed glued to the ground, a hand grabbed my ankle.

I looked down. The shadow-man was conscious. He was in bad shape, but as I watched he found the strength to stand, his slayer weapon shaped into a small dagger and held loosely in his hand.

CHAPTER
TWENTY-TWO
DADDY DEAREST

I met the shadow-man's eyes and there was no one home with even a shred of sanity left. Ragnar was delusional, but even he was nowhere near this far gone.

"Can I finish her?" the shadow-man asked my cousin, grinning madly at me.

"Cut her up and take her out of the fight, but don't finish her," Ragnar said.

My back was to him now and a loud noise accompanied his words, but I couldn't see what it was. One thing was clear though, someone had managed to move beyond his spell.

I was taken effectively out of wondering who it was as the shadow-man brought the dagger close to my throat.

The spell loosened on me due to whoever had attacked Ragnar behind me, I surmised, and I grabbed the slayer's wrist, pushing the dagger away an inch, then another.

With a laugh, he drew a second glowing blue dagger and slashed at my stomach with it.

Just great, I thought. He could dual-wield.

I moved back and he missed me by a hair, only lightly shredding my tactical vest but not touching my skin.

I dropped Torst, he was useless in a fight this close, and drew a dagger out of a thigh sheath, bringing it to the madman's neck. I was pushing it in right as he left my reach and my sight in a quick, furious rush.

I blinked briefly at the sight of Monster Dom ripping his intestines out but made myself turn and pick up Torst, heading determinedly back to Ragnar, who was now in a four-way fight with Caleb, Cam (a bear now) and Sloan (a tiger). At least I thought that was the order of their beast-calls.

Harvey and Christian and the whole second team were still MIA, but we had no time to worry about it. Ragnar was fending off three of the deadliest fighters I'd ever met with one long sword and a few spells. We had our hands full.

I tried to flank him and was about to sink Torst into him when the air grew hot.

"Take cover!" I screamed as I buried the axe into my cousin's thick back. He went to his knees, and I didn't have to think about it, Torst took over, hacking at him like a tree trunk.

A torrent of white flame bombarded us, and Cam and Sloan had to dive for shelter as my father lit the world around us on fire.

I looked up, still hacking away, and took in his glorious visage. He was beautiful and terrible, all glamour gone, his true form revealed. He was silver and glorious, the size of a large barge, his massive wings spread wide as he roared out more fire.

I took inventory of the others. Caleb was still there, hammering at Ragnar's front, a wicked little dagger in his second hand, whittling at the dragon's stomach between hammer pounds.

We were making good progress against Ragnar considering all of our slayer weapons were otherwise occupied but, *ah fuck*, Caleb was on fire.

"Caleb, you're on fire!" I shouted at him. He didn't seem to hear, and I raised my voice. "You need to stop, drop, and roll!"

He ignored me, still hammering and stabbing with gusto, totally on fire now.

Okay, then.

The heat receded, Daddy dearest taking to the air again.

"Where the *fuck* is the other team?" Caleb asked no one in particular, batting the flames out of his clothes rather casually.

To be fair, I was doing the same, but *I* was immune to fire.

Ragnar was limp now, effectively decommissioned for the near future, and I glanced around. "We need a fucking slayer," I added, also to no one in particular.

Sloan and Cam came slowly out of the palace, and we went in search of Dom.

We found him quickly by following the sound of carnage.

Harvey was there, cradling his brother's jaggedly severed head in his hands and crying like his life was over. I'd hated his twin and even I was moved by the raw emotion of it. It had clearly not been an easy death. Having your head literally ripped off equaled some suffering.

Monster Dom was still ripping into the rest of the shadow-man with gusto about twenty feet away. Full druid berserker mode.

With a sigh I approached. "Domhnall," I said firmly when I drew close.

He froze, straightened, and turned. He was eating a heart and at least twelve feet tall now with massive antlers growing out of his head.

I'd never seen anything like it, but I just stepped closer and reached my hand up high, palm open to him. "He's dead, my love," I told him. "He'll never hurt me again. Now back to the fight, soldier. We're not finished yet and we need you."

He dropped the heart and touched my hand with a bloody claw with absolute delicacy.

I caught his eyes, ascertained that it was still Dom in there. He lowered his head close to me, and I stroked his beastly face once before moving back to Harvey. The other three were trying to get his help to slay Ragnar but he seemed lost to grief.

"Can someone just use his weapon?" I asked the group loudly.

It was a silly question, no one but a slayer could wield one of the dragon slayer relics, but it got Harvey's attention.

He set his twin's head gently on the ground and stood up. Tears were still running down his face but his voice was clear enough. "Lead on."

I wasn't the only one cursing when we went back to the spot where we'd left Ragnar in and found nothing there.

Dom and Cam tore into the main building to search for him, I presumed.

"Could we fuck this up any more?" Caleb asked no one in particular.

"Where is the other team?" Harvey asked.

Question of the day.

"Take cover!" I screamed as I felt the air shifting again.

This time my father didn't rain fire down on us. He merely landed gently, but it was worse, much worse as I saw what was hanging out of his mouth.

A pair of legs hung from the side of his mouth, familiar black boots dangling lifelessly. The silver dragon looked directly at me as he spit them out. There was no torso, just some entrails hanging out of the top of the pants.

"No!" I screamed. Oh God, *please no.*

Caleb didn't make a sound, but he was at the legs in a flash, gathering them up, emotions running over his face in a way I'd never seen before. I'd never seen him move so fast, didn't know he could. Didn't know he could look grief-stricken either.

He ran out of the dragon's reach in a flash and bent down, grabbing one of the attached feet to look at something.

I glared at my father, tears streaming down my face, and charged with a scream. I was crying even as I hacked at him. He swept me away easily and I was up again, throwing myself at him again, getting thrown again. I felt nothing physically, I'd become numb to everything but what I felt inside, and there it was all sorrow, all pain.

I was thrown even farther and this time as I made my way back I spotted something moving on the dragon's back.

As I processed what I was seeing, relief flooded me utterly, head to toe.

I heard Caleb's voice shouting at me. "It wasn't Christian!" he said as he pounded the hammer against the dragon's side. He looked tiny against the huge creature. "The legs weren't Christian!"

I pointed up at the dragon's back. What looked like a small figure, but was actually a large man was clinging to it, twisting its bright blue sword between scales with vigor.

He wasn't just alive, he was fighting his heart out.

With renewed effort, I charged at my father again.

The battle was a revelation. Every slice between the creature's diamond hard scales and into its flesh seemed to heal almost instantly. It was exhausting and demoralizing to realize how little damage I could do in my current form.

We'd killed one easily. My uncle Villi. It hadn't fazed me then just how weakened he'd been before we even entered the fight. It did now. My father was much stronger than Villi and even with Christian hanging on to him and piercing him on the back with his slayer blade, he was hardly weakened.

Dom was fighting beside me, his claws raking between the scales, pulling out handfuls of flesh at a time and even that was healing.

And then we had a break in the case. The other team arrived and joined the fray.

Fucking finally.

We didn't ask questions and neither did they, just tore into the beast with relish.

It felt like we were making progress. My father was screaming in agony, and at least three of the slayer weapons were digging deeper into him slowly but inexorably.

The day was cloudless and bright but just then a shadow fell over us like an ominous raincloud and I looked up. A large green dragon had arrived.

Everyone else misread it.

"Fucking finally," Christian yelled.

"About damn time," Cam growled.

The monster swooped low and everyone just stared at it.

"That's not Sven!" I screamed. "Take cover! That's Ragnar!"

The creature lit the world up around us as it swept past, but the slayers and I stayed put as the rest took cover. Christian had dropped down to his belly now and had teamed up with Hamish to start digging straight for his heart. I thought they were close.

So did my father, apparently. Without further ado, he pushed off hard from the ground and took flight.

This time there was no determined Christian holding onto him. Gods dammit, he was going to escape.

As though they'd coordinated it, Ragnar landed right as my father was leaving and before we had a chance to brace for him.

He landed right on top of one of the bear druids, crushing

him with a splat into the ground.

"Fuck!" Cam shouted.

Without word, without having to so much as think about it, we fell on the green dragon hacking, hammering, slashing at it.

This one was smaller and dumber. Instead of defending himself right away, he shifted off the body he'd just crushed, picked it up, and ate it with a loud chomp.

That only served to piss us all off even more.

As though the first, stronger dragon had just been practice, Christian and Hamish, now joined by Harvey, started digging into a spot in its belly with coordinated effort. Soon Helen caught on and joined them.

I could tell right away they'd make better progress this time if we could just keep the dragon from realizing what they were doing.

I moved to its face where Dom, a step ahead of me, was already taunting it.

I was a better target though as the dragon focused on me as soon as I was in view.

It was still chewing on the dead druid as it glared at me.

I glared back, crouching, axe ready. "Come closer, you coward!" I screamed at it and the motherfucker fell for it, lowering its head, still chomping away. When it was close enough, eyes glued to me, I leapt, burying Torst in its eye.

It screeched, a terrible noise, and shook me off. I fell away, but Torst stayed, sinking deeper into the eyeball and holding on as though it was in love.

Ragnar just kept making that terrible noise, and Dom was pulling out his tongue now, shredding deeply into it with both claws. I drew a long knife out of a thigh sheath and joined him, hacking away.

The dragon was still healing fast but not as fast, and we kept working at it relentlessly.

Dom had pulled the tongue out so far that Ragnar's head was low to the ground now and he couldn't use his own teeth without helping us to sever his tongue. It was brilliant. And a perfect distraction.

When he was close enough I jumped up and grabbed Torst from his eye. It was a struggle to pull him out, he was buried nearly to the hilt now. When I was free, bloody axe in hand, I lunged up again, going for the other eye. The first one was slow to heal, I already saw. I'd found a vulnerable spot and I took full advantage.

I took a step back to study where next to do damage (Dom had the head covered at this point.) when things changed suddenly.

A slayer's blade, Christian's I saw by the fact that he was the only slayer that had gone *inside* of the beast, pierced its heart. Everything changed. Dragons are creatures of magic, and whatever was keyed into those damned blades cut off the flow. Immortality gone in a blink.

No one was immortal. Not even me. What magic made strong magic weak? What unnatural thing had made the slayer blades in the first place? I didn't know but whatever it was, it was damned effective.

Immortality is unnatural. That's why my kin was trying to kill me. It's why I was trying to kill them. It's why druids could live forever, but often maintained the same lifespan as a normal human. Nature finds a way.

"The neck!" I screamed at the slayers that weren't inside of the beast digging its heart out. I started hacking zealously, and Helen and Hamish joined me straightaway with their slayer weapons. Harvey had followed Christian deeper into the beast.

The flesh was giving way satisfactorily to my axe. We were actually killing it now.

Fucking finally.

It took a lot of wet work but at last the head came off, slopping limply onto the ground. The tongue had been clawed clean off a while go, Dom finishing the job on both of the eyeballs for good measure.

Christian was grinning, every inch of him covered in blood and gore, Ragnar's huge heart hugged to him like it was his favorite giant teddy bear.

"How do you finish it?" I asked him. "Without casting it, what exactly is the death spell?"

"Avada cadavera!" Christian grinned. "Just kidding. It's top secret. You need to get clear out, so we can finish him."

I was nodding and moving into the main building before he'd finished speaking. I started searching for my sister's eyes, but only made it two rooms in before I felt the shockwaves of the death spell reverberate through the land.

CHAPTER TWENTY-THREE
WATCH THE WORLD BURN

I stepped outside just as the shadow of an enormous dragon appeared above the compound. It was dark as a shadow, and I felt dread curl in my gut. It wasn't silver but dark gray and even larger than my father, its head about twice the size.

Holy shit.

"Thanks for nothing," Christian yelled up at the sky.

"That's not Sven!" I screamed for the second time that day just as my grandfather unleashed hell on us.

When I could see again the hellish black dragon had landed and Dom was already going for his pitch black eye, Hamish and Christian at his gut.

The rest were slowly coming out of the spots they'd been thrown at or run to for shelter.

I took quick inventory of everyone as I moved into the new battle.

Jasper and James were missing. I was pretty sure those were our two casualties so far.

Everyone else was in decent shape, considering.

I noticed that Henri and Helen looked like they'd each taken a good beating, Harvey and Christian were covered in drying blood and gore, and Corbin and Caleb seemed almost cheerful. Figures.

I joined Dom at the dragon's head as another shadow fell over us.

Oh, c'mon, I thought as I looked up.

"That one is Sven!" I shouted. 'Bout damn time.

My brother swooped low, landing claw first into our grandfather's back. Sven was about a third of his size. Not good.

"Where the fuck have you been?" I shouted at the beautiful iridescent blue dragon as our grandfather tried to bite me, and I tried to dig his eyes out of his head.

Grandfather attacked me while I was shifting. It was a close thing.

Well, hell. That *was* a good excuse.

Just then the larger dragon *breathed* on me and it wasn't fire, it was magic that sent me to my knees.

I felt the blood in my veins light up. Flames flared deep inside of me, and I was suddenly on the ground against my will as my body took the choice away from me.

Something he'd done to me, some errant spell he'd breathed at me was forcing me to shift mid-fight.

My grandfather then whipped around to snap at the smaller dragon on his back.

Giant monster Dom crouched beside me, looking worried.

I waved him off, tried to speak, but I was already too far gone. I started crawling away, trying to cover as much distance as possible to give myself room.

Dom was following me. I couldn't speak to tell him he

could go back to the fight, but he'd see what was happening soon enough.

The shift took me all at once, like catching fire, the flame traveled over me a flash. Whatever old magic my grandfather had used was changing me faster than I'd ever experienced before.

My wings snapped out, and I got a brief glimpse of them out of the corner of my eye. They looked like they were made of pure light, so blinding I could scarcely look at them.

I didn't wonder about it for long as my other self took over completely.

I joined the fight with glee. They hadn't gotten to his heart yet, not even close, so I focused on helping to hold his head down while Dom clawed at his eyes.

He tried to flap his wings out to take off, but Sven was holding his body to the earth as I pinned his head. Obviously I'd underestimated the potential of the two of us working together in dragon form. He was much bigger than us, but he was only one and he didn't have even one slayer on his side now.

Helen and Hamish were chopping at his neck as Christian and Harvey dug into his chest. Only one dragon down but they'd developed a sound strategy in the killing of it.

Another shadow flew over us, and I looked up to see my father circling overhead in an irresistible taunt.

Don't go after him, Sven projected into my mind. *It's not worth it.*

My father roared into the air, and it was like a siren's call to me. I could not resist it. My dragon took over and I was flying, chasing after him before I'd realized it.

He was faster, bigger, stronger. All I had on my side was sheer determination and blinding hatred, and I used that to follow him as he raced across the sky. He veered straight up and I shot into the clouds after him.

It took me awhile to see his plan, his intention in drawing me out.

I chased him through the sky for some immeasurable beat of time until he suddenly took a dive, and I followed that too, right on his tail now.

I was slow to see the settlement of small houses until we were almost over it. I stared as it began to catch fire and deep inside some part of me should be horrified, but that part was buried deep from where I was looking now.

I was following my father for a second sweep before I even realized it wasn't me setting the quiet town ablaze, I was that mesmerized by it.

I could just let go, I realized for the first time. I could let the fire take over. That was what the madness was. But in the madness was freedom from responsibility, from care, from pain.

My whole life I'd held back. I didn't want to anymore.

I wanted to watch the world burn and glory in it.

Even in my altered state, with my other nature in control, I saw the problem right away.

It would be hard to step away from the urge. It was hard to remember why I should want to.

I only saw what my father was doing then. He wasn't drawing me away so he could attack.

He was showing me, tempting me with something I'd never let myself consider before. There was another path when you left the human part of you behind, when you let the draak rule you as my father had and his father before him, and it was one short fork in the road away.

In the end it was taken out of my hands as another dragon shrieked in the distance, a distress call that drew me away from the destruction my father had wreaked and that I had been hypnotized by.

I simply had to see who the other dragon was. If it was a call to victory or defeat.

When I saw that it was my brother whatever had kept me fueled through this mad dash seemed to fade from me all at once, and I went down hard.

Of course it was Dom that found me. Who else?

I was laying on my back, in human form, naked, limp, my stomach an empty pit. I'd never felt more helpless, more hopeless in my entire miserable existence.

It had taken me a long time to see it.

Centuries.

But I saw it now. I was a monster. One good panorama of what I could really do, of how I could truly let my true power loose, and I'd nearly helped my father raze an innocent village to the ground. I'd wanted to do it. I'd *craved* that power; the dark, twisted power of ruling over a burning ruin. The only way you could truly own something was to *break* it, to cleanse it with fire.

Destruction ran in my veins, and it was more powerful than any other trait I owned.

I was as sick as any of them. As dangerous.

Dom, in human form now and even clean, covered me with a blanket, his expression very carefully blank as he did it. He lifted me, tucking it completely around my body, trapping my arms.

We were alone in the back of an armored vehicle, driving before I could find the words to speak.

"Dom," I whispered hoarsely.

"Shh," he soothed, stroking my brow but never glancing down at me.

"I've lost it, Dom. I see it now. I'm just like the rest of them. I need you to do something for me."

"Shh," he said again, still without looking down.

"I need you to finish me, Dom. I'm too much of a danger

—"

"Stop. You're weak and delirious. You need to be silent and rest."

"You don't understand. I almost didn't stop. I wanted to keep going, to burn—"

"Silence, I said! We're not doing this now, and you need to quit talking such nonsense. My temper has been tested enough this day."

"It will be better if you do it. You and Christian. I'd prefer —"

"I'm only going to tell you this once, Jillian." His voice was low, but his tone was so sharp that it cut. "Don't speak these words again. This is out of your hands. If you go behind my back, convince some other poor sucker that they need to kill you, just imagine what will happen to them. Just step back and think about this. Do you honestly believe I could ever kill you? That I would *allow* you to *die*?"

"My life is not worth more than an entire city's worth of people, Dom. I've seen into the black void that is my power, and it cannot be allowed loose. I need to die."

"Never." He was squeezing me so tight that I could barely breathe. "That is not an option. We will find a way to control this, but you need to quit speaking this way. And I repeat, if you try to go behind my back with this, don't say I didn't warn you. If you think I have one fucking qualm about killing Christian, you're deluding yourself. He'll be dead before he can lay one pinky on that fucking sword of his."

I closed my eyes, giving up. His furious speech, as much as I hated to admit it, had comforted me.

This was out of my hands. I had tried my best to do the right thing. I knew this man well enough to understand that he was incapable of budging on a thing like this.

I'd been holding it in for a while, and, completely spent, lacking all self-control, I unloaded, "I love you. Always have.

Never stopped. Wouldn't know how."

His breathing became ragged, his tight hold got rougher. He started speaking Druidic in a furious flood into my ear.

I couldn't understand that fucking language, but I thought I got the gist of it. Still, I made him repeat it in English.

He loved me, he always had.

I was the bane of his existence and his reason for breathing.

Still closing my eyes, smiling, I said, "Ditto."

CHAPTER TWENTY-FOUR
MAGICAL EYEBALLS

W e were almost back at the compound before I said, "My father got away, but I watched him burn a whole village to the ground first." I took a trembling breath, trying hard not to cry. "How about ol' grandpa? Did you guys finish him?"

Dom stroked a hand over my hair. It was down now, out of its braids and falling in waves down my back.

He hadn't looked at me, and I knew he was still struggling for control. The chaos and carnage of the battle combined with me disappearing and coming back suicidal had taken their toll on him.

"We did," he said laconically.

I didn't want to ask, was scared to know, but, "Any more casualties on our side?"

"Harvey is dead. He died at the last, taking a bite meant for Hamish. It was an honorable death that he would have been proud of."

"So James, Jasper and Harvey?" I asked in a weak voice. It was too many.

"It could have gone better, but we learned a lot and we'll be better prepared in the future. Your father won't get so lucky next time."

"We're down two slayers now."

"We'll get more, as many as we need," he said, a special sort of relentlessness in his voice that only someone truly powerful can state and implement with absolute authority.

And he would, I had no doubt.

Dom had clothes for me, but I refused to dress until I had a shower, which he showed me to as soon as we got back to the compound. I wore a blanket from the armored vehicle to the bathroom, but no one said anything about it.

It had been a hellish day, half of our team was inconsolable about the ones we'd lost, the other half gone to dispose of the dragon remains properly.

The last thing I wanted to do was search the half burnt down compound for my sister's magical eyeballs, but I got started on it right away, doing a quick, unsuccessful sweep then settling into a longer, more detailed one.

The druids had already gone through various seeking and detection incantations—Sloan was a veritable encyclopedia of all the druid spells—but none had born fruit. They thought the place was too covered in Ragnar the Spellbinder's stink, and it was skewing their results.

So looking very carefully with our eyes it was. The druids were doing druid things, planning the trip back, cleanup, blah blah blah.

I noticed that Cam was missing an arm. He seemed downright chipper about it, the most cheerful I'd seen him in years.

I asked about it but no one seemed particularly concerned about it, especially the man himself.

In fact he seemed proud of it.

"He bit it clean off!" I heard him telling Corbin. "And did you see the size of his teeth?"

"Why is he so unbothered by it?" I asked Dom in passing, still hunting for eyeballs.

"Growing back his own limbs is a specialty of his," he explained.

"That's horrifying," I said slowly. This was news to me. "How often does he lose limbs?"

Dom looked thoughtful. "Not often, but a few times tends to leave an impression."

"I imagine it would."

The remaining slayers were disposing of the two dragons they had managed to slay, so it was me, Henri, Corbin, and Caleb going through the property with a fine-toothed comb.

It was on the third sweep that Corbin sniffed out a break in the trim along the floor of a study, and we moved half of the things in the room from one side to the other until a piece of the wall opened up. Secret passage. Jackpot.

I went first down a dank, creepy stairway into a dark, foul-smelling passage that led to an underground dungeon.

I had to pause and collect myself as I took it all in.

God, my father was a bastard.

Several people were chained to the wall, and some were even still alive. If we hadn't been looking for Lynn's eyes they likely would have rotted here.

Henri, Caleb, and Corbin started freeing and checking the pitiful creatures while I searched for the eyes.

I found them pretty swiftly since they were just sitting on a metal tray next to a collection of bloody torture devices. By the exact shade I knew they were my sister's right away.

God, I hated my father.

The eyes didn't look great, not to mention the unsanitary conditions I'd found them in, so I spent some time finding a proper container to store them. For some reason I wanted them in liquid but not in an airtight container. They needed to breathe? I didn't know, but I went with my gut and hoped I never had to do anything like this again. I washed them and put them away in a leak proof pouch with water but didn't close it tightly. It was beyond strange to deal with eyes that I was used to seeing exclusively in my sister's face, but I muscled through it by sheer will alone.

Someday we'll tease each other about this, I told myself, a form of self-comfort.

"Why didn't her eyes just grow back?" Caleb asked when I had them secured.

"I'm not sure if it was an active spell or if it's just that the hammer was used on her when it happened. She'd have to walk me through how she lost them and there's been no time. Villi was the one that took them out, though, so if I had to guess I'd say it was some combination of the two."

It was beyond strange to be carrying my sister's eyes around, and I did so with excruciating care.

I texted the number that had originally contacted me that we had them and hoped that she saw it.

There were three survivors in the dungeon and six dead bodies. The druids were healing them and trying to figure out what they were—chances were it wasn't strictly human—but they were too traumatized to communicate much.

"What will you do with them?" I asked Dom when we were finally traveling home again, our surviving task force and new guests in tow.

"We'll take care of them. Rehabilitation, therapy, whatever's needed."

That was the upside to the druids. They were elitists, but they had the infrastructure in place to take care of whoever was in need in the supernatural community when it was necessary. Certainly no one else was organized enough to do it as well.

"What color was my dragon?" I asked out of sheer curiosity. I remembered catching a glimpse of a blinding light when I'd glanced at my wing but that was it.

"You were like white but like shiny," Christian said. He was wired and jittery and way too cheerful, and on top of that he'd taken on most of the burden of dragon body disposal so he was still covered in gore. It was nasty.

"Pearlescent," Dom said quietly. He was sitting next to me and had his eyes closed as though sleeping. "A kaleidoscope of colors reflected off of you as you moved. It was exquisite."

Christian tried to ruin it by making retching noises. I stuck my tongue out at him. "I was always wondering if you could remember things when you came back from being a man-bear-pig," he just had to add.

I laughed, glancing at Dom and even he was smiling a bit, eyes still closed.

"It sounds like you have a crush on my dragon form," I said quietly, teasingly, into Dom's ear. He smiled wider, eyes still closed. "I can't say the same about your new druid form. That thing is terrifying. What's going on there?"

"I'm experimenting with it. You don't think it's cute?" he asked, deadpan.

I laughed harder, hugging his arm. What a roller-coaster of a day.

Helen caught my eye a few rows away. Her seat was facing me, and she was glaring.

I didn't glare back, instead ignored her. She'd just lost her brother. She had a right to glare at whoever she wanted. I don't think I'd spoken one direct word to him, but I felt terrible for her. Sibling bonds could be as powerful as anything, and they'd seemed close.

"We keep going like this, Torst will stay quiet forever,"

Caleb remarked.

"Way to look on the bright side," I told him, tone sardonic. Though the axe was mercifully silent again. All that magical dragon blood, buckets of it, should keep it quiet for a while.

We made it back to Vegas without a hitch.

The group parted ways at the private airport but our work together was far from done. There were several draak still wreaking havoc across North America, and we were a team that now had an effective method to kill even the oldest and most powerful. I still had a score to settle with my father and several slayer weapons with his name all over them.

Corbin left us with some cryptic words about keeping us posted on a lead about a vampire kiss near Phoenix.

I wasn't sure he understood the assignment, but vampire hunters tended to be fixated on vampires, so no one thought too much of it.

Henri made some noises about returning to France right away, but Corbin dragged him, unresisting, along for the vampire hunt.

Dom sent Sven and Hamish to take the jet to check out a lead in Quebec he'd received while he was sleeping on the plane. The poor man couldn't even get a cat's nap worth of rest.

Sven pulled me aside before he departed. He said he needed a private word right as we got back to the casino.

He'd returned in human form from who knows where right as we were loading up and heading from the compound to the airport in Mexico and had barely spoken since.

Sloan heard his request and directed us into a small meeting room and gave us privacy.

I glanced around. The room didn't even have windows, but I clocked at least three cameras. Damned druids. "Nothing you say in here will be private," I told him.

Then just listen, he sent the thought.

Oh yeah, telepathy.

Grandfather had a spell he used that caused madness. It also forces you from human to dragon form against your will. Do you understand?

"I think so," I said, my brain piecing it together slowly. It had been a very long day.

It's called the breath of darkness. And taken only once it has a temporary effect. Much like taking a drug, it is a temporary high. Taken many times, though, it is permanent. Do you understand?

"*Grandfather* was what sent them all mad?"

He certainly helped. Him and their own predilections toward destruction and indulgence. You felt it, it is a heady thing. Imagine if you had no qualms about the things you did or saw in that state. You'd go back for more, time and again, as so many of our kind have. Like an addiction it goes from a choice to an inevitability over time and usage.

But you are not the urges you felt back there. You don't own any part of them now that the breath of darkness has faded from your body. That was his spell, and he is the only one who could cast it. It did irreparable damage to our clan, but he is gone now and we are free of him at last, and of the madness.

Relief was a weak word for what I felt then. The thing I'd most feared my whole long life was banished from this earth. It was a lot to process.

Dom found me sometime later. Sven had left for his next mission.

I was alone, laying face up on the ground, and I wasn't sure I could make it to our room on my own strength alone.

Dom seemed to pick up on that right away, lifting me easily and cradling me like a child, my head on his warm, firm chest. I moved my head until my ear was over his heart, listening to the beat, and closed my eyes.

I didn't fall asleep for a long time. My mind was too

active, still taking in all of the ramifications. I couldn't wait to tell Lynn that we weren't ticking time bombs anymore.

"What did your brother need to tell you in private?" Dom asked me in the elevator. "Was it bad news?"

"No. It was very good. The madness was a spell, and it died with my grandfather."

He squeezed me closer. "Now we just need to get your sister's eyes back to her and all will be right in the world."

That sounded just great, but of course it was easier said than done. Story of our lives.

A few days passed and different members were sent in various directions to scope out some draak leads but still no word from Lynn.

Caleb and Christian went to Florida to check out some disturbances that fit the right MO.

Everyone was to investigate and report. No one got to engage without backup, but it still made me twitchy to split up like that.

I had Dom attempt to set up another meeting between me , Drake, and Lynn. If we could get a moment alone like last time, I should be able to handoff her eyes, hopefully without being detected.

Of course there was a good chance Drake knew we already had them. How else had Lynn gotten the intel on my father's location if he didn't have someone in there? In that case we might need to take more. . . aggressive measures if Drake became uncooperative. I would do whatever it took to get my sister's eyes back to her.

CROSSING FIRE

CHAPTER TWENTY-FIVE
TIME STANDS STILL

I was a fool. A masochist. A glutton for punishment. I was the type that kept picking at a scab, keeping the wound open until it scarred, though my scars were on the inside.

Knowing all this, with a few days to kill, I found myself seeking out The Grove, yet again.

"More," I spoke to the blood red water, before I even saw the creature emerge.

It didn't take long to present itself. A white body, that odd, wrong, creepy as hell presence, was out of the water and nearly to me in the strangest move. It never looked like it was moving fast, but it covered ground between one blink and the next.

It paused when it reached me, and I clenched me teeth.

I felt like a junkie looking for a fix, and perhaps I *was*. My fix just happened to be pieces of my past, *our* past.

"Don't draw it out," I told it, my voice harsh. "I don't have much time."

"You know how it works here, first-born," it breathed on me. "Time stands still."

Wasn't that just the brutal truth of it?

Without another word, it took me under.

I was on shit duty in Denver with Cam. It was a punishment from the Arch, but I didn't mind it. It consisted of traveling constantly and investigating possible supernaturals that weren't on the registry. Two things I was interested in anyway, but I'd never share with Declan that I was more than happy with the punishment. Then he'd move me for sure.

Declan, the North American Arch, had nearly as much of a problem with Cam, so here we were at some random private investigative firm checking things out.

The receptionist was human, I could tell right away. An unexceptional middle-aged woman that looked at us with wide eyes and just stared for a beat.

We were unusual—bigger than most men, our coloring similar and striking, my eyes outright strange. We wore impeccable three-piece suits and moved with proud purpose.

We were used to this reaction so we just waited for her to gather herself.

"How can I help you?" she asked eventually.

"I have an appointment with one of the P.I.s here," Cam said, looking down at his paperwork and listing off the name.

"Oh," the woman said. "She's running a few minutes late. I'm terribly sorry. Just have a seat and I'll tell you when she's ready."

"I also have an appointment," I told her, and glancing down at my own paperwork, I read off the name of the second investigator listed by the agency. We had to check out both to see which one wasn't blending in as strictly human.

"You. . . both have appointments?" she asked slowly. She picked up her phone. "Let me just tell my boss."

I reached over her desk and hung her phone up. "That's not necessary. Just point me in the right direction."

"She won't like—"

I smiled and she couldn't seem to look away from my eyes. "Where's her office? I'd rather go in unannounced."

I didn't want our quarry warned ahead of time. The receptionist could well have instructions to look for anyone of our description. The proverbial men in black. I wanted to keep things nice, quick, and simple. I hated when these things turned into a chase.

Finally she pointed down a hallway to the left. "Second door. At least knock."

I didn't. I found the door and pushed it open.

And my world tilted on its axis for the second time.

Decades had passed, but she was unchanged, though her white-blond hair was longer, her clothes different. She was the same age and still the most beautiful woman I'd ever laid eyes on.

She froze mid-motion and stared.

Joy filled me. Elation. Unadulterated relief. Sharp comfort.

I'd been waiting for this since the day she'd disappeared. I'd known it would come. I hadn't known the when, but fate would have its way. She was always my destiny, I knew it deep in my soul. And finally the wait was over.

"Jillian," I said her name like a prayer.

She stared at me with tender gravity. "Domhnall." It was a soft, astonished utterance, but it spoke the world to me. She hadn't forgotten anything. Our love affair had only lasted a few months before she'd disappeared but in that time I'd given her my very soul, and it hadn't left her unscathed, either.

"Do you believe in fate now?" I asked her pointedly.

"How?" she asked. Her lips were trembling and she bit them.

"I've been looking for you this whole time," I told her. And it was true. I took every case I could with two women involved, knowing she always stayed close to her sister. "I would have searched forever. I'll always find you. You swore I'd outgrow my

obsession with you. Well? What do you have to say for yourself now?"

She took a step closer, then another, her hand touching my face, finger tracing delicately along the brow above my wolf's eye. "I never thought I'd lay eyes on you again." I don't think she meant to, but she said it with wonder.

"Why did you leave me?" I hadn't intended to ask the question, it had been torn out of me, a world of longing in my voice.

She traced her finger over my lips. "I wasn't leaving you. We'd been discovered. I think one of your friends turned us in. No one told you?"

It was a blow I wasn't expecting. "I didn't know. One day you were just gone without a trace. You said goodbye with a note that I found weeks later in a random pocket. It's haunted me."

She moved closer, her hand on my jaw. "I'm sorry. I didn't want to leave you, couldn't stand the thought that I'd hurt you, but it was out of our hands. They raided our place, tried to take us into custody. There were some. . . unsavory allegations against us. We couldn't even take anything with us. We just fought them off and ran and didn't stop. We're good at disappearing without a trace. We've had a lot of experience."

I leaned into her hand like it could hold up the world. For me it could.

I closed my eyes and just breathed, letting that special something fill me, that something I'd only ever felt when I was near her.

Everything that had ever kept her aloof from me, every obstacle in our path was gone now. Everything I'd ever wanted from her was within my grasp now, and it was a heady feeling.

I was hesitant at first to touch her, I didn't know where to begin, I wasn't prepared, but while her unapproachable beauty and stoic demeanor had always made her look a bit untouchable, she wasn't that.

Hers was a cold beauty, but inside I'd always known there was fire. Fire that felt like only I had ever truly touched it, like it was mine alone.

Her arms slipped around me, hugging my back, her face lying softly against my shoulder.

I touched one hand to the top of her head, the other stroked her back but I almost recoiled at what that simple touch did to me.

I drew back, pushing her away.

She looked at me, puzzled, then studied my face.

I stared at her and she saw it then, the raw, primal animal staring back at her. I was holding onto my civilized self by a single thread.

This place was too public. I couldn't so much as lay a finger on her the first time without absolute privacy.

"Where are you staying?" asked Jillian softly, grasping the situation. "Let's go there and talk. I'll take the rest of the day off."

"No," I said, and it didn't come out friendly. Everything would not be on her terms like before.

"No?" she asked, our gazes locked, and it was pure enigmatic seduction.

There was something dangerous about her, it had always been there. One pointed look from her was like a weapon bared. She was transformed in a blink from a beautiful woman then suddenly you knew you were really in bed with a tiger. It was a special sort of rapture for me to view it again after all these years.

"It won't be all your way this time," I told her gruffly, taking her hand. "We're going to your place. I want to see where you live."

On our way out, I saw Cam was still waiting in reception. If I knew anything about Jillian's sister it was that he would be waiting for a very long time.

"You can call this one off," I told him. "I'll work on the roster myself; do all the paperwork. If anyone asks about it, have them report directly to me."

His eyes went from my hand, locked with Jillian's, to studying the woman herself. I saw swift recognition in his eyes, then deep disapproval.

I had a thought and felt disloyal for even having to ask, but I couldn't seem to keep the question in. I had to know, to see his face when he answered. "Someone turned her in last time, it's why she had to run. Do you know who did it?"

He looked appalled, and I was instantly assured. Cam was volatile and headstrong, but loyal to a fault, and what you saw is what you got. "Of course not. I would have told you right away. I know how you feel about her. How could you think it? I don't like her, but my loyalty is and always has been first to you. I would never betray your trust."

"I apologize. I know that, I'm just a bit. . . overcome at the moment. Listen, I'm going off the radar for a few days. Don't worry about it. I'll see you at our next assignment."

We took her car, an unassuming black sedan, and I left Cam the rental we'd picked up at the airport. He'd have a lot of questions later, but I'd deal with that reality later.

Her house wasn't far away, a small attractive one story, white house with blue trim on the edge of downtown. It was just the sort of idyllic spot I'd once fantasized about sharing with her.

She unlocked and opened her door and I followed her in. I took in the place. It was nice, neat but sparse and practically nothing was out of place.

That made the large signet ring, obviously a man's, laid out casually on a side table catch my attention right away.

I froze. My whole body zoned in on this little thing like a hound on a scent.

She caught on to something in the air and followed my eyes until we were both looking at the same thing.

"I don't want to know the details." My voice was cold as a grave, and it took restraint for me to be even that civil. "But you need to end it. Never see him again. He won't survive it, whoever he is."

"Oh, Dom, no," said Jillian. "Stop that. It's not anything like you're thinking."

She looked half-amused which calmed me a bit. She wasn't into games.

"Not a boyfriend," she amended, "or anything like that. Just a friend."

"A male friend. One that gave you a very expensive, personalized ring. Care to explain?"

"I don't care to, no, but I will to get that fatal look out of your eyes. I won a bet with a friend, and that was his wager."

"Must have been some bet."

"It was. That's all I'll say about it."

"So there's no one?"

I didn't think she'd answer when it took her so long to respond. The strain of waiting had the tips of my fingers trembling, and it wasn't only rage. Fear was in there too. The thought that she could have moved on from me, that she could prefer some other man, weakened me greatly.

"I'm not seeing anybody," she finally said.

The dark tension slid out of me like a sickness being purged, and I moved, crowding her now, everything back in its proper place. "Except for me," I corrected.

"What are you trying to get out of me?"

"That this is something, that you're not just going to disappear tomorrow or even next year."

She moved into the kitchen, maneuvering around me like it was a dance, waving her hand at a small table set into a breakfast nook. "Have a seat. I'll make tea."

Frustrated, I sat and watched her.

"I missed talking to you," she said without looking at me, her hands busy measuring out tea.

"Oh yeah?" I asked dryly. "Is that all you missed?"

She didn't respond to that. A first impression of her would have you think she was a little apart from the world, a bit above it by the way she held herself. But I knew her better, knew exactly what was underneath all of that cool armor of hers, and I knew without her *ever having told me that I was the only one that ever had.*

I remembered well exactly how it was with her. Her chilly exterior, her walls, her straight back, and unruffled manner as though nothing in the world could shake her composure. It was such a lie; the dichotomy of what she presented to the world. What others saw versus what I knew her to be forever fascinated me.

She brought me a cup of tea just how I took it and sat down with hers across from me. The table was small, our legs would touch if she pushed her chair in a bit more.

"How have you been?" she asked, locking her pale ocean eyes with mine.

"Fine," I said shortly. "You?"

"Fine," she repeated back, amused. "Are you Arch yet?"

I shook my head, one sharp motion right to left, rejecting the question. "No."

"A lieutenant, then?"

"I don't care for the current North American Arch, I wouldn't work to be one of his lieutenants, and I have no plans to move to Europe, so no."

"I'm surprised. I always knew you'd take over the world." She said it with a certain pride of ownership in her voice and that was what caught me more than the words themselves.

"I think your ambitions for me outmatch my own," I told her softly.

"We'll see," she said enigmatically.

I'd be annoyed by it if I wasn't already feeling too many more overpowering things to name.

"I always just wanted to settle down and be a family man," I told her softly, but it was nothing she didn't already know.

Something about that made shadows move in her eyes, but she hid it quickly. "Perhaps I'm not your girl, then."

"You know better than that."

"Kids are out of the question with me, Dom."

"I don't care. I'll take you as you are, whatever that means. I

just want you."

"You're impossible," she said affectionately.

I just stared at her, equal parts frustrated and desperate. "What will it take to get you to take me seriously?"

"I've always taken you seriously." She paused. "It's me I can't take seriously." She paused again. "And it's very much mutual. I just want you, too." Another pause and we ate each other with our eyes. "You don't have to go easy on me, you know," she said in her raspy, silken voice, "I can take it. Do your worst."

My mind did filthy things with that. "Excuse me?" I was gripping the table, braced and trying not to pant as I battled for an ounce of control.

"Yell at me. Curse me out. Say whatever else you need to say."

"Raging at you is not the first thing that comes to mind at the moment."

She smiled, a tender smile that belonged only to me, and the knowledge of that was powerful enough to break me. She set her tea down and sat back in her chair, spreading her arms wide, "What I said still stands then. Do your worst."

I was afraid what I had to give her might be just that for a few rounds at least. "Don't say that unless you mean it."

"You think I don't mean it?" It was a challenge, issued in her sublimely velvet voice.

I stood so violently that it sent my chair back crashing into the wall.

She stood more slowly, nonplussed, never breaking our locked gazes. "I'll show you my bedroom," she said and smoothly made her way to the back of the house.

I followed, breathing down her neck like the big bad wolf.

"Where do you live now?" she asked me without turning or stopping. "Not in Denver, I assume."

"I'm between places. On the road, mostly, staying at druid crash pads between jobs."

"Is that by choice? Are you able to live in one place or does your

job not permit it?"

"It was a choice."

I followed her into her bedroom and instantly went to the bed, sitting on the edge of it and staring at her, studying her some more in large, hungry bites.

She was dressed much differently than the last time I'd seen her, in slacks and a blazer. Almost like a man except that her curves and graceful, lithe figure made it all hyper-feminine, the masculine attire accentuating the fact that she was anything but.

"I like your hair long," I told her.

She moved closer to me, reaching behind me and freeing my hair from its tie. She ran her hands through it with long, slow strokes, and I closed my eyes with pleasure. It hung just past my jaw now. "Yours is long, too. I love it. Remember how short it was when we were together?"

I didn't answer. She knew I remembered everything from when we were together.

She was close to me, her standing, me sitting. I opened my legs and she fit herself between them, hugging my head to her soft, heavy breasts. I inhaled her, palms flat on the bed. I knew the second I touched her it was lights out, and I was hanging on by a thread.

She bent down, her chest moving unfortunately away from my face, her lips coming to my ear. "Are you feeling particularly beastly right now, lover? I meant what I said. Do your worst. I won't break."

I snapped and thoroughly lost it for a while. She meant what she said. She could take it. She could take everything I had to dish out, which was fortunate.

I had her flat on her back on the bed, our clothes gone, when I came even a little back into my own control. I was kissing her like she held the air I needed to breathe as I pounded into her with deep, devout focus.

She took it all with shuddering, encompassing submission. She went against her very nature to yield to what I needed, which was *to lower her guard and give me her total, abject surrender.*

I had the enormous urge to do absolutely everything to her, but for the first few times it would just be this, my body consuming hers, hers giving way, embracing mine, unfolding to my brutal attention until I finished with deep pulses of choking pleasure that crescendoed into sweet, overwhelming oblivion.

I came wholly back into reason in stages, but I never stopped, never subsided for the duration of it. I was a passenger to my savage devouring of her for hours, spending my body in hers until there was nothing left to give, her body receiving mine until it was topped up and overflowing.

She was smiling at me when I finally went still, and it was a relief. It had been many rounds of me being less than gentle, being mindless enough to do damage without realizing.

I was still on her and in her as she fingered the ends of my long hair. "I love your hair," she told me, "I can't get enough of it. If you love me, you'll never cut it again."

"I won't cut it again." It was a promise. "You don't get to cut yours either," I told her. "And I love you more than life, but you know that."

"I won't cut mine either," she agreed. "And you know I love you, too. I'm sorry I left you like that."

"Never again," I told her softly and fervently. "You're mine now, and I'm keeping you this time."

CHAPTER TWENTY-SIX
JUST A BLINK

I was yanked out of the past unceremoniously. On my hands and knees, I looked up at the creature.

It had changed.

It was less humanoid now, the shape of it harder to make sense of. From the bottom of its chin to the top of its head, to the spot where its ears should have been, it had wicked little mouths all over.

I wondered exactly how much damage I was doing. How much power was it gaining from this?

Still the first thing I said was, "I want to go back."

It made a terrible noise out of every hideous mouth that I thought was supposed be a laugh and struck again.

Some part of me remained while I was in his head, in his past now, and the more I did it, the stronger it was. I could form thoughts as a watcher now, cohesive ones.

And as I came into his body for this memory, I thought, *Oh no, not this one. My heart can't take this memory. It's too much.*

I was looking at a very somber Sloan. She had a manila envelope in her hand, but she was shaking her head, over and over.

"You don't need to see this, Dom," she told me, a weak thread to her voice I'd never heard before.

I held out my hand. I had to see. I already knew it would be bad. My lover had left me, breaking all ties, leaving chaos in her wake, and the harder I looked for her, the more damage I found.

That was Jillian for you. She never did anything in half-measures.

She should have known me better. I'd never stop looking for her, no matter what she'd done. She needed me as much as I needed her.

She'd broken our blood bond, parts of me breaking with it. What could be worse than that? What could a manila envelope hold that was more profoundly detrimental to me than the loss of her, *the only woman I had ever loved?*

Sloan handed me the evidence, and I asked her for a moment alone.

"Please, Dom. Don't look."

I shook my head, and she left. She knew me better. I was resolute.

I sat for a long time before I opened the envelope, time bracing myself, staring at the thing like it held horrors I could not bear to stomach.

It did, of course. I'd known it as soon as I heard there were pictures, had it reinforced when I saw the defeated look on Sloan's face.

My hands shook as I pulled out the stack of photos and began to flip through them.

I was three pictures in when I began to shake so badly that I fell to my knees.

Six pictures in when began to wretch.

Ten pictures in when I began to weep.

Not only had she left me, broken oaths, severed bonds.

She'd been unfaithful, done the thing she knew would break me the most, and with a man I despised. She'd shared her body, all of that beautiful flesh that belonged to me, with my enemy.

I was blind in my agony, lost in my pain, but even crippled and broken, I knew there was calculation behind this thing she'd done.

Why? How could she? It was so uncharacteristic. So wrong.

It didn't matter what she'd done. And it didn't matter why she'd done it. I'd still never stop looking for her. What I'd do with her when I found her, well, that didn't bear thinking about just then.

But him. Declan. To him I'd show no mercy. Not an ounce of it. I had a target now, a focus for the unadulterated rage that had gripped me from the moment she'd broken our bond.

When I came out of the spell, I stumbled to his room, to his bed, on trembling legs.

My own pain had been bad enough, but to shoulder his as well, to feel it unfiltered and fresh like that.

I couldn't stand it.

He wasn't there, of course. It was the middle of the day.

I made my unsteady way out to the hall, then a bank of elevators that I knew were guarded.

The druid there gave me a startled look.

I knew I was a sight. Blood on my neck, likely on my clothes, wild hair, wilder eyes, breath ragged. Tears running down my face.

"Are you hurt?" the guard asked. "What's happened?"

I shook my head, feeling disoriented but determined. "Get Dom. Tell him I need him."

I didn't wait to see what he'd do, just went back to Dom's room.

I meant to strip off my bloody clothes before I climbed into the bed, but couldn't find the energy.

It was less than five minutes later, and I was laying on my back, knees draped off the side of the bed, tears running in unhindered rivulets down my cheeks, when Dom burst into the room.

He was at my side, hand at my neck, eyes scanning me for injury.

"What happened? Where are you hurt?"

Everywhere, I wanted to say. Every part of me hurt.

"Dom," I gasped, reaching for him.

He resisted at first when I tried to pull him to me, still concerned that I was injured. I kept pulling.

"I've done something terrible, and I'm sorry. But I've been punished for it, and I *can't take the pain*. I'm sorry. I'm so sorry."

"What are you sorry for?"

"So much. But mostly for leaving you like that, for the way I made you suffer, for making you think I'd betrayed you. It hurts. It hurts so much."

He was kissing my tears away and soothing me. "We've been over that again and again. I forgive you. We're past it. You want another bit of comfort to help you work through it? Even all the years we've lost are just a blink in the expanse of our eternity together."

It *was* a comfort. And I felt all the more guilty for it.

"You don't understand," I told him. "I *felt* it. I felt your pain as you did, and it was more than I could *bear*."

He froze, raised his head as horror filled his eyes. "Jillian, tell me what you've done."

"It's The Grove. . ."

"What about it?" he asked and anger was mixing with the horror now.

"It's been taking my blood."

"How?"

"I let it."

"Why? Why on earth would you put yourself at that thing's mercy?"

"For memories."

"Memories? What memory could possibly be worth that

kind of price?"

"There were several, actually. *Your* memories."

"I don't understand. What use did you have for *my* memories?"

I didn't ever want to look at him, I was so embarrassed by my answer. Because it was the naked truth. The truth and I had never been close. "They were memories from before. . . Before I hurt you, and I could feel how you loved me. It was so pure, absolute, and uncomplicated. Unassailable. I felt the raw emotions that you did, and I kept going back for more. I know how idiotic it was, but I couldn't seem to help myself. I wanted to live in that world for a bit, that world where I had your love like that again, with no reservations at all."

In spite of the horror and anger he was experiencing at me specifically, his eyes softened. "That's the world you still live in. Just open your eyes and here we are. Now tell me how many times you indulged in this."

I told him and his expression did not comfort me then.

"Every time it took your blood it gained power over you and its range to reach you increased," he explained. "It's not good. I need to think on this, and we need to get you away from The Grove."

"Does this give it more power over *you*?"

"I think that was its intention, but not how it will work now. It's good you told me. I can use that against it to draw the power into myself. It's a burden, but one I'm familiar with. It takes a dark thing to guard a dark thing. To contain it. It is a dirty job, for a dirty soul. It is cursed, and so am I. We're all cursed, those of us that guard The Grove."

"Is that how you've become so powerful? You draw it from The Grove."

He looked at me like I had it all wrong. "Yes, I draw from its power, but not for personal gain. Don't you see? It's the only way to weaken it, to take it into yourself. What do you think an Arch is for? To rule? That's not the half of it. We're a vessel. A vessel powerful enough to contain a darkness that cannot be ended.

And no, it's not the reason for the increase in my power." He pointed at his wolf's eye. "This was my mother's legacy, but there was much more. Once I became Arch, my uncle gave me her journals. She was more than a druid, she was also an enchanter from an ancient line, and as I've studied her powers, I've become something more, as well, though I still have a long way to go. I also think all the years of you feeding me your blood didn't hurt."

"This room is warded against everything. What we share here cannot be overheard, but you must never speak of any of these things again, do you understand? I can't bear to think what they'd do to us if they knew that I was sharing these secrets with you.

"Who are *they*?" I asked, but only because I couldn't help it. I didn't want to interrupt him when he was sharing so much information I'd been so avidly fascinated about for so long.

"The Circle. It is our druid council. Any druid that's been burdened with this knowledge themselves would see what I was doing as the ultimate betrayal. They'd do more than take my head. They'd make me an example the likes of which the world has never seen."

If that's what they would do to their beloved, pure-blood son, he didn't have to utter what they'd do to an outsider like me.

"I'll take it to my grave, I swear it," I said solemnly.

"Don't talk to me about a grave. Swear on something else. And also. . . the fact that you've shared your blood with it willingly. No one can ever know that. Are we clear?"

"We're clear. And I have to leave now?"

"The Grove, yes, and as soon as possible. I'll find us other accommodations, but in the meantime you need to stay in my quarters or with me at all times while you're in the building.

"Is Conan safe?"

"Yes. He's warded as strongly as we are, but when we move, we'll take him with us. It's going to be complicated to guard him as closely when we're remote from the property, but I'll arrange it all. I just need some time, and I ask for your patience."

CHAPTER TWENTY-SEVEN
REPTILE LIKE YOU

P atience has never been a virtue of mine so that was easier said than done.

I was ready to climb the walls within a day.

I shadowed Dom some, but he had too many super-secret druid meetings that I couldn't attend, and I visited Conan several times, but he mostly slept since he was still an egg and no matter how hard I stared he showed no signs of hatching anytime soon.

And of course waiting for word from or about Lynn was adding exponentially to my restlessness. Her eyes were burning a hole in my pocket, I wanted them in her hands, or rather her eye sockets, so badly.

The longer it took the more daunting of a task it seemed to find a way to see her again.

In an effort to keep me from going insane while I waited, Dom found a dragon lead for me to check out that wasn't too far away.

I needed to be close in case Lynn or Drake made contact.

It was in L.A., which was convenient. It was a short flight or a manageable drive away. The task force had two hard rules at this point.

1. Don't investigate leads alone.

2. A dragon slayer must be with you.

This was bad news because at the moment the only one of those not already otherwise occupied was Helen.

Just my luck.

But I went without hesitation. Anything to stay active so I didn't lose my mind with the waiting.

This meant a lot of time spent with Helen, and of course, she still hated me.

I was past hating her. I more felt sorry for her but didn't enjoy her company. It wasn't nearly as much fun as the hate had been.

We drove. It was five hours but by the time all the arrangements were made with other transportation it just seemed easier to get on the road right away.

Helen wanted to take the wheel, but I took the first shift just to be contrary. "You can drive on the way back," I told her.

She had a whole file with her, an actual physical copy, and she read through it to brief me on the way.

"So much wasted paperwork," I remarked.

"Can you take this seriously?" she snapped at me.

"I am serious. Why'd you have to print it out? Don't you have a phone?"

She fumed for a bit then went back to the briefing.

I couldn't see Dom dating someone so totally without humor, someone who took themselves as seriously as she did. She was no fun at all. Then again, he probably hadn't *dated* her, and I knew he hadn't exactly been picky in the years I'd abandoned him. But it was hard not to think about it when I found it taxing to spend even a few hours with the woman.

I had a hand on the wheel, eyes steady on the road, and I didn't know I was fussing with one of my earrings until Helen brought it to my attention.

"I'm surprised you let him track you like that," she said, her tone poisonous.

I raised my brows. So she knew what the earrings were, and she was trying to get a rise out of me. Malicious teasing was almost like joking so I went with it. I was bored. "I see he didn't bother to track *you*. Jealous?"

She didn't take the bait, instead hung on to the topic as though she'd change how I felt about it if she just brought it up enough. "I thought you had more pride, more independence than to let him keep tabs on you."

"You're trying to imply I'm not an independent woman?" I asked with an eye roll. "How dare you," I said, deadpan.

"*I'd* never put up with it."

"He definitely didn't ask you to," I shot back. I could have told her why, the way I felt about all I'd done to him and how that made me put myself in his shoes and try to be more sensitive to his worries, but I'd be damned before I explained myself to her.

"It's a useless gesture anyway. If you wanted you could just take the trackers off and leave them anywhere or even send them somewhere else."

"Is there a point to this?" I asked her in a perfectly reasonable tone. "Or would you like to get back to business?"

"I just don't understand you."

"It's mutual. I don't understand why you don't have a sense of humor or a personality. Was your slayer training so vigorous that you didn't have time to develop one?"

"English slayers are efficient, or *most* of them are," she sniffed and I knew she was alluding to Christian, and I wanted to slap her. "We don't have time for frivolity like *some* people. There's a reason *our* dragon kin have been extinct for centuries."

I didn't tell her that my kin had killed all of our slayers and a good portion of theirs. I didn't have the stomach to even tease her about something like that when she'd still so freshly lost her brother.

Holding my tongue was a chore and a muscle I was learning to exercise just for Helen. Personal growth was good for the soul and all that.

"I'm sorry about your brother," I said. I'd wanted to say it since it happened and now seemed as good a time as any.

"Can you really say you're sorry one of your natural enemies is dead?"

"I am. And I'm sorry you had to go through that. I know we aren't friends, but no one should have to lose a brother in such a way."

"I don't want your sympathy. It's misplaced and inadequate and frankly I don't believe a reptile like you can even conceive of what a family bond consists of and what having that severed feels like for someone warm-blooded. You're helping us to hunt your *own kin*. Save your condolences for someone else. It means less than nothing to me coming from a creature like you."

Ouch. Okay. I almost defended myself but even that seemed pointless with someone so dead set against me. "Copy that, loud and clear."

"I can't believe Dom is so attached to you of all things. He seemed like a perfect man other than that."

I just rolled my eyes, letting her see it. I wasn't being drawn into this. She was lashing out, and I'd gotten the man in the end so I could take a few jabs and stay pleasant. I had to repeat it to myself in my head a few times, though.

"You know he can never be satisfied with only one woman

though, don't you? He's insatiable, needs a new lover every night. It's only a matter of time before he falls into his old, natural patterns."

Okay. That was it. I took her bait. It's just that she was getting it all wrong, selling Dom short, and I felt the need to set her straight. "Those aren't old patterns for him. They're new ones, and they only emerged after I left him. Ask around and you'll see that he's never had a problem being faithful to me. If anything he's devoted to a fault. I'm sorry you developed feelings for him when he was clearly on a bender to get back at me, but that's the past and you're going to need to find a way to get over it. He's just not that into you. It's not you, it's me and all that. Even when I was gone and he hated me, he was still madly in love with me. Now, would you care to get back to the briefing, or should I turn on some music?"

I could feel her glaring at my profile for a good long while. I looked straight ahead and whistled a cheerful tune until she finally sighed dramatically and got back to her paperwork. "The lead we're following is flimsy at best, to be frank," she said. Oh ho, she was improvising now instead of reading straight from her notes. Some hint of a personality aside from petty jealous bitch might be in there after all.

"Why send us out to check on it in person instead of having local druids do it then?" I asked, honestly curious.

"I guess we're more qualified to eliminate the lead, flimsy as it is."

"And what does this flimsy lead consist of?"

"Some mysterious fires set off in the warehouse district. Sightings of something big in the sky at night. A missing female supernatural creature in the same area, which seems to be your dad's M.O."

"What type of creature?"

"It's unclear. Some sort of half-breed."

"Well, that's certainly not much to go on."

"We have an address for the missing girl. We'll interview her family first, see what they know. Perhaps they saw something, though the druids are usually thorough, and it's not in the report. From there we'll investigate the locations where the fires were set. Obviously either one of us can determine whether or not it was dragon fire though it most likely isn't or it wouldn't have been extinguished so easily, as we both well know."

She had a point. "And do we have the location of whoever saw something big in the sky at night?"

"We do not. I'm disappointed in their sloppy work, but one of the witnesses was a homeless man and it seems he got away."

"Were they supposed to hold him hostage until we got there?"

"Ideally," she said without a trace of humor. "The other claim came from the creature before she disappeared, so that's a dead end. Ah, here is a note about her. They say the people who adopted her believe she's half-angel."

"Does it say why they think that?"

"I'm looking." She went through the paperwork for a good long while and I drove. "They say that the being that brought her to them was divine and from that they assumed she was half-angel."

"That's all it says? How did they know it was divine? And how did they know the child was only half? Seems like we're missing pieces of the story."

"I'm looking." A good half an hour later she said, "I'm not finding any more information about it."

"Well, I guess we'll just have to ask when we get there."

We stopped to refuel about halfway and as though he were tracking me, which he was, Dom called as we paused.

"Everything okay?" he said as soon as I answered.

"Just Peachy. And you?"

"Please be careful."

"We both know we probably won't even see any action. You just sent me on this mission because you knew how bored I was, and you didn't want me to do anything stupid while I wait to hear back from Lynn."

"That's only part of it. Now tell me you'll be careful. I need to hear it."

"I'll be careful."

"Has it. . . been terribly unpleasant, dealing with Helen?" he asked tentatively.

"Are you worried we'll compare notes about you? Are your ears ringing?"

He paused, and I thought I could feel the pulse in his temple pounding in irritation as though it were my own.

I misread it though.

"I apologize that you're in that position, that I ever—" he began in an agonized voice.

"Don't," I said quietly. "I was just giving you shit. It's in the past. We both have regrets, but none of it matters now, right?"

"Yes," he said succinctly and then something impassioned in Druidic that made my toes start to curl.

"Ditto," I told him.

A few hours later found us at the address we'd been given with no one answering the door.

"Do we have a phone number for them?" I asked, pulling out my cell.

She checked her paperwork, rattled it off and I called.

No answer and still no response at the door.

Well, that was annoying.

Time to break in. It was a quiet neighborhood, and there weren't a lot of people hanging around outside and we walked casually to the back gate, tried it, found it unlocked, and kept going.

The back door was locked, so I went to try the windows.

As I did so Helen kicked the door in and looked at me pointedly.

"Unnecessary," I told her right before she pulled a gun out and charged in.

Okaay. We were going to have a talk, and if she got trigger happy with some humans, it was going to get ugly fast.

Turned out it didn't matter right then, though. No one in that house was alive anymore. The half-angel's adopted parents and their daughter were all facedown, dead in their beds. They'd been killed execution style, bullet to the head.

It distracted me from giving Helen the lecture she deserved.

We searched the small house, but found nothing but the bodies.

I had a gun drawn by then too, in case whoever had assassinated this poor family was still around.

I let Helen drive to the next lead so I could call Dom. I updated him.

"I don't like this. I'm sending you backup."

"Some local druids? That's fine. Tell them we're checking out the sites of the fires. It's pretty much the only lead we have left over here. I really don't think this is my father, but I'd like to stay and find the girl that was taken, especially since the poor thing is an orphan now."

"You're letting him saddle us with backup?" Helen asked after I hung up. She looked angry and disgusted about it. Way too bent out of shape in general.

"They'll be fine. They won't get in the way. Druids are unfailingly competent."

"Perhaps compared to *you*."

"Really? Miss bashes doors in and charges into a civilian house, gun cocked, with no communication. Didn't look too competent to me. Sloppy is the word I'd use."

Oh, she was fuming now. "I don't have to answer to you," Helen said disdainfully. "And the last thing we need is a bunch of druids on our case. Our job is simple and easy and yet you still need backup. You truly are unimpressive."

"How can you be surprised Dom's sending backup? I'd almost think you've never worked with him before, but you have. You're being completely illogical, actually." I studied her, but didn't know her well enough to read anything on her face. "What's going on with you?"

She sneered but at least kept her eyes on the road. "Let's just finish up and head back, and don't think we're spending a bunch of time looking for some random lost child."

"I'll tell you what we're doing and when we're leaving, and if I have to pull rank to do it, I will."

She muttered something very unflattering under her breath, and I ignored it.

The druids were already there when we arrived at the site of the first fire. There were eight of them, and Helen glared daggers at me as soon as she saw them.

Helen stayed in the car to make a phone call while I followed the druids to the spot. It was a large square hole where a building used to be.

"This is arson, not dragon fire," I told them after a few seconds. "On to the next spot."

"We'll ride there with you," one of the druids said. I just shrugged and led two of them back to the car. The rest of them headed to their cars.

Helen was just shutting her door and glared at the two druids with me like they'd personally offended her. "Why are they riding with us?"

I was sick of her, so I just said, "Doesn't matter. This one wasn't dragon fire, and we're headed to the next. Best to be thorough."

"Perhaps I wanted to check it for myself."

I waved behind me. "Then do it, princess, and make it snappy."

She got back behind the wheel and off we went. We were nearly to the next spot when I saw that one of her hands was shaking.

"You okay?" I asked her. "Need me to drive?"

Her lip curled. "Of course not. And we're nearly there."

We arrived at the next spot and investigated and again it was very obviously not dragon fire.

I was annoyed when I realized Helen was on her phone again and had wandered off a few blocks, but I just called her back and off to the next spot we went.

We eliminated them all perfunctorily, but my mind was more on steps to find the missing girl than on the fires, which were clearly simple arson. Those were a dead end, and none of this was dragons, but the mission had turned into a search for the missing girl.

At the last site we finally hit upon something but again, not dragons. Someone was calling out for help from the building next to the one that'd burnt down here.

It sounded like a young girl, and I was in the building and up a flight of stairs before my mind even caught up to what I'd heard.

In a strange twist we found the missing half-angel girl tied up in a room by herself next to an open window facing the spot where the building had been burnt.

It felt like a setup, and I told everyone to be on alert, but we extracted the girl with no trouble at all.

The druids searched the building thoroughly and found nothing.

The girl seemed shaken, with no memory to speak of, but she was unharmed and was, in fact, half-angel. I'd seen an angel once, and this girl had enough of that aura to confirm the connection. She was blond, beautiful, and delicate, but that's not what made her angelic. It was the subtle gold glow that surrounded her, head to toe.

There was some resemblance to me there, especially if I was fresh from a long dragon trance. I could almost see how Dom's loving eyes had made the mistake in thinking I was one.

I left the poor thing with the druids, knowing they would take care of her as much as anyone could a young girl who'd been kidnapped and freshly lost her adopted family.

I relieved the team Dom had sent us and told them to brief him and that we were headed home. I knew he had a lot of meetings, and I had a knack for calling him right in the middle of them. He'd always answer me no matter how important the meeting was or how trivial my call. Better to delegate the task to them.

The whole day was depressing, what a waste of time and that poor girl. I was still ruminating on it, so I didn't protest Helen's insistence on driving home.

Maybe I'd pretend to sleep so we didn't have to talk to each other.

We didn't make it far before I noticed that there was something wrong with her.

She was acting strange, shuddering at odd moments. Turning on her signal to go one way then veering the other.

"Are you okay?" I asked reluctantly. I told myself I only cared that she seemed to be having small seizures because she was behind the wheel of a car I was currently sitting in. I could not be this big of a softie. "Why don't you pull over? I'll drive."

She waved me off. "I'm fine. It's just adrenaline."

"Adrenaline? W—" I asked but was cut off as our car sideswiped hard into a wall.

CHAPTER TWENTY-EIGHT
ORGAN DONOR

The impact left me stunned, but otherwise unharmed. I'd been looking at Helen, hadn't seen the crash coming, and so hadn't braced myself.

I was stunned enough that I just sat there after we came to a stop, turning my head slowly to look at Helen. There was simply no way on earth I wouldn't be giving her shit for this.

"Did you forget which side of the street you're supposed drive on here?" I asked her wryly. The bitch couldn't take a joke, so I knew it would piss her off. All the better.

She bared her teeth at me in a snarl. "We've just been in an accident. If you can take a break from making sarcastic comments about absolutely everything, maybe you could think about getting out of your seat and checking on it with me."

I rolled my eyes, opening my door.

She stopped me from getting out with a hand on my arm.

"Wait," she told me, her accent extra crisp. "I must tell you something, but it can't go beyond this car."

She waved me over as though she wanted to say it in my ear. It wasn't my favorite idea, but I did it, if only to hurry her up.

This motion put my back to my now open door.

She seemed to have another small seizure, but that didn't keep her from speaking into my ear, "I hope this hurts like hell, you bloody cunt." As she spoke, something sharp stabbed hard into my back.

I should have seen it coming, the signs were there, but I was as stunned as I'd ever been in my entire long life when I looked down to see a slayer weapon in all of its shining blue glory protruding from my chest.

I looked up at Helen, confused at her smile.

"You'll die for this," I explained, every word agony as I somehow tried to be reasonable with a glowing sword gutting me.

She shook her geas at me, laughing. "I didn't do it."

"Everyone knows that I'm with you. Who the hell do you think they'll blame?"

She let out a disgusted sigh. "A sword's been buried in your back, one that can *kill you*, and you still won't shut up. What he sees in you, I'll never know."

"Maybe you should take some notes. He's never turned *me* down." That was the last crack I could manage before I lost my hold on consciousness.

I came to with my arms chained above me, feet dragged below. Everything hurt. Even my earlobes burned. Of course they must have ripped out my earrings/trackers, likely sent them in the opposite direction as a decoy.

How would Dom find me? When?

My entire mid-section was the worst of it, on fire with a

bitter, insidious pain. It was unbearable, the worst agony I'd ever born and even knowing it might be the end of me, I prayed for oblivion to take me under until mercifully it did.

When I came to again, I was strapped on my back to a metal table. My arms were still pulled above me, and there was a pretty decent-sized hole in my chest. Sharp pain in my neck and each of my wrists had me pretty sure I was being drained of blood. One mercy, though, the slayer weapon had been removed. So they weren't going to kill me right away. Good to know. Unfortunately, I knew what they *were* going to do and that was harvest me for parts, and *that* was going to be hell.

I heard a little snipping sound somewhere above my head, out of sight. I wasn't sure whether to make my wakefulness known or pretend to still be sleeping. It was anyone's guess which would serve me better.

The choice was taken out of my hands as I was already made.

A strange little man scuttled to my side. He held up a handful of pale gold locks from my hair tied with little black ribbons. He grinned at me, a harmless kind of grin with no malice in it. Insanity, hell yeah, malice, not at all.

"I won't take it all at once, you understand." His accent was British, his voice soft and melodious. He was freaking strange. "I mustn't flood the market. Wouldn't be wise. If we can keep you alive for a while, we'll all be rich. Stinking rich!"

He said it in a way that made me think he assumed that I should be happy about this. For once, I kept my mouth shut. I didn't begin to know how to deal with that level of crazy.

And this was me we were talking about.

Luckily I didn't stay conscious for long.

I awoke again to agony and despair. The slayer weapon was back in my chest, set in there like a placeholder. Cruel but affective.

I realized there were more slayer weapons impaled in me somewhere, smaller ones, I could feel them, but there was so much pain everywhere that I couldn't place where they were, but I knew they were doing their job, albeit slowly.

Every moment I spent there it felt like there was less of me. I was being diminished with every minute I spent in this exceptional piece of purgatory.

I could catch just the barest glimpse of my skin from the way they had me pinned, but what I saw was gray flesh with glowing runes flaring bright white.

"What the fuck are those?" a male voice asked in a crisp British accent somewhere close to my right.

"Those are druid runes," another male voice answered. Also British.

"Why the fuck is she covered in druid runes?"

"She's the druid Arch's ex. He must have placed them on her at some point."

"She's not his ex anymore," a third voice joined the fray. "They reconciled shortly before we took her."

There was what sounded like a roomful of cursing at that.

"Why the bloody hell didn't Helen tell us that before we took her?"

"It doesn't matter," the third voice said. He was calm and his voice held authority. I pegged him as the leader of this little crew of slayer psychopaths. "We covered all our bases. And don't worry about the runes. In fact, they might have helped. She'd be dead without them. You've been overzealous. One slayer weapon would have sufficed to sedate her. Three would have finished her without those runes, and we're nowhere near done with her."

I found that far from reassuring.

At one point I thought they were going to take my eyes out. It was a close thing, some sort of scoop shaped object being dug into one of my eye sockets before whoever was doing it was stopped with a shout.

We're about to be twins, Lynn, I thought to myself. Gods, I didn't want to go through this.

"Wait until we finish the bidding," the leader was speaking.

"Why rush and not get as high of a price as possible?" another voice added.

"Can't we just take them out now and hold onto them?" Still another horrible voice. "No matter what we do, she doesn't stay under. It could be a problem and if she's blind it's *less* of a problem."

"Does she really look like she can cause us any trouble now, conscious or not?" the leader asked sardonically. "The buyer will want it fresh, perhaps to even take them out themselves. Imagine how high we can get the bidding to with an offer like *that*?

"You have a good point."

I blacked out then, and it was a mercy.

Helen was there the next time I came to, and I could see just enough to catch her waving her arm around and cursing at me I noted vaguely that her geas had turned from shiny black to a dull gray. No wait. Not just the geas. Her whole arm was gray. Gray and rotting. She may not have directly defied the geas by letting others do the dirty work, but clearly it had turned against her anyway. Go Dom.

I came to again, more in pain than before, weaker.

I had lost a lot of blood. They'd been draining me the entire time I'd been here.

Just when I thought I couldn't be more miserable, I made the mistake of looking down to see my insides spilling out of my chest and stomach. No one should have to see a thing like that. Really. It was a whole new kind of wrong.

"—about the rest of her parts?" a male British voice was saying, the one that had almost taken my eyes.

"The bidding is concluding as we speak," the leader said with satisfaction. "They're bidding on everything from her skin to her teeth and her nails."

It's just a pity we can't let her shift to her other form and take her apart like *that*," another voice said. "We'd fetch a higher price for sure. Imagine full-sized dragon eyes and teeth!"

"That's too dangerous," the leader said flatly.

"I still think we're overlooking a good opportunity for extra money by just renting out her body while the auction runs," one of them said animatedly, "but nobody's going to want her when she looks like so much butchered meat."

All of their voices were measured, very British and as casual as if they were discussing tea and scones.

"I wouldn't say nobody," the attempted eye stealing bastard said, "I'm sure we could find someone that would pay extra to have her while she's like this. How about we offer both in either order and see what happens? We could always sew her up and split her open again. Perhaps we could charge extra if they want to take her apart themselves."

Hate is a funny thing. Sometimes it takes years to build to full strength and sometimes just a few hellish sentences will do it.

"Can't hurt to try," another seconded the awful idea.

"Let's not overcomplicate things," the leader said disdainfully, "there's not time for any of that. As I've said, the bidding is finishing up as we speak."

I was hurting so bad from the physical and mental torture

that I wasn't even plotting revenge anymore. I just wanted escape. I didn't have to kill them all on the way out. I could always come back and bring friends.

One of the men was standing over me then, his hands moving around inside my chest. I had no idea who he was, but I really didn't like him. In fact, I'd put this up there as the worst introduction of all time.

"You'll die for this," I told him with what was left of my voice and my bravado.

He shot me a look. He was handsome, in a clean cut kind of way, and his eyes would have been a nice blue if he wasn't moving my organs around with his fingers. "You think so?" When he spoke I clocked him as the one with the horrific ideas that had almost taken my eyes. "We've covered our tracks pretty well. You'd be surprised what a well thought out plan will let you get away with."

I opened my mouth to contradict him, because, let's face it, that's what I do, and if ever there was proof, this was it.

It was official: literally nothing on earth could shut me up.

But I never got a chance to say another word to him.

There was power in the air. Scary power. Make every hair on your body rise power. It was electric, and pervasive, and I had no clue where it was coming from.

The man was frozen, looking at something out of my eyesight that seemed to have terrified and immobilized him.

Suddenly and shockingly the man's head exploded, raining bloody bits of flesh and gore everywhere. There had been another man working to my left, and I turned my head just far enough to look at him right as his head popped right off.

No, that wasn't right. It had blown to fucking bits, just like the other guy.

I had no idea what was going on, had never seen any power that did that, but I couldn't say I didn't love it right that second.

With reservations, of course. If my head exploded next, I would fucking *hate* it.

"Help!" I called out weakly. I was really hoping that the scary power in the room was on my side, or at the very least, not my enemy.

I only realized it was Dom when I saw him with my own eyes. I didn't know about this ability, couldn't wrap my mind around it.

"Have you been hiding this, or have you just gained that much strength?" I managed to gasp at him as he approached my prone figure.

He was in no shape to answer, fury and anguish in every line of his shaking body, madness in his eyes.

I didn't imagine he liked seeing my organs spilling out of me much more than I did.

He was fully in human form, but threw his head back and howled. Like an animal. Like a beast on a rampage. Like he'd lost every ounce of sanity he ever possessed. And that howl went on and on.

Even broken, even turned inside out, the terror-inducing sound of that howl made my hair stand on end. I supposed that was the purpose of it.

I felt a tear slip down my cheek when he finally stopped. It was a tear of relief. I could not take one more horrible thing, not even on the tail of my rescue. My mind was at its breaking point.

His hands trembled as they lowered to me. One went to my cheek, the other to a part of my body I couldn't see and didn't want to.

A sickeningly wet sound told me that he was moving some organ back into place, his breath shuddering out in horror. I couldn't even look at him directly, couldn't face his unbearable eyes.

He was in a state. Who the fuck could blame him?

I think that a person's reaction upon being rescued from the most dreadful experience of their lives tells you a lot about their nature.

What did one express at a moment like this? What priority had taken precedence in my near-broken mind? With agony singing through every inch of my slaughtered body, what did I reach for?

Call me what you will, but I am not indecisive.

I reached for vengeance.

"It was Helen," I gasped out, no part of me numb, each syllable working its way through what was left in the ruins of my lungs. "She betrayed you. She handed me to them."

That was all I had left. I closed my eyes and let the darkness take me.

CHAPTER TWENTY-NINE
THE RIVER

The passage of time is a funny thing. In the darkness, it felt to me like a flowing river, growing wider in places and narrow in others. The darkness brought time to its narrowest point and spilled me gently into its widest. I floated along, mind racing aimlessly through the many years of my existence.

I still don't know what it was, this darkness. Sometimes it wasn't even dark. Sometimes it was so bright and warm that I found myself basking in it.

It was benevolent, this outer realm, letting the recent horrors filter far enough away from my consciousness to let me breathe, to let even the broken parts of my mind begin the healing process.

All I know for sure is that the darkness took me from the earthly realm, and that being there meant that I was near enough to death for me to question my mortality.

It was a bit like the place I went when my dragon takes over completely, but it wasn't that because that place still gave me a sense of the familiar. When I'd given birth to the egg that would one day be my son, I'd drifted for what felt like days, and turned out to be months, the monster inside of me sheltering me from a natural pain.

I came back to my body knowing I'd been in a fight for my life, and that I must have won.

I was in a familiar bed, which was a good sign. I couldn't move, which had to be a bad one.

Shifting my head down to glance at my body was a chore, but I caught enough of a glimpse of bloodied bandages covering just about everything to let it go, for the moment. Maybe I'd try again in a few days.

I moved just my eyes to look to my right. Dom was there, decked out in full combat gear, still as a statue, head in his hands.

Not good.

I tried to speak, and it was better, at least, than trying to move, though still an effort.

Again, I couldn't help thinking it's a sort of twisted personality test, your first words coming out of a near-death experience.

"Did you kill her?" I asked, my voice a pitiful rasp, my eyes still craned far to the right to study Dom.

He shuddered, a great wave of it rocking his body before he could lift his head, and when he did, I looked away, pure instinct making me recoil.

I hurt enough, without shouldering his terrible pain, as well.

"Yes," he said hoarsely. "I killed them all."

The darkness took me again.

Countless peaceful flowing miles later, I opened my eyes.

I moved my head to look down. Still bandaged, but not

bloody now. That had to be good. A glance to my right showed I was alone. Not good, or at least, not what I'd wanted.

Another blink, gone and back, and Dom was beside me again, watching me intently this time, looking much less haggard, much less devastated.

Another tally in the column of good. If each time I returned, I found a bit more good, well, I'd be myself again in no time.

He leaned forward to lightly touch my cheek, his eyes still too much, still more than I could face. "Stay with me for just a moment," he said softly and got up.

He left the room, but came back within seconds, holding some sort of satchel with both hands.

His right hand shook as he reached into the bag and pulled out a gory prize by its long blond hair.

I stared at Helen's severed head with gimlet eyes, a sense of relief flooding me. Her eyes were wide, glassy, and black as though some dark terror had overtaken her right before the end.

It had clearly been a horrific death.

"She suffered greatly," he told me. "The geas tortured her relentlessly before I found her and finished it.

"Thank you," I mouthed, eyes already drifting closed again.

The next time I roused I remembered a bit more about the current timeline than revenge.

Sloan was at my bedside now, and I figured Dom must be setting trusted guards on me when he had to leave.

She was reading a book, but when I started to speak she straightened and looked at me. She reached for her phone and started texting.

"Any word on Lynn?" I asked her. I sounded pitiful, but at

least the words were coming out faster now. My lungs must be healing, a healing that would have been slowed exponentially by the slayer weapons they'd kept impaled in me.

"Dom managed to get her eyes directly back into her hands," she said without looking up from her phone. "But we haven't heard from her since. We're working on it."

The matter-of-fact way she spoke to me was infinitely reassuring, as though things were normal, just business as usual, and I was myself and whole.

I nodded. It was better than I'd hoped for, honestly. "How long have I been out?"

"Two months."

Worse than I'd hoped for there. "How is Conan?"

"The same. He was unsettled, but we let his friend in to see him whenever she wants and that seemed to help soothe them both."

"Have we learned anything else about her?"

"She claims to be half-dragon, and I'm leaning toward believing her. Do you think you're up to having more visitors?"

"Is Dom close?" I asked. I wanted to set eyes on him before the darkness took me again. I could feel it coming like an invisible hand pressing down on me.

"He's two minutes away. He started heading here as soon as I texted him that you were awake. He rarely leaves the building now."

"Is he okay?"

She paused, and I knew she was choosing her words carefully. "Are *you* okay? I would say he's however okay you are, perhaps. . . a few steps below that."

I'd been afraid of that and I was not surprised. "Two minutes?" I asked, but I was already fading out.

The next time I woke Dom was there. He was fully dressed in a suit, sleeping on the bed beside me on his side, facing me, his hand reached out to me but not quite touching as though he was hesitant to.

I reached out to touch his cheek but was distracted by the sight of my hands. My skin was gray and my nails were gone, and the nailbeds were pink and soft.

"They ripped your nails out," Dom's voice was hoarse and a bit too raw. "I felt it when it happened. I felt quite a bit of it, through the runes I placed on you. The runes didn't keep you from harm, but they mitigated it, somewhat."

I couldn't look at his face, his eyes were too much to take, but I touched his hand. "I didn't realize. So many other worse things were going on. I'm surprised they haven't grown back, though. And my skin doesn't look so good."

"The slayer weapons' effects are still at work. You're healing human slow. I've been able to take most of your pain away, but nothing seems to work towards healing you faster. I'm consulting with every type of supernatural creature with healing powers I can find to speed it up but nothing so far has worked. I had hoped Sven could help, but he has no specialty in the healing arts."

"How are you taking most of my pain away?" I asked, but I already knew. I was familiar with a lot of druid spells after our years together.

"However I can," he answered.

"You're hedging," I pointed out.

"I take it into myself, as you know. I wish I could take it all." His voice was full of pain and regret. I could hardly bear to hear him like that.

"You don't need to do that."

"I do. I need to and I want to."

He was a lost cause here, but I'd known that the second I opened my mouth. "Lynn could help," I said. "Is there any way we could get Lynn?"

"I'm working on it. Drake was—" he cleared his throat, but the hoarse quality remained, "*displeased* by the trick we played on him. Hopefully he will move past it and see reason soon."

"How'd you do it? Get Lynn's eyes back to her?"

"Caleb couldn't fool Lynn or me by mimicking you, but he managed to convince Drake for long enough to hand the eyes off to your sister."

"Thank you. It brings me a lot of peace knowing she has her eyes back." Now we just had to get *her* back.

"Of course."

"How did you find me? I know they ripped the trackers off as soon as they captured me." I touched the torn ruins of my earlobes. Even those weren't fully healed.

I caught him staring at what I was doing and stopped.

I couldn't take how broken his eyes were, couldn't look at them directly for even a *second*.

It was like standing at the edge of a void I couldn't save myself from, let alone both of us.

"Helen's geas," he said, his voice even worse now. He said her name like it was a curse. I could feel him still staring at my mutilated earlobes. "She went on the run not knowing we could find her with it. We were following her, checking every location she visited. It was a few days before she went to the building where they were keeping you. I think she was looking for help with the geas, it was slowly killing her, rotting her from the inside. I assume she learned then that there's no reversing it, and though she didn't stay at your location for long, it was enough. You know what happened after that. They're all dead. Helen's entire bloodline has been wiped from the face of the earth, and everyone involved, whether they were there or helped plan it. We've wiped out a good percentage of the English slayers. Hopefully the rest of them got the message."

"How was she able to plan it, restricted as she was by the geas?"

"She must have made the plans before she touched down in Vegas, before the geas was placed.   It will be my everlasting sorrow that I overlooked such a possibility."

I reached over and touched his cheek and even that was still a struggle. I studied his face. His eyes were closed so I didn't have to meet them. It was a mercy. "Not everlasting. No pain lasts forever."

"Speak for yourself."   His expression didn't change, but tears were running down his cheeks.   "I'll *never* forgive myself."

"Don't say that. I forgive you. I survived. I'm here. And I think your runes helped. I think they saved my life. Days with a slayer weapon imbedded in us is not something I think even dragons normally survive."

He opened his eyes, and I looked down at our hands.

"Don't let them take more from us than they already have," I told him.

I was trying to convince myself as much as him, and I think we both knew it. Still, I took the fact that I was even trying as a good sign.

"Was I imagining things or did you storm the place where they were keeping me all by yourself? I know there were a lot of slayers there, but I only saw you coming in."

"I brought a large force with me. They just couldn't keep up. I didn't stick to the plan, stormed the building before they were ready. I was. . . unruly. I wasn't entirely myself. I wasn't thinking clearly."

"I figured. Where did all of that come from? The head. . . exploding thing?   One of your mother's enchantress powers?"

He paused. "More or less. More accurately I suppose it

was my version of it. I was very upset. I had recently taken all the power The Grove had gained from your blood into me to weaken it and keep it from expanding. It was an. . . intense colligation of things with results I'm not sure I could repeat if I tried. I still have a lot to learn."

"I see."

"In my mother's journals she wrote that many generations ago the Druid Circle decided that our line was cursed. The wolf's eye is too strong combined with beast-call. An individual with that much power can't be controlled. The Arch himself went to seize the head of our house for execution but ended up marrying her instead and making her Arch in his place soon after."

"That tracks," I said wryly.

"I thought that would amuse you. And it was an enlightening story. I can see why she kept the nature of our other powers so secretive, even from me, though it will be hard to do the same with Conan."

"Telepathy, huh?"

We were quiet for a time. He had moved closer to me on the bed and held my hand like it might break. "How long was I out this time?" I asked him.

"It's been just over a week since you were last conscious. Sloan told me I only missed you by *two minutes.*"

I squeezed his hand comfortingly. "I'll try not to stay away so long anymore. I think it's just my mind's way of trying to heal from the ordeal."

"When my parents died, they died together. I don't know the details, no one alive does. All that was found of them were their heads mounted on spikes side by side at the gates of the enemy's keep. But I always wondered if they really died together or if one was taken from this life and the other followed willingly. If they let themselves be killed to stay together.

"That's how I felt when you were taken, when I felt some of what was happening to you, when I thought I might be too late—"

He had to pause for a moment to collect himself.

"And then I saw you like that, so close to death, and I knew. A true tie of fate is a noose, and I felt it tighten as you became more mortal at their hands. If they'd taken you from this realm I would have *followed you into the next one.*" He was weeping quietly.

"Don't say that. What about Conan?"

"Someday he would have understood, as I have come to. He'll find his mate, and they will be the other half of his soul and he will understand that this life isn't worth living without them."

"Well, we'll both just have to stay alive then, won't we?" I said emotionally just before the darkness pulled me under again.

When something truly horrific happens to us it is more than the memory of pain that remains at first. It is anguish. It is the feeling of it all over again with just a thought, triggered easily by just the wrong word or memory. It was the sad reality of reaching for a smile and finding it forced, of reliving it all again with one short blink. I'd born many unpleasant things in my long life, and so I knew that this sort of thing would fade for me with time, but that made it no easier to bear in the real raw reality of the now.

I tried to hide it, tried my hardest, in fact, because the fact was I was mortified that spending a few days with my body inside out may have broken my spirit.

I was healing, though, slowly as it was, and I took heart in that. I was awake more and more, even started receiving visitors, though Dom limited it to short visits, one at a time.

It was never more apparent than when Christian came to see me that I just wasn't myself. His unfailing good nature, his endless sense of humor, made my fragile state impossible to ignore, at least on the inside.

"I guess you haven't heard, being unconscious and all," Christian told me, his voice pitched low like someone was listening in and he didn't want to be heard. "Dom went on an *unholy rampage* against the English slayers. No, scratch that, it was more like a *holy war*."

I was a bit surprised to hear it named like that, an all-out war, though I shouldn't have been. The way Dom had found me, I might have been more surprised if he hadn't gone to war over it.

It was during these visits with Christian that I remembered bits about myself. Like, oh yeah, I used to be funny. Humor was a thing I used to enjoy.

And so I would throw out a few obligatory insults, jokes, and get the reaction that made me feel better, because if I could fake it, then it was still in there somewhere, that old me, and I'd find her again, eventually.

Caleb was, ironically, easier to take. I didn't have to pretend things were normal in front of his dead, judgement-free eyes. Being friends with a cold-blooded alien had its perks.

Sven was somber, and it seemed to pain him a bit to even be in my vicinity. He squirmed in the chair beside my bed, could hardly look at me.

Being a telepath could be brutal, I was sure.

"Don't let Conan near you until you're better, okay? Just trust me on this."

I had already figured as much, so I just nodded.

Company was good because I felt helpless if I had any free time awake. I tried to plan a way to rescue Lynn, but I just didn't know enough about Drake and the way he operated to think of a way in. If he was too upset to even deal with us now we were at an impasse I didn't know how to cross.

CHAPTER THIRTY
CHAOTIC NEUTRAL

The problem solved itself a few trips back from the darkness later.

Or I should say Lynn solved it. Typical Lynn. We'd given her the tools—aka eyeballs—and she'd rescued herself.

Rumor was she appeared inside the casino like nothing had happened, Drake on her arm like he was her beautiful, harmless eye candy.

Ha.

More like her seeing eye dragon.

I didn't witness that part, just heard about it later from Sloan, but I was fortunately awake when Lynn came to my room to see me.

Her hair was its natural color now, a silver blond a full shade lighter than mine; true platinum.

Her eyes were still healing, but unless Drake was willing to take them out himself and keep them (Which he hadn't done yet, so I was hopeful he didn't have that in him), they were no longer an effective bargaining chip for him. It had been enough to tip the scales in her favor, and she was more or less free to wander the earth again.

I couldn't hide a thing from Lynn, not even from her reforming, unseeing eyes.

She sat beside the bed and patted my hand. "You'll be okay," she told me.

"I know." I said, trying to mean it. "So you're free now?"

"More or less. Drake's agreed to stay in the States, and I told him I would keep considering his proposal if we live together for a few years first and I get to stay close to you."

"A little easier to get him to negotiate with your eyes back?"

"Well, yeah. He fights dirty, but don't we all? I'm not sure I'd know what to do with someone that didn't. A clean fight is an oxymoron to me. What would even be the point? At least I understand him."

"Fair enough. So no war with the Chinese dragons?"

"Not as of now. Tianlong is not happy. He has a half-human daughter, a young girl, that's chosen to stay with the druids rather than follow him home, and he struck out with you, which shook him to his core, but he's retreated back into his lair for now. Being ancient breeds a special sort of patience. And arrogance."

I connected the dots. The little girl I'd found before I left. The one Conan was so attached to, was Tianlong's daughter. "Yinlong," I said.

"Excuse me?"

"Tianlong's daughter is Yinlong."

"You're mixed up in that? Of *course* you are." She sounded a perfect combination of vexed and amused.

"She and Conan are very close."

"Of *course* they are."

"I thought they didn't believe in diluting their bloodline. Isn't that the whole reason they were looking for *us*?"

"Someone like Tianlong doesn't make rules because he plans to follow them *himself*."

Figured.

"But Drake isn't like him?" I asked hopefully. "He's not, ya know, totally evil?"

"They're not good or evil. They're kind of like nature. Often benign but also capable of terrible, wondrous, and unpredictable things."

"Are you telling me they're chaotic neutral?"

"Yes, that. But more than that they're a law unto themselves."

"Checks out. Is Drake really his name? It doesn't quite suit him."

"Drake is the name he uses in the west. In the east he is Shenlong."

"That tracks. I like the hair. Back to your roots, huh?"

"For now. So I heard Dom's found you a compound of epic proportions and you're moving there soon."

This was news to me. Kind of. It made perfect sense so I wasn't exactly surprised. "Am I?" I asked.

"That information was from the man himself. Is he okay, by the way? He seems. . . a little off."

"I don't know how much you've heard about what happened, but he's the one that found me at the harvesters. I was in bad shape. It was a lot for him. For me, too. It was my first direct, personal run-in with what a slayer weapon can really do to us. I haven't been that helpless since childhood."

"I've heard enough to know it was bad." Her voice was measured. I knew her as you can only know a sister. Enough to know her perfectly neutral tone was hiding a world of concern. "Wanna talk about it?"

"Not really. So where are you going to live with your betrothed?"

"Don't call him that. And I was going to ask you to go house hunting with me for a place close to your compound."

"You want me to be your eyes?" I teased her. "Can you see at all yet?"

"I can some but they're still healing. And if anyone can figure out what I'll like, it's you."

"I'd be happy to help as soon as Dom lets me out of bed."

"And when do you think that'll be?"

"Probably when I can stay conscious for longer than ten minutes at a time."

"It's that bad, huh?"

"Because of the slayer weapons they used—"

"*Multiple* slayer weapons?"

"Yes, at least three," I said matter of factly. "Some of the harvesters were slayers themselves—"

"I heard the druids went to war with the English dragon slayers," she interrupted like she'd been dying to talk about this subject. "I was surprised, but now it's beginning to make sense."

"I wish I could have been there," was all I said.

"Same, sis, same. I heard it was quick, over in a few days, a few vicious battles, and that most of the English slayers were wiped out clean."

"That part I can confirm."

"Dom, huh?"

"Him, yeah."

"Nice that you have a king at your beck and call, ready and eager to avenge you."

"Don't start," I began.

"I wasn't joking. It makes me add more pros in Drake's column when I consider a match, ya know?"

I couldn't tell if she was messing with me, but that was what was so amusing about Lynn. Even after all these years she still kept me guessing, kept me smiling and baffled as I tried to figure her out.

"Okay," I said slowly, waiting for anymore punchlines. When she was quiet, I continued, "Well, because the slayer weapons were impaled inside of me for so long, for close to three days I think, I'm healing human slow, and I had some gnarly wounds."

"I think I can help a bit with that."

"That would be nice. Oh yeah, I meant to tell you we were nearly missing eyeball twins."

"That sounds heinous."

"You would know. At the time, though, it gave me a weird sort of comfort."

"Glad I could help," she said wryly. "Well, I got mine back, and you still have yours so I guess things are looking up all around."

I opened my mouth to respond with something pessimistic I think, but I slipped back into the darkness before any words came out.

When I came back this time, my body felt markedly better. A glance at my hands showed me that my skin was a normal, human color again.

Dom was there. It was dark out and he was sleeping beside me. He wasn't even wearing a suit. He was letting himself rest at night again like a normal person. Things were looking up.

For the first time in months, I was able to turn onto my side. Yes, the wounds were finally healing faster, I was positive of it now.

I touched his hand and he woke instantly, turning to face me. "I'm healing faster," I said. "Was it Lynn?"

"Lynn and Drake. He did something strange that made this entire wing of the casino fill up with red smoke and then black smoke and freaked a lot of people out, myself included, but if it helped it was worth it. He also claims he has a way to make you more resistant to the power of a slayer weapon, but that the price will be steep if he's to share it. We're in negotiations now."

"I bet Lynn can talk him into giving it to her as a wedding present."

"Perhaps. They're an interesting match, but somehow it makes sense to me. They remind me of ornery cats circling each other."

I thought about it. "I can see it. I heard you found us a compound to live in."

"I did. We're just waiting until you're well enough to be moved."

I gripped his hand. "I think I'll be there soon," I said, and let the darkness take me again.

When I came back from the darkness that time, I kept absolutely nothing with me that I didn't need. No extra burdens to shoulder in terms of pain. The river had washed me clean.

I met Dom's grave, tender eyes squarely for the first time since I was taken. "I'm better. Can you bring me the egg? I think my mind is clean enough that I won't hurt his with it now."

EPILOGUE

The compound was completely ridiculous. It was more like a mini resort complete with an exterior of mirrored, blue, bullet-proof glass and an inner courtyard with a pool circled by a lazy river.

Christian, ever the kid at heart, would be stoked.

It was less than a mile off the strip, an oasis of privacy in the thick of things, except that we had so much extra security that I wasn't sure how the druids were sparing the manpower.

I didn't fight it, I wasn't up to it yet, but I would muster the energy to someday, I was sure. For now I let Dom be as insanely overprotective as his obsessive heart desired. It seemed to make him feel better.

The entire place was furnished and ready to move in the second Dom pronounced me fit enough to be moved.

I was able to walk the short distance from Dom's rooms in the casino down to the valet without assistance, but Dom was close at my side, watching me with anxious eyes the entire time.

He had Conan in an unobtrusive backpack held to his chest with one arm and a small troop of druid soldiers following us every step.

"It's just because we're moving the egg between secured vaults," Dom told me when we were alone in the back of a limo and driving to our new home. "It won't always be like this. I know I can't send a contingent of soldiers to follow you everywhere indefinitely. Perhaps just a small detail."

I wasn't sure if I needed to nip this in the bud or let it lie while he worked through his trauma, but whatever the answer I decided to leave it for another day. I was healing faster now, but still not at a hundred percent and the small walk had close to exhausted me.

Dom gave me a tour of the place when we arrived, and I got through it slowly. It was a lot of space, but Conan's vault was closer to our bedroom here, and I was farther from The Grove so I was happy with the new conditions in general.

I only realized along the tour that Yinlong had a room in the compound as well and then only when I saw it, the little girl already settled into a reading nook in the corner of her giant lavender princess room. She was a gorgeous little thing with light brown hair and violet eyes.

She rushed to Dom and threw herself into his arms. He hugged her with familiar affection. They must have spent some time together while I was recovering. They acted like old friends.

"Daddy," she called him.

I raised my brows.

She turned to me next, giving me almost the same treatment. We'd only met once before, but it had made an impression, and she was very happy to see me, hugging me like I was a long lost relative. I hugged her back, sending Dom a warm look over her shoulder, and let her talk my ear off about Conan.

"I take it we're adopting her?" I asked Dom later, not at all displeased with the notion. Just the opposite. I'd badly wanted children for most of my long life, and Dom knew it well.

"Conan already has. I just made it more convenient for him. I meant to tell you, but it was hard to keep you conscious long enough to relay the information. I knew you wouldn't mind adding to the family when it meant rescuing a baby half-dragon. She's a darling and she and Conan are hopelessly attached."

"Is there any chance Tianlong will try to get her back?"

"Not unless he wants a war."

"Thank you for taking care of that, for taking care of them, for handling *everything* while I was indisposed."

"Of course," he said like it was his job and I knew he saw it as such. He had for far longer than I'd ever been willing to acknowledge before now.

It was later and we were ensconced in our new bed when I said, "Quite the little family we've developed all of a sudden."

He stroked my hair. He was still handling me like I was made of glass, but I'd managed to coax him into letting me use him as a pillow. It was progress.

"About that." He cleared his throat, sounding suddenly nervous, which was a very new Dom to witness. "I'd like to make things official. Legally and spiritually. I want every vow from you before our child is born. I'm old-fashioned, as you know."

I wasn't expecting that and I reeled for a bit, taking it in. "You knocked me up so now you have to marry me?" I finally asked. Making light was my coping mechanism when I didn't know what to say.

"The opposite. You're the mother of my child so *you* have to marry *me*. It's not a question. I was informing you."

A rush of joy straight through my body surprised me. I'd wanted this, somehow wanted a thing I'd never even let myself consider before. "Well, I guess I won't answer you since it wasn't a question."

He made a sound like a big cat purring and squeezed me tight. "It's settled then. I'll make the arrangements."

I did end up helping Lynn look for houses close by. Even though she still couldn't see well, she didn't like anything.

"I don't like the aura on this one," she said at the fourth house.

I couldn't tell if she was messing with me. Was this some new blind trick she'd learned in her time with Drake? "What's its aura doing?" I asked her in the tone you'd use with someone less than sane.

"It's hard to explain but it's like it's playing music I don't like. Something like that but nothing you can hear or see."

"You're fucking with me, aren't you?"

"Like I have time to go house to house just messing with you."

"Now I *know* you're fucking with me," I told her.

"Next house, please!"

Christian threw a pool party at our new place pretty much the second he could.

We were all settled in and I was finally healed, and that was all the excuse he needed to invite everyone over like it was one of *his* houses.

Caleb in swim trunks swigging a beer bottle was always a trip, so the sight of that alone was worth the price of admission. The fact that he was chatting almost amiably with Corbin and Henri, who seemed to be a package deal these days, took the amusement a step further. Our resident sociopath chameleon alien was adapting more and more to being human-ish.

Lynn and Drake were there, and Drake went out of his way

to be kind and gentle with Yinlong, even sitting down to have a tea party with her beside the pool. She had Conan's egg cuddled close beside her in a nest of soft blankets, as she often did. She poured Drake a perfect, tiny cup of tea, and I saw him send a warm look in Lynn's direction.

I shot Lynn a look and she glared. The glare was because my look was pointed, and in sister language she knew what I was pointing at was that her man was baby-crazed. I knew well all the signs firsthand.

Drake had found a house for them less than ten minutes away from us with an aura that Lynn could 'tolerate.' It was a black, gothic monstrosity, unlike anything I'd ever seen built in sin city, as though Drake had conjured it out of thin air and specified to Lynn's preferences.

I was pretty sure he couldn't do that, though. Ish.

Sven was there, he was living close for the time being, at least as long as our father was still at large.

He joined Drake and Yinlong and Conan's egg for the tea party. It was pretty damned adorable.

Lynn was near them watching, and I knew it was only a matter of time before she caved and joined them, as well.

I was fine sitting out to give someone else a turn. I'd spent the latter part of my convalescence attending similar tea parties.

Sloan and Cam were on the lazy river in a double floaty and Christian, who was hitting on the pretty bartender he'd hired for the occasion, kept shooting meaningful looks from me to them as though I couldn't see it myself. They looked like they were getting along, perhaps even permanently reconciled, though neither were speaking a word of it.

Dom had me cornered in the pool, arms braced around me like I might fall down without them. I let him, even leaned into it. Perhaps we *both* needed it.

It was some time later, all of the adults having joined us in the pool, when Lynn asked me, "So you've like adopted her?"

"Yes," I said, still getting used to the idea but very happy about it.

She was referring to Yinlong, alone now at the tea party table with Conan, but she seemed content as could be pretending to help his egg sip tea.

"So they're like siblings?" asked Christian.

"Not at all. They'll be raised together, but will marry when they come of age," Sven said.

We all just stared at him.

He shrugged, looking unbothered. "It wasn't my idea, it was theirs, and they won't be deterred. I dare someone to try to come between them." He laughed like he found the idea of that was very amusing.

It was a lot to take in. I caught the look on Dom's face. "You *knew*?"

He gave me an enigmatic glance. "I've told you about the stars," was his response.

The wedding was as ridiculous as the compound Dom had found for us.

It was an extremely formal druid affair, upholding all of the customs and traditions his people held dear.

Dom wanted to make a statement with it and he did.

It was romantic and beautiful, extravagant and huge.

We'd had to wait until the stars were in an exact alignment to his liking. I took his word for it. I wasn't the stargazer in the relationship, though I did occasionally let them run my life.

The vows were held in the druid casino's impressive atrium.

It was the pretty Hollywood version of the real Grove, so similar that I found it a bit disturbing, as though a flip might be switched and the soil beneath turned to squishy flesh, the water to congealing red blood.

It behaved itself though. Mostly.

We were barefoot, our skin touching the earth was part of the ceremony. We both wore crowns of flowers and antlers, much smaller than the ceremonial one Dom wore as Arch. I wore a flowing ivory lace and silk gown. He wore white druid robes.

We stood inside a sacred circle marked with flowers that only the couple and officiator—in this case, Sloan—could step inside of.

Sloan stood on the other side of a heavy altar made of stone. She spoke in Druidic, but I'd been told beforehand what the vows were, so I got the gist of it.

It was a promise, and pact, of forever. For better or worse, our fates were intertwined in perpetuity.

For druids, and now for me, mating was for life and even in death, we would follow each other to the next realm.

If I went down, he went down. We'd go down together, as a too young Dom had once told me.

With one shared athame, we cut each other's palms and let it drip into the soil beside the altar, an offering back to the earth.

I wondered if that part was such a good idea with all that had happened between me and the real Grove, but held my tongue. Didn't want to ruin the mood.

When the soil was sufficiently bloodied, we brought our wounded palms against each other and Sloan tied our wrists together with a colorful crios.

We made our blood oath and hand-fasting, my solemn eyes on his shining, mismatched ones.

All but one of Dom's seven lieutenants attended the ceremony.

Sloan was officiating and the rest stood directly outside of the circle, spaced out evenly to further reinforce its power.

Siobhan wasn't there. In spite of being one of his lieutenants, she wasn't invited, for obvious reasons.

Later I heard she'd tried to disrupt the wedding but was stopped before she succeeded and had to be detained and sedated for some time afterward.

The news didn't make me happy. I could be spiteful and I did hate her, but I wanted her just to get the hell over it and move on. Dom had been telling her very clearly (since she'd expressed her love to him as a teenager) that he did not and would never have those kinds of feelings for her. I would have felt pity for her if she wasn't such a raging cunt.

The bride's half of the wedding guests was significantly smaller than the groom's, just a handful in fact, but when we were pronounced wedded, they cheered the loudest, Christian, Lynn, and Sven being particularly boisterous.

I glanced back and smiled at my little crowd.

Drake inclined his head politely when our eyes met, and Caleb appeared bored. Corbin was there, looking uncomfortable in his suit, but he smiled affably at me.

Henri was there, standing very close to Corbin. He'd forgiven me, and we'd become tentatively friendly again. Dom was still in heated negotiations with him to buy all of his Jillian inspired art.

Even Luke was there, still giving me doe eyes when Dom didn't send him murderous looks for it. Lynn and Drake had rescued him from Tianlong's household, and he seemed none the worse for wear.

Yinlong was there. We'd made her a flower girl even though it wasn't typical for druid weddings. She was very happy with the role. She threw petals around enthusiastically every time I looked her way.

She was a frail looking thing, tall for her age but painfully thin. It was a deceptive delicacy, though. She held Conan's egg in a baby carrier against her chest without showing an ounce of strain for the entire day.

He was tucked away in a blanket, a little hat clipped to the top to make it look like Yinlong was just very attached to the idea of playing with an oversized baby doll.

There was only one small snag during the ceremony, but it was a doozy.

We were close to the end of the vows when Sloan paused and shared an enigmatic glance with Dom. A rumbling noise shook the entire massive building.

They both looked down at the ground next to the altar at the same time, like they'd heard something the rest of us couldn't.

I followed their eyes.

A strange, ominous object pushed up out of the dirt.

I hadn't known about this part, but as I saw Sloan and Dom's reaction I realized that it was a shock for them too. I didn't take that as a good sign, and the look they shared then was not reassuring. Whatever this meant, it had shaken them both.

"She has to pick it up," Sloan finally said after a prolonged staring contest with the strange little thing. "There's no escaping it."

"I'll take it myself," returned Dom.

"It is closer to her and you know what that means. There cannot be a proxy for this, not even if it's you."

"You're right," Dom said, and each word felt like a nail in a coffin. "I don't want her burdened with this." His voice was almost pleading.

"It's not for you to decide. There's no question that it is for her to take. Even you can't control everything," said Sloan. "You will just have to coach her on what to expect when the offer is made."

Dom looked at me and there was something in his

expression, a bracing sort of regret that made my breath catch in my throat.

I touched his cheek, a comforting gesture.

"I'm sorry, but you must pick it up," Dom told me, and the words were torn from him.

"Okay," I said, and bent down to take it, operating on the blind trust that Dom knew more about what was happening than I did and had my best interests at heart.

It was attached to a piece of twine the color of the dirt, and gingerly I took the string between two fingers. The object was a dull red I saw as I started to pull it out, and roughly the size and shape of a small chicken egg. It was still mostly buried, but when I applied the slightest pressure the whole thing came clear as though it was throwing itself at me.

I didn't want to touch it directly so I lifted it closer, still on a tie, to study. Several little faces were shaped into it. Their expressions made it look like they were in some sort of acute agony.

"Hold it in your palm, count to seven, and then put it away," Sloan told me.

I placed it in my hand and immediately had to stifle the urge to recoil, to throw it far from me. It felt like flesh, perhaps like an organ dried on the outside, but still filled with a bit of blood.

I counted to seven.

My dress had pockets and I placed it in one, wrenching away from it as soon as I could. I shook my hand as though that could erase the feel of it from my skin.

Sloan nodded decisively. "Good. Keep it safe, and don't speak of it again until Dom brings it up. He'll know when it's safe to discuss it."

Ookaay.

And then the ceremony concluded like nothing bizarre had just happened.

Countless hours of celebrating later, he brought it up again.

"If it tries to bargain with you, you will turn it down, no matter what it offers. If it begins to vibrate or move in any way you must tell me right away, and I'll give you further instructions. If it speaks to you, stay silent and come find me. Other than that, we'll just put it somewhere safe, in a room with no windows. It must *never* see an eclipse, and it is better if it is kept from sunrise and sunset, as well. I wish this wasn't your burden, but if The Grove had ahold of something like this, it is good that we have pried it away, whether or not that was its intent."

I was as lost as ever, but his instructions seemed easy enough to follow, at least. "Are you going to tell me what it is?"

"When the time comes I can, but not yet. Just trust me and don't veer from those instructions."

I rolled my eyes. Fucking druids.

A few weeks later, we had another ceremony. One for just the two of us.

We hiked five hours to a spot in the Rockies we'd found years ago.

It was no one but us and the land and the sky.

We were on a mountain summit, a rare slice of land between heaven and earth where the clouds met a pristine lake that was surrounded by fields of wildflowers.

He laid me down among the riotous blooms. Purple, red, orange, yellow glowed around our bodies, framing us, my flaxen hair pooling around us like mantle.

He was braced over me with a warm smile so wide his arresting eyes wrinkled up at the corners.

He touched a spot above my head.

"What is it?" I asked him.

"The way your hair fell, the way it's glowing in the

sunlight, it almost looks like a halo."

"You know I saw an angel halfling on my mission with Helen, before it all went south. I have to say there was some resemblance there, but I think you know me well enough by now not to accuse me of having even one angelic tendency."

He smiled and kissed my nose. "You might have a few."

We swore a blood oath there, alone together at the edge of the world. This was a heart oath, the cuts deep into our chests and pressed together to mingle while we pledged ourselves.

The multitude of vows might have been overkill at this point, but overkill was a specialty we both shared.

"There will be no one but you until my last breath," I vowed to him.

"Until the stars fall," vowed Dom.

R.K. LILLEY